Rescues, Rogues & Renegade

Mary Seifert

Books by Mary Seifert

Maverick, Movies, & Murder
Rescues, Rogues, & Renegade
Tech, Trials, & Trouble (fall, 2022)

Rescues, Rogues & Renegade

Katie & Maverick Cozy Mysteries, Book 2

Mary Seifert

Secret Staircase Books

Rescues, Rogues, & Renegade
Published by Secret Staircase Books, an imprint of
Columbine Publishing Group, LLC
PO Box 416, Angel Fire, NM 87710

Book layout and design by Secret Staircase Books
Cover images © Viktoria123, Patrick Dufour, Scott Cummings

First trade paperback edition: July, 2022
First e-book edition: July, 2022
* * *

Publisher's Cataloging-in-Publication Data

Seifert, Mary
Rescues, Rogues, & Renegade / by Mary Seifert.
p. cm.
ISBN 978-1649140920 (paperback)
ISBN 978-1649140937 (e-book)

1. Katie Wilk (Fictitious character). 2. Minnesota—Fiction. 3.
Amateur sleuths—Fiction. 4. Women sleuths—Fiction. 5. Dogs in
fiction. I. Title

Katie & Maverick Cozy Mystery Series : Book 2.
Siefert, Mary, Katie & Maverick cozy mysteries.

BISAC : FICTION / Mystery & Detective.
813/.54

ACKNOWLEDGMENTS

A huge thank you to Stephanie Dewey and Lee Ellison for your professionalism and your attention to detail. Your help has been invaluable. Much gratitude to the many friends who took time to support my dream and a few who went beyond the call of duty: Colleen Okland, Sandi Unger, Margaret Sullivan, Evy Hatjistilianos, Molly Silbernich Johnson, Deb Van Buren, Dr. Ali Schollmeyer, Ruth Neely, Hal Neely, Joanne Haugen, Dr. Anne Bruckner, Stephen Bruckner, and my lovely family: John, Kindra, Charles, Danica, Thomas, Adam, Mitch, Jack, and Leo. Work with Reedsy was funded in part by a grant from the Southwest Minnesota Arts Council with funds provided by the McKnight Foundation.

Hiraeth: (noun) a homesickness for a place to which you cannot return, a home that maybe never was; the nostalgia, the yearning, the grief for the lost places of your past

CHAPTER ONE

Maverick smelled trouble, and a Labrador knows what a Labrador's nose knows. Maybe I didn't appreciate his habit of lugging dirty laundry through the house or stealing my dinner when I turned my back, but he howled on key when my landlady played piano, and he read me like a book.

Maverick dragged me through the streets near my apartment and as we finished our speedy trek on the sidewalk lining Maple Street, my breathing returned to normal.

With one yard left to pass before landing home, an energetic preschooler toddled out to greet us or, more to the point, to greet Maverick, arms upraised and all smiles. "Hi, lady. Here, doggy," she said around her giggles.

I watched in amazement as Maverick sat in answer to the "sit" cue I offered. He didn't respond to many cues and I quickly dug out a treat. As the pink-and-white gingham ruffles on her pinafore flounced nearer, I stepped between the girl and my dog and scanned the yard for someone to give permission for them to meet.

In the blink of an eye, the toddler skirted around me, grabbed Maverick by the collar, and nestled her blond curls into his muscular black chest. Maverick cocked his head and glanced at me with a polite grin tugging at his lips. I signaled him to "stay," and I handed him another treat. I kept one eye on him and the little bundle as I searched the yard for a guardian.

The woman on the porch might have been stunning if her face hadn't been red bordering on purple. She stepped outside and I flinched when the screen door slammed, sounding like a gunshot.

"Get that mangy mutt away from my Emma!" The woman hurtled down the steps onto the cluttered lawn and tripped on the raised basket arm of a rusty yellow Tonka trencher. She grabbed her ankle, winced in pain, and limped in our direction.

She tried to wrench the child away from Maverick, but tiny fingers squeezed his blaze-orange collar. Maverick struggled to stay next to me, shifting his weight from paw to paw. The woman peeled Emma's fingers off the collar one by one and shuttled the little girl behind her amid cries of, "Good doggy," and "No, Mommy."

"Did he hurt you, baby?"

"No." The little girl squirmed to get back to Maverick. "Doggy!"

The mother's hand took a wild detour through her

tangled mane. She dropped her hand to her side, and growled, "Keep that mongrel away from my daughter."

"He's not—" Maybe he was. But even before I could finish, she spun on her heels and towed the girl toward their front door. Emma glanced back at Maverick with longing in her eyes. I wish I could've read Maverick's body language. Maybe everything would have turned out differently.

"Heel, Maverick." When he followed the cue, I scrounged up another treat.

I rented the back half of Ida Clemashevski's stately Queen Anne-styled home. Maverick waited for me to open the gate and then pulled me into our yard, where Ida sat on the porch.

"Here, Maverick," Mrs. Clemashevski said with open arms. I stumbled behind Maverick as he raced up the steps. He burrowed his head into her lap and she rustled his ears. His tail thumped the decking.

"Join me for supper tonight?" Mrs. Clemashevski elicited a smile and a satisfied groan with the promise of her stupendous cooking.

"I'd love to, but shouldn't I make something for you?" I said.

"I've had your cooking—thank you very much—and until you expand your repertoire beyond charred macaroni and stringy cheese, I'll pass."

I feigned hurt. "You like my peanut butter and jelly sandwiches."

She rolled her eyes.

"I don't think our neighbors like us much."

"Patience, Katherine Jean Wilk." Mrs. Clemashevski sounded like a Zen Master but looked a little like a gypsy with wisps of her freshly dyed red-orange hair peeking out around a multicolored silk scarf. "Your students like you just fine. They just need to get to know you."

We looked for kind faces when out on our walks, but at sixty-five pounds, Maverick was a somewhat large specimen of British Lab, and residents who didn't know him tended to bolt when his powerful figure padded nearby. A lot had happened in the two months since I'd moved to Columbia to teach high school math, and Maverick had gained a well-earned reputation as a rather frightening resource-guarding dog, me being the well-guarded resource.

Or it could have had something to do with the bodies he'd found.

CHAPTER TWO

A fter I spent thirty minutes plucking soggy streamers from our tree limbs, Ida warned me about the pitfalls of homecoming, the week when students' attention focused on the next rousing event. Rather than compete for quality study time, I assigned a logic problem for the weekend.

"In honor of the Cougar/Pirate football game tonight, please riddle me this. Twelve pirates aboard a ship each have a coin to identify their authenticity. One of the pirates is a phony and holds a fake coin. The only characteristic that distinguishes the fake coin from the real coins is its weight, which is a tiny bit lighter. The captain has a perfectly balanced scale. What's the least number of times he must use the scale to ensure he finds the fake coin and the imposter?"

Two students shadowed me to my desk, gripping the homework sheet on top of their pile of books. Before they could ask any questions, I said, "It's just for fun. Give it your best shot."

They exchanged confused looks, shrugged, and left. I sat down and took a deep breath before turning to work on my lesson plans.

A door opened and running footsteps broke the tenuous peace. Rounding the corner and out of breath, one of my students blew out her words. "Come on, Ms. Wilk. We're already late and you don't want to skip your first coronation. Carlee's sister could be the next queen."

Lorelei Calder looked so hopeful; I couldn't escape this homecoming tradition without hurting her feelings. "Let's go."

We raced to the auditorium. I couldn't hear Lorelei over the blaring music, but she waved then wound her way through the crowd into the bleachers to sit with her friends and watch the action unfold onstage. I found a space and pressed against the people-packed wall, blinded by the swirling lights.

Each toe touch for the eight candidates' final promenade had been choreographed. The fidgety girls marched across the stage in step to a pulsing fanfare, trailing the lively patterns of assigned spotlights, their gowns floating behind them. Flowing tresses rippled in their wake. Vibrant colors outlined bright white teeth clenched in broad grins. Coronations were ceremonial affairs: vivid lights, glittering dresses with matching shoes, chic hairdos, manicured nails polished in complementary colors, and makeup applied in smoky hues.

One by one the candidates lined up, and nervous energy bubbled among them. One grasped another's hand, and soon all eight were tethered for good luck, giggling neophytes teetering on their sky-high heels.

The newly crowned Homecoming Prince and King sat on makeshift thrones and tried to remain indifferent but failed, with their constant high-fives and smiles breaking through forced nonchalance.

I scoured the sea of students, looking for familiar faces. Carlee Parks sat in the third row and beamed as she caught her sister's eye. She wriggled her fingers under her chin and then her brow furrowed. Beautiful, blond, blue-eyed Ana looked lovely in her teal mermaid gown overlaid with mocha-colored lace, giving it a vintage flair, but Ana's smile seemed forced, her movements stiff. More than nervousness flickered across her face.

The emcee flapped an envelope above his head to quiet the audience, but they ignored him. The young man whistled and exaggerated his movements to attract their attention.

The girl standing next to him scanned the results then sashayed behind the expectant candidates. She paraded back and forth, drawing the process out as long as possible, stopping behind every candidate, assessing each young lady's claim to the crown, brandishing the tiara over each head, tormenting all of us. I couldn't imagine how the girls felt. When the crowd's gasps turned a bit menacing, she terminated her torturous teasing.

The crown descended, and Ana's mouth formed the words, "Oh, no."

CHAPTER THREE

After the coronation, I returned to my classroom and ran my hand over the engraved nameplate delineating professional ownership. It read, Ms. WILK. I closed my eyes and inhaled the light lemony scent left on the desks, courtesy of the cleaning crew.

After my husband was killed, I gave up a career in cybersecurity, and to secure my first teaching contract, I agreed to take on the extracurricular supervision of science club and mock trial. Columbia High School seemed like a good place for me.

The celebratory week of homecoming would culminate next Friday when the Columbia Cougars football team took on the Sauk Rapids Storm. If I'd been paying closer attention, I might've seen the storm brewing. In the middle of all the goings-on, my principal had scheduled an open house four weeks into the year, providing an opportunity for teachers to communicate concerns early enough to be able to make a positive difference for their students. And I planned to be prepared.

I had just finished reviewing my notes when a group of students swarmed my room. "Do we have a meeting today?" I wondered aloud.

Lorelei printed the words SCIENCE CLUB FORMATION in large black letters across the top of the SMART Board. Underneath the words, she wrote Ashley next to president, Brenna next to vice-president, and Brock next to by-laws committee chairman.

"What time will we be done today, Ms. Wilk?" asked Ashley.

"What time will we *finish?*" said Lorelei, a sometimes-too-smart-for-her-own-good junior. She surprised me by repeating one of my favorite lines. "Cakes and pies are done; people are finished. And that would be when we have completed our agenda." The wheels of her mind whirred behind those dark eyes, magnified by her bookish glasses.

She wrote secretary but before she turned around, the unified voices shouted, "Lorelei!"

"Ms. Wilk, look at my new shoes," Brenna said, pointing the toe of one of her patent-leather ruby-red pumps.

Lorelei rolled her eyes.

"Don't you just love them?" said Ashley. "We went shopping in New London, the perfect place for our retail therapy. And I picked up this sweater." She modeled a hot-pink cardigan and Brenna cooed.

Brock's newly acquired homecoming crown set rakishly over one eye. "Hey, Carlee, tell Ana congrats for me. I didn't catch her after the coronation."

"Tonnenson, are we working out after this?" he asked the other young man in the room.

"Yup," said Galen Tonnenson. He'd realized the damage that was done to his system by the steroids his coach had provided and turned himself in. The coach was awaiting trial for various charges and Galen lost wrestling eligibility until after Christmas. But he looked happier and healthier than he had when the term began.

Carlee Parks joined us for her second meeting. Her raven-black hair hung straight to the middle of her back, and her gray eyes kept Galen in her sights.

You wouldn't know it at first glance, but these students worked hard and surpassed expectations in science, technology, and math.

With the friendly banter out of the way, Lorelei said, "We're thinking we might want to change the way we do things here."

Alarm bells clanged in my head, and my heart raced. Our club already had undergone a thorough examination after one of our inaugural members had been arrested for arranging drug parties. I didn't want everything to fall apart now.

"We'll have officers, a meeting agenda, and committee assignments," Ashley said. "We want to use our participation in the science club on our résumés. If you hold an office or take on leadership responsibility in an official club, it's more impressive on a college application."

I released the breath I'd held.

Lorelei continued matching names and offices.

"Snack chair*person*," Lorelei wrote. Prone to seriousness, her laughter sounded like tiny bells.

"That falls to Galen," said Brock. "But we're still one

job short," he said, tilting his head toward our newest member.

"I'd rather just sit on a committee until I see how this works for me," Carlee said in a rush.

"Then all in favor of accepting this slate of officers, say aye," said Lorelei.

After the unanimous vote, Galen grabbed Carlee's hand and raised it. "We volunteer to choose the next geocache."

Carlee snatched her hand away. "What's a geocache?"

"A high-tech scavenger hunt," Brenna said.

And for her first official act, Ashley said, "Meeting adjourned." And just like that, they were gone.

My phone buzzed. I checked the caller ID and a smile grew on my face. "Hi, Pete."

I met Dr. Pete Erickson the first time I ended up in the ER. We were trying to figure out our future, which meant we needed to share a bit of our past as well. Old fears resided in the nearest shadows, and I wasn't quite ready to shine a light on all of them.

"How about a picnic before the cross-country meet?" he said. "The weather channel's predicting an awesome day. I'm on call tonight, but I can meet you at Sibley State Park at eleven a.m. tomorrow."

"Sounds perfect. I've heard it's a great place to hike."

"It is." We both waited for someone to say something. The silence made me anxious. I added, "I'll bring lunch."

"Great. See you there."

Why on earth had I volunteered to bring lunch? I could do that, couldn't I?

I jumped at the knock behind me.

A curtain of black hair covered her face. She looked up

with worry in her eyes.

"What can I do for you, Carlee?"

"Have you seen Ana?" Carlee asked. "I can't find her."

I assured Carlee that her sister would turn up. With the crown came responsibilities and celebrations.

CHAPTER FOUR

More anxious than I guessed, I tossed and turned through the night and woke to the slimmest thread of peach sewing the night to day. I opened my current bedstand reading material and plunged so deeply into the cryptograms I missed the dawn entirely.

When I finally emerged from my morning ablutions, panic set in. I checked my fridge and cupboards. I found a jar of olives, a bottle of ketchup, and two cans of chicken soup. With no ideas forthcoming, I hoped I could persuade Mrs. Clemashevski to provide some insight into what would constitute a proper picnic lunch. I knocked on her door, then heard a pounding, a rattling, and an unexpectedly terse, "What?"

With trepidation, I answered, "It's Katie."

"Come," she called imperiously.

I opened the door to a room upended: piles of pots and pans on the countertops, empty drawers, overturned appliances, cupboard doors hanging ajar, leaning stacks of bakeware, and the microwave door standing open. Silverware clattered to the floor. Her kitchen provided ideal accommodations for each and every article of cookware she'd ever need, but she'd scattered everything all over.

"I can't find it," she lamented. "You know there's been a rash of burglaries. What if someone stole it?"

"What are you looking for?"

"The brown-checked tea cozy that fits over this." One hand gripped the filigreed handle of a buffed silver teapot while the other clung to its spout. She carefully set it in the microwave, protecting it from the chaos.

"It'll be here." I waded into the kitchen.

From my vantage point, half a foot taller than her just-under-five feet, I could see into the back of the highest shelves and found a mound of light-brown checked quilting. On my toes, arm fully outstretched, I snagged the ribbon tie and pulled it down.

"Oh, my." Relieved, Mrs. Clemashevski grabbed the tea cozy and crushed it to her ample bosom. Then she held the fabric up to the light as if examining clothes for an infant, judged it fitting, and snuggled it over the teapot, returning it to the cupboard.

"This is a family heirloom." She took a satisfied breath. "Thank you."

"Mrs. Clemashevski, could I borrow a picnic basket?"

She eyed me with suspicion. "Call me Ida. And why do you need a basket?" She was aware of my culinary ineptness and her curiosity was well founded.

"Pete and I are going to Sibley State Park, and I volunteered to pack a picnic lunch. Do you have any suggestions?" She stared at me. I turned toward the door.

She snorted. "When is this supposed picnic to take place?" she said as she hung a pan from the hood above her industrial stove.

My face flushed when I answered. "Eleven today."

She cleaned off a small area of the workstation and bustled to her refrigerator, swung open the heavy door of her stainless-steel Wolf Sub-Zero, rummaged through the shelves, and pulled open the drawers. She snagged a colorful armload of fresh produce. Hands full, she bumped the door closed with a wild hip swing and poured the fixings onto the counter. She grabbed a cutting board and a knife, which she offered to me, handle first. "Narrow slices," she ordered, wagging her forefinger and passing me carrots, radishes, tomatoes, celery, red and green bell peppers, and jicama.

I sliced carefully, but when slamming cupboards and rattling dishes made me turn my head, she scolded, "Keep your eyes on your work."

By the time I'd completed my task, I sighed. The room held a place for everything and everything gleamed from its place.

Ida examined the results of my assignment. "Not bad for someone who can't boil water," she said in jest, I hoped. Before I could utter a smart reply, she said, "Remember when you melted a spoon on the edge of your saucepan making pasta. I'll finish. Go."

For a hike in the woods, I chose a comfortable long-sleeved flannel shirt and donned a pair of worn Levi's, which possibly would, after a few more of Ida's luscious meals, fit well again. Her hearty food tasted marvelous, a superior change from the institutional fare I'd consumed when I'd stayed at the Center for Traumatic Brain Injury while my dad recuperated. I brushed on some tinted mascara to bring out the blue in my eyes and dabbed a little pink onto my cheeks.

Ida delivered a green-and-tan wicker picnic basket and heaved it onto my kitchen counter.

"What's in there?"

"Plastic place settings, a tablecloth, a baguette and olive oil, pasta salad, a Ziploc bag of crudités, dip for the veggies, and shaved parmesan cheese with croutons. I would send wine," she said and winked, "but it's a little early in the day." She handed me the beverage cooler and a detailed map with directions to the park entrance.

"Thanks. I couldn't have done it without you!"

"I know," she said, her eyes sparkling.

I packed a collapsible bowl, two bottles of water, and one of Ida's homemade dog biscuits for Maverick.

* * *

If I hadn't pulled over to count the deer in the field, my Jetta would have been crushed by the idiot van driver rounding the corner at top speed. I vented for a solid minute and still arrived with five minutes to spare. I purchased the Minnesota State Parks permit from the unmanned registration kiosk and followed the instructions on the self-registration envelope. Harboring a tiny bit of ill will at the driver, I ripped off the user copy to stick on my windshield, but before I slid the payment envelope into the wooden slot, gravel crunched under the tires of another vehicle.

A door clicked open, and I heard a lighthearted, "Hey there, pretty lady."

I turned, and batting my eyelashes, asked, "To whom are you speaking?"

Pete bounded from his royal blue Ram truck, a toothy grin beaming on his delectable face. "Sorry. I forgot to tell you there'd be a fee. Let me get that for you."

I chuckled at his belated chivalry. "I'm valid for a year. Thanks." The envelope finished its journey into the slot. We drove in through the open gates. A variety of trees, just beginning to change color in the autumn warmth, hugged the gently curving road. Skinny streams of sunlight sliced through the thick canopy. The drive ended in the nearly empty parking lot in the shadow of the Interpretive Center.

I grabbed my lightweight jacket and clipped the leash on Maverick. We joined Pete in front of an engraved wooden map that outlined the walking paths.

"We have a four-mile hike beginning here." He pointed, tracing the route with his forefinger.

"It's gorgeous," I said, taking in the surroundings.

"It's perfect."

My face flushed when I caught his brown eyes looking at me instead of the park view.

The trail opened onto a field of native prairie grasses, waving in the slight breeze. I turned my face to a periwinkle sky and drank in the intense beauty. "I have lunch in the car," I murmured.

"I'll believe it when I see it," he said and laughed.

The first one hundred yards began with a steep incline and I skidded on the grass. Pete stepped in front of me and put his hands on my waist to steady me, smiling all the way down to his toes.

"Thanks," I gasped, and too soon he released me.

Thick, crisp vegetation encroached on the well-worn path, making it difficult for Maverick to heel.

"I think you can let him off-leash here," Pete said.

Freed, Maverick darted ahead of us, zipping from one shimmying leaf to another, circling back to verify our whereabouts, then dashing to the right or to the left, investigating the territory. He flushed songbirds and chased a few gray squirrels foolish enough to show themselves.

Pete took my hand. Our threesome seemed perfectly natural for Maverick, but as nice as it was, I struggled to keep my burgeoning anxiety in check. I liked spending time with Pete but I knew he wanted an explanation about my dad's accident and the death of my husband. I've heard silence is golden, but in this instance, the silence was also painless. I feared summoning the monster in my memories.

We both spoke at the same time. I said, "I suppose you'd like to know about…"

And Pete said, "I have some exciting news to tell you…" We stammered our Minnesota niceties, but Pete won with the old cliché, "Ladies, first."

"Should I go chronologically?" He shrugged in answer. "I was born—"

"You don't need to go that far back. Tell me about your cryptanalysis career."

"I finished my studies at—"

"Wild Thing" burst from Pete's pocket, the mechanical ringtone completely out of place. He threw me an apologetic look and tipped his head to check the phone screen. "Sorry. I wasn't expecting any calls. I took the day off. But it's the ER. Excuse me?"

Saved by the bell! I really didn't want to tell him how sadness had enveloped me the entire flight home from London, nor the conversation I'd had with the flight attendant who'd asked with sincere gentleness, "Are you still in love or have you forgotten?" I'd loved Charles and discovering the love was reciprocated was a dream come true, until it became a nightmare.

Pete's right hand brushed his wayward locks away from his forehead, a familiar gesture while concentrating, and then he quickly pocketed his phone. Pain clouded his eyes.

"I'm sorry. I have to go, Katie. It's my dad. Susie said he's been admitted to the hospital for observation and a workup for some chest pains."

My grip tightened on Pete's arm reassuringly. "Let's go."

"You and Maverick stay," he said distractedly. "I'll call you when I know more." And off he ran.

I'd met Pete's dad a number of times in his professional capacity as the chief of police. He was very good at his job and a nice man, to boot. I hoped he'd be well.

"It's just you and me, Maverick."

Researching the activity for my science club students, I opened the geocaching app on my phone. I chose the easiest cache for Maverick and me to find. Time spent outdoors on the hunt gave us a purposeful trek while waiting for Pete to call. We hiked to the top of Mount Tom. A breathtaking panorama equal to any in Minnesota lay before us. We looked down on colorful fields that crisscrossed farmland and took in the water towers of three nearby towns. Against the blue sky, the few cottony clouds seemed within arm's reach. Small birds somersaulted energetically, and a few larger birds swooped and plunged in and out of the treetops. Pete was right, of course; the park was a wonderful place to hike.

We found the geocache in a camouflaged ammunition canister hidden just off the walking path. After letting Maverick sniff the container, I signed the log and started back to the parking lot.

Maverick increased his pace and also increased his distance away from me, his attempt to keep us outside. The sun slid behind a cloud, and the air chilled.

I called to him. He ignored me. I couldn't hear him rustling through the underbrush, so I backtracked and spotted him about twenty yards off the path, silently on point, having stalked some unsuspecting quarry.

"Maverick." My call garnered no response. "Nice try, Maverick. Let's go home." I whistled to no avail and trudged up the hill to fetch him. I made plenty of noise to roust Maverick's prey and release him from point. I saw nothing but large birds diving above us. "Maverick," I called again.

He finally acknowledged my conspicuous approach with an infinitesimal head turn. My gaze was drawn toward the object of his focus. Glistening in the intense sunlight, partially hidden from view, concealed by a tangle of leaves, was a collection of sparkling stones, twinkling and reflecting so brightly that I had to shield my eyes for an instant. Caught in a maple embrace, maybe ten feet off the ground, flickered a ring of crystals.

"What did you find, big guy?"

The stones resembled gems, and since diamonds are a girl's best friend, or so I've heard, the scintillation drew me in.

"No, Maverick! No!" I cried. I squeezed my eyes closed and dropped to my knees.

CHAPTER FIVE

I clipped the leash to Maverick's collar and ruffled the fur on his neck. "Now what do we do?" I asked rhetorically and punched in the number I knew by heart.

"Hey, Katie. Dad's doing great. Sorry I didn't call. I've been busy seeing to his every need."

In the background, I heard a deep voice growl, "Liar!"

"Pete?"

"How was your walk? Are you on your way back to town?"

"Pete, I found a body."

He chuckled. "Yeah, right." He'd been very understanding the day we first met when Maverick and I had found the body of the School Board Chairman in the wetlands slough near Ida's home, and now he calmly awaited a punch line that wasn't coming. "Katie?"

"Actually, Maverick found it."

"Where are you?"

"What's going on?" the deep voice bellowed.

I described standing near enough to make out the edges of the parking lot and the building roofline, partway up a hill. "We're northwest of the Interpretive Center."

"I'll be right there, Katie. Don't move." I expected a reprimand but instead I heard, "Are you okay?"

"I'm alive." My left eyebrow twitched. "Pete?"

"Yes."

"There's a crown."

"And?"

"Carlee Parks was looking for her sister Ana, who was just crowned Homecoming Princess."

"I'm on my way."

A kettle of turkey vultures soared and circled overhead, swooping scavengers intent on ravaging carrion. I hoped they hadn't yet found this source—a body with long blond hair and bare legs dotted with fiery red spots, splayed and unmoving. I quivered, listening to the awful drone of black flies buzzing in the dry air. A tiara dangled in the tree above the body.

I thought I'd steeled myself with a protective anesthetic armor, but Maverick turned to me and swiped a sloppy tongue against the tears streaming down my cheeks.

After what seemed an interminable time, Pete's truck sailed into the lot and slammed into a parking space next to my car. He jumped out of the cab wearing his navy County Coroner windbreaker, carrying a small black bag. He searched through the trees. When he looked in my direction, my hand rose in a limp greeting. As he jogged up the hill, the passenger door of the truck opened, and Susie slithered out.

Nurse Susie Kelton assisted Pete in the ER and worked with the County Coroner's office. They'd dated for a while and I think she still had a thing for Pete, but he seemed oblivious to her charms, or so I hoped. As she exited the truck, she closed the door and stepped up to the side mirror, reshaped her auburn hair, then gestured to the emergency vehicle and two sheriff's cruisers that had followed them into the park.

Although I'm certain there was absolutely no way for him to know it by the look on my face, I couldn't have been happier to see anyone. Pete inspected the terrain as he neared Maverick and me, investigating scientifically, looking for an anomaly, evidence of death by accident or foul play.

His voice cut through the heavy silence. "How do you react to poison ivy?"

I remained kneeling, petting Maverick, waiting for instructions. "I don't know."

"You're surrounded by it. Don't move." He called down to the emergency crew. "This hill is covered with poison ivy. We need to lay Tyvek."

After donning white paper coveralls, which made them look like workers in a nuclear facility, they clanked open the rear of the ambulance. From the back of the blue-and-white emergency vehicle emerged a thick roll of white paper, which they spread in sections of ten feet, two swaths wide.

The paper suit looked good on Susie. I'm not sure what wouldn't. She delivered a second suit to Pete. Mindful of the greenery, he shoved his booted feet through the elastic encircling the ankles, elbowed his arms and torso in, and zipped up the front. Then he pulled on purple nitrile gloves and helped settle the last few sections of the safety paper trail between tree trunks and over brambles to Maverick and me.

"Leaves of three, let it be," he muttered. "This is all poison ivy, Katie."

Duly chastised, I said, "I wasn't paying attention. I followed Maverick here."

Pete continued to lay sections of the paper toward the body. "Susie, take her down the hill."

I rose and edged onto the protective tarp. "We can do it," I said, exasperation thrumming in my throat at the sight of her smirking face. Her laughing eyes pierced my confidence.

We'd taken only a few steps when I heard Pete sigh. "Oh, no."

Maverick and I stopped in response, and Susie took a forcible step toward us to propel us down the slope. Not relishing her escort, I shook my head. "We can do it," I said again, and continued toward the parking lot, silently acknowledging the crime-scene photographer as he made his way to the body.

At the bottom of the hill, one of the EMTs handed me antibacterial wipes for my hands and an unopened box marked Tecnu Poison Ivy Scrub.

I scrupulously washed my hands. When I finished, he handed me a damp towel to wipe Maverick. Neither of us appeared to have any adverse reaction to the urushiol oil, but I'd be careful to wash Maverick again, launder my clothes, and sanitize my hiking shoes.

When they finished with the on-site examination, Pete

beckoned the techs, who rolled in a metal gurney, and gently lifted the body, placing it into the forbidding shroud.

The officers removed their caps. With profound silence and respect, punctuated by the rattling of the gurney, the team moved the metal carriage down to the ambulance and loaded the body into the rear. With a final collision of metal to metal, the door slammed, burying the body in a mobile tomb.

CHAPTER SIX

Ma'am?" A resonant voice wrenched my gaze from the retreating strobing light.

A rumble from Maverick brought me to attention. "Yes."

"You called in about the body?" I nodded, and he took out a notepad and pen. He was an older trooper with hazel eyes and light-brown hair peppered with gray. His tan uniform blended in with the surroundings. On his head sat a brown felt campaign hat with a gold-corded band. He searched my face before asking, "What brought you out here?"

"I was hiking and geocaching."

"Geocaching? I don't remember one being placed out this way."

"We found it near Mount Tom, and on our way back to the car, my dog wandered off and discovered the body." *Again,* I thought.

"Did you touch anything?

"Nothing near the body."

"Did you see anyone? Notice anything out of the ordinary?"

I shook my head.

"Why did you call the coroner before law enforcement?" The question caught me off guard.

"I know Pete--Dr. Erickson." When I'm nervous, I sound annoyed. "In fact, he was here with me this morning before he was called to the hospital to look in on his dad." I'd have to ask Pete about his dad.

A flicker of amusement kindled in the trooper's eyes. "How did you know the victim was deceased?"

With a start, I realized I didn't have an answer. "I guess I really didn't know."

"Name?"

"I don't know who it is." When his eyebrows shot up, I understood my mistake. "Katie Wilk."

"Address?"

"3141 North Maple Street in Columbia."

"Thanks." He snapped his notebook closed, tapped the brim of his hat, and strode purposefully toward Pete. They shook hands. Pinioned with both sets of eyes, I felt like the subject of their prolonged conversation and focused my attention on Maverick.

I could have lost myself in the green thicket, buried the sadness, and hidden from the anguish brought upon some unsuspecting family. I'd experienced the abrupt, sudden loss of a loved one when my husband of seventeen days was killed and never would wish to inflict that heartache on anyone else. Almost two years ago, Dad, Charles, and I had been biking on the trail near my home town when my dad had been taken down by a bullet. He still suffered the effects of his traumatic brain injury. The second shot took Charles. I missed him. And we still didn't know who'd pulled the trigger.

Susie stripped off the white spacesuit and gloves like a professional and meticulously balled up the used outerwear then added it to a huge bin positioned at the bottom of the hill. She flashed a smile at Pete and the trooper and joined them in her professional capacity. She and I might have been at odds where Pete was concerned, but when some students had gotten a bad combination of drugs, she'd proved her worth as a good nurse and we'd found a common enemy. Susie and I had declared a truce and did all we could to protect the kids. That tragedy averted, I think we again held conflicting intentions. I envied her involvement in the discussion until I remembered why everyone was here.

When their conclave broke up, Pete shook the trooper's hand, and he and Susie walked toward me. "Katie, let me drive you home."

"I can drive myself home," I said with a little defiance.

"I have something I'd like to discuss with you," he said.

There it was. "How will you get your truck home?" At that moment, the truck jumped into gear and pebbles sprayed as it raced from the lot as if on fire, Susie owning the wheel.

"Pete? Was it Ana?"

He shook his head as we walked toward my car. "No, not her."

"Thank God."

Pete opened the doors. Maverick jumped into the rear seat, his private domain—a perch from which to observe everything going on around him and still keep an eye on me, and I took the passenger seat. I dug my keys out of my pocket and dropped them into Pete's outstretched hand.

Pete started the car and cleared his throat. I cut him off with a stern look. "If this is a 'You should have been more careful' speech, I couldn't have done anything about what happened and if it's a 'What's with your bad luck?' speech, I'm not in the mood."

He gritted his teeth. "She suffered before she died. Her hands were bound."

"It wasn't an accident?"

"It couldn't have been. She had an adverse allergic reaction. Her airway closed and she slowly suffocated. Someone let her die. That's one deviant I'd like to put away."

The car rumbled on the bumpy blacktop as we rode in silence to Ida's home.

Pete's truck sat on Maple Street and Susie revved the engine as Pete drove my car down the long path to the detached garage. "Do you want me to come in for a while?" he asked with genuine concern.

"No, thanks. I know you have work to do," I answered, looking down at my hands clasped in my lap. "Sorry for the way I acted. Is there anything I can do?"

A tapping at the window startled us, and we looked into Susie's mischievous eyes. Pete pressed the button to lower the window.

"What do you think?" she said with too much enthusiasm.

I glowered at Pete with disbelief.

"Now isn't the time, Susie." Pete's face turned crimson. He crawled from the driver's seat, reached around to the back door, and released Maverick into the yard.

"Time for what?" I called as I pulled my door release and stepped out of the car.

A high-pitched voice rang from the next yard. "Petey!" I almost didn't recognize my cranky neighbor without her glaring red face. She waved at us through the scrollwork of the rails in the black wrought-iron fence. "Is that *your* beautiful dog?" Maverick's transformation in her eyes was nothing short of incredulous.

"And here we go," said Susie, rolling her eyes.

I gawked, and Pete followed a scampering Maverick to the front gate, where my neighbor and her little girl Emma closed in to lavish hugs and kisses on a dog extremely intent on pleasing.

I jostled Susie out of my way. "Sorry." I halted Maverick's progress toward the tiny outstretched fingers, much to his bewilderment. "He needs a bath!" Pete, realizing the danger the residual poison ivy oils posed, stepped out of the yard and closed the gate behind him.

"Pamela, this is Maverick. He belongs to Katie."

"Petey and I go way back, Kathy. He let me get away before he went off to college and has regretted it ever since." She giggled.

"It's Katie," Susie said through clenched teeth with precision befitting a surgeon. Sparks flew in the air, and it looked like a hockey face-off.

Pamela placed a hand on Pete's arm. "Why don't you come in for a cup of coffee? You're still addicted to caffeine, I assume."

"You assume correctly," Pete said, "but I have work

to do. Maybe some other time we can all get together for coffee." Susie shook her head and stomped toward the truck.

"Well, Kathy! Any friend of Petey's is a friend of mine." Pamela bared her teeth in what I'd hardly construe as a smile, gently picked up a distressed Emma, and pressed the adorable child into her shoulder, kissing the top of her curly head as she walked away. Emma wiggled her fingers in farewell.

Susie tossed Pete's keys over the truck. They landed in his outstretched hand, and I thought I heard her say, "You have to tell her soon."

CHAPTER SEVEN

The Friendship Center buzzed after the Sunday service. I snagged a chocolate doughnut from a tray bearing a hand-printed sign that read, PROVIDED BY THE FELLOWSHIP COMMITTEE—LOOKING FOR YOU TO VOLUNTEER. We had coffee with one of Ida's jovial dance partners, Cash Schultz. The clean-shaven man had a round face, full pink cheeks, and the most sparkling sapphire-blue eyes in the room, which helped distract from his balding head. He furrowed his normally smooth brow and leaned toward us conspiratorially.

"They found a body in Sibley State Park yesterday," he said with true sadness, my own part in the discovery undisclosed. "It was Lorelei—"

I inhaled sharply and choked on bits of doughnut.

Coughing into a paper napkin, I couldn't believe it. I saw the body. I would have known. Pete would've told me. Maybe he couldn't tell me. Lorelei had a brilliant future, full of classes, dances, dates, graduation, and college. She had a life to fill with girlfriends and boyfriends and late nights and beautiful days. A flood of tears came unbidden, and I labored to breathe.

Ida gently rubbed my back as I urged him to continue. Mr. Schultz knelt on the floor next to me. "I should have been impeccable with my word choice," he said. "She is not your Lorelei."

The spasms in my throat abated, and he continued, "She was identified as Lorelei Therese Fiorillo, twenty-two, of Center Valley, a little town north of here. Her death was caused by exposure to an allergen. That poor girl died a horrible death." He dropped his head to his hand.

* * *

Once home, I took a call from Pete.

"Could we get together this afternoon, maybe walk Maverick and make up for yesterday?"

"I'm expecting a call, but any time after one works. And come with an appetite. I owe you lunch."

Ida promised to teach me to use my oven, and today we were going to make a dish she called Hawaiian Lunch for Company. The bulging bag of groceries sat on my countertop next to a glistening new aluminum nine-by-thirteen-inch pan, a shredder, two lethal-looking knives, a set of black measuring spoons, and white measuring cups. Brightly colored three-by-five-inch index cards were curled inside nested Pyrex glass bowls.

My lesson began with a brisk knock on the door and a

grand entrance. My whole being grinned as this diminutive woman rescued me once again.

For the next hour, we cut and shredded, measured and poured, whisked and stirred, melted and sprinkled, and set Swiss cheese and honey-ham sandwiches drenched in a buttery sugar glaze to bake. We shredded cabbage for slaw and dressed it with a homemade vinegar mixture. A banana bread pudding baked in the oven, and what Ida called a hard sauce bubbled on the stove.

I smiled when my phone rang. My dad's physician hinted that in anticipating his needs, I'd made my dad overly dependent on me, so Elizabeth had banished me from the step-down unit at the TBI center. They were right; without my interference, his recuperation was remarkable. Ever since, he'd begun to check in on Sunday afternoons, when his wife took a break after her lunch visit. He told me how hard he worked to get out of there, but I kept the call short so he wouldn't tire.

After our talk, Ida put me to work. She directed me to squeeze lemons, muddle strawberries, sprinkle sugar, and add water to an ornate glass pitcher. The doorbell rang just as I finished setting the table for three. Ida mimed removing my apron, which I did, as well as primp for a moment in front of the mirror in the hallway between the kitchen and the living room. My face had regained some of its fullness, and the pink in my cheeks wasn't entirely unbecoming. I ran my hand through the waves of light-brown hair that tended to do its own thing, wiped a speck of poppy seed from my chin, and swung open the door.

Pete looked up from his black cowboy boots, his dark brown eyes appraising. A black sport coat over a black T-shirt covered the broad expanse of his shoulders. He wore pressed blue jeans and his customary leather belt with a big silver buckle. A white grin flashed as he held up a bouquet of pink carnations. "For you." As I reached out to accept them, the bag he carried in his other hand clunked to the floor. He took my hand, causing immediate heat but before he released his grip, he stopped and sniffed the air. A question clouded his chiseled features. "Something smells great."

We entered the kitchen, and all trace of my fairy godmother had disappeared along with the dirty dishes. The table had been magically reset for two, side by side on the mismatched chairs, a lighted candle in the center of the table. The pleased look on Pete's face belied my surprise.

The timer on the oven dinged, breaking the spell.

"Sit," I ordered.

"Look at that," Pete said with a hint of pride. Maverick sat in answer to the request. "What ya got, boy?" Pete walked over, and Maverick dropped a pair of lacey red panties into his outstretched hand. My face burned. I was a second too late figuring out that Maverick had raided my laundry hamper again. I wished I could melt into the floor when Pete grinned and handed me the bundle.

After our first bite, I asked, "How's your dad?"

"Doing well. Resting in the hospital," he said, around a bite of ham sandwich. "Ronnie Christianson is in charge now."

"Does he know what to do?"

"He will. He has Dad on speed dial."

Pete nearly licked his plate clean. "This is great!"

"You do know I had help," I confessed as we cleared the last of the dessert dishes from the table.

"Could you do it again?" I nodded. "Then you've

learned lesson one." *It was about time.*

"Mr. Schultz said the woman we found was from Center Valley," I said. "Do they have any suspects yet?"

"No, but Katie, promise me that you'll stay out of it."

He squeezed my hand, and I responded, involuntarily curling my fingers around his. *If I can,* I thought.

Maverick loved retrieving. Pete grabbed a Frisbee from the bag he'd left near the door and headed outside. "Do you think he can catch it midair?"

In their first attempt, Pete simultaneously tossed the disc and asked Maverick to fetch. The dog raced like a bullet, and before the Frisbee hit the ground, he snatched it and commenced his return. After a few more throws, Pete tossed the disc higher, and Maverick's powerful legs sent him soaring. "Maverick can almost fly," Pete said, putting the discs away.

"We didn't get to finish our talk yesterday, Katie."

"It's all right."

We sat next to each other on the two blue Adirondack chairs on the patio, but before Pete could continue, a voice dripping with honey called over the fence, "Petey."

I treasured the astonished look on his face as much as I hated welcoming my nosey bleached-blond neighbor. She wore a lightweight lacey top over tight white leggings. Bright red bangles accented her slim wrists, and long red earrings dangled from lobes peeking out beneath a swirly up-do. She strutted through the gate in shiny red stilettos. Carefully following the pavement, Pamela and Emma invaded our space.

"I heard the awful news," she said, dragging Emma into the yard. "You poor thing, having to work on all those dead people."

Emma's eyes lit when she spotted Maverick. She pulled away from her mother and skipped up to Maverick, who sat properly, tail beating the grass behind him. "Is she okay with that dog?" Pamela sought permission from Pete, who directed her question to me. I nodded.

After an uncomfortable moment, Pete stood and offered his chair. Pamela sat. I asked, "Would you like some strawberry lemonade, Pamela?"

"Certainly. And do you have any apple juice for Emma? Citric acid isn't very good for teeth, and hers are so new I don't want to destroy her chances at having a winning smile. We know how that works. Don't we, Kathy?"

"It's Katie," Pete said.

When I reappeared a minute later with a tray of lemonade and an apple juice box from my lunch hoard, Pete occupied the seat next to Pamela. She leaned forward, laughing and drawing a manicured talon down the length of his arm. I felt like an invisible waitress as I held the tray in front of these two people who snatched glasses and napkins and continued to reminisce.

"Thank you very much," Emma said politely, reaching for the juice box.

"You're very welcome," I replied, settling next to her.

Parts of their conversation drifted toward us. "I hear her hands were tied behind her."

Pete's confounded voice came through. "Where did you hear that?"

Pamela whispered something unintelligible, and then she remarked, "So she was a queen too."

Emma's little hand touched mine. "Can he shake?" she asked.

"Yes, and he's learning to do more." For the next

few minutes, Maverick sat, raised his paw in greeting, laid down, rolled over, played dead, and retrieved his tennis ball to Emma's heartwarming giggle.

Pete rose from his chair and helped Pamela stand.

"Inside, Maverick," I cued. Maverick had practiced opening the patio door by pulling at a towel wrapped around the handle. He raced between an unsuspecting Pete and Pamela, upending the glass in her hand. Pink lemonade spilled down the front of her white ensemble.

Emma applauded as Maverick slid the door open. Her golden curls formed a bouncing halo around her head, and her emerald eyes crinkled into narrow slits behind chubby cheeks. I almost clapped with her, almost.

CHAPTER EIGHT

Pamela clutched Emma's hand and stumbled out of the yard, furiously dabbing at the front of her shirt with a paper napkin. Her spikey heels sank into the lawn each time she missed the pavement. When she'd disappeared through her front door, Pete burst into laughter. I heard a rapping on a window and looked up to see Ida's mirth-filled eyes contradicting her shaking head. I joined them.

"That went over well," Pete said. As our chuckles subsided, he said, "Sorry about that. We dated a long time ago. I just don't get it. Pammy dumped me. Now she acts like it was my idea. Either way, it was for the best."

Pammy?

"She made the right move. Adam truly loves her. And he's a great guy."

He looked uncomfortable, his eyes traveling to the rose trellis over the entry. *Oh, oh,* I thought. He turned to look me in the eye. *This is it.* I sighed. *I can take it. He just wants to be friends.*

"I wanted to tell you I've been accepted into a specialized fellowship program through the university, to improve emergency room techniques and help me learn the telemedicine technology more efficiently. We're one of three outstate hospitals that were awarded a grant for new equipment and the education to use it."

"Congratulations. That's great!" The look on his face was pained. "Isn't it?"

"Sure. But it's a twelve-week part-time commitment with HCPH because they use the most up-to-date equipment and have the most diverse and serious emergent cases. I'd be trained to use state-of-the-art technology, how to apply Telestroke, and how to monitor cardiac resynchronization therapy devices or gastric neuro-stimulators. The process will improve our patient treatment." The word "ebullient" sprang to mind as his excitement waxed. But an abrupt alteration on his face stopped me short as he took my hand in his. "It runs Friday evening through Sunday afternoon three weekends a month."

My mouth formed an O. "Sounds like a great opportunity. You can't pass it up, Pete." His energy regained a foothold.

"Thanks!" He took my other hand and, facing me, said earnestly, "I love spending time with you, Katie. We'll have to make good use of the time we have together."

I smiled demurely. I'd thought it had been *my* life secrets I needed to share. Now I wasn't so certain. "Let's take Maverick for a walk?"

For the next hour, Pete explained how much Columbia Hospital would benefit from everything he could learn and the improvements to patient care. He'd also be allowed to work in a superior forensic laboratory, sharpening his skills as county coroner, wherein he concluded, "And the nefarious guy goes behind bars."

On our walk through the wetlands refuge, I located a few patches of moss I could use for our next science club experiment. Although we'd had relatively dry weather, the slough hosted a number of florae which survived in the damp environment. I scooped the slightly browning mass into a bag Pete held open for me.

"This is a great opportunity for you." I could only wish the best for him, but it also justified my relationship reticence. "What?" I asked.

He smiled and worked up a goofy grin before making a biking date with me for early the next evening.

* * *

Our scheduled science club days were Tuesday and Thursday, but my students seldom missed the opportunity to harass me after school, all in great fun, and today was no exception. They arrived unexpectedly, en masse, and requested an impromptu meeting.

"Can we borrow the GPS units?" Brock asked.

"*May* we," corrected Lorelei. I noticed her smile with relief.

"And *may* we also use the SMART Board and your computer to locate another geocache?" he added.

When they finished explaining geocaching to Carlee, Galen asked, "Do you have anything else we can do?"

"How about a terrarium you don't have to pay attention to?" I replied.

"Plants can live and grow without any care at all? No green thumb necessary?" said Carlee. "I might even be able to do that."

"I have everything we need if you'd like to try it."

Brenna and Ashley lined up the pea gravel, the activated carbon, the gauze, and the Super Glue. Brock opened the bag of organic soil and the seed packages. Lorelei divided the moss I'd collected. Carlee filled the spray bottle with water and when Galen waved the wooden craft stick like a tiny sword, she squirted him.

Each student grabbed an ornament and instruction sheet. "The magic ratio is one-third filled to two-thirds empty space to allow for adequate circulation," I told them. "Cover the bottom with pebbles. Then sprinkle enough carbon in each ball to coat the gravel."

Brenna had read ahead and busied herself cutting four-inch white gauze circles to fit over the carbon and stones.

"The soil follows," I said. I stirred the dirt, and the rich loamy aroma brought back wistful memories of springtime in England. "Stuff a small clump of moss into the ball then gently tamp it into the black medium with the craft sticks. You can sprinkle parsley seeds, alfalfa sprouts, or bean sprouts on top to give your terrarium an additional dimension. Dampen the layers with two squirts of water." Carlee giggled when Galen squirted her as well. "The last step is to seal the ball. Squeeze a wide bead of Super Glue around the top of the ornament and make sure the tin clamp is air tight and won't allow air or water to escape."

"When's Ms. Mackey coming back?" asked Brock while dropping in his seeds.

"Soon," I said, and I hoped it was true. My friend Jane Mackey had gone home to Georgia to recover from a near-fatal poisoning, and I missed her.

When they finished, the students returned each glass ball to a depression in the ornament box. I replaced the lid and secured it with packing tape so the ornaments would remain upright and untouched until the glue dried. Brock slid the box on top of the cupboard, keeping it out of harm's way and also prying eyes. And then they were gone.

On my way home, I planned my biking outfit.

I rounded the corner onto Maple Street and my mouth fell open as I passed through a gauntlet of cars and trucks lining both sides. I drove slowly, rubbernecking into the empty neighborhood yards beyond the vehicles—no people, no kids, no dogs, no cats.

More cars blocked our driveway and I thought Ida might be entertaining. We had yet to divulge birthday particulars. However, I thought I would've been invited to her party. I parked on the street and grabbed my briefcase. My car door clanged in the eerie silence and reverberated between the quiet houses.

I marched onto the porch and called for Ida, but she didn't answer. I searched my apartment for Maverick and he too was absent. It appeared I'd missed out on spending quality time with both of them. I thought about walking without Maverick, but that thought fell flat when I heard a door slam and I dashed outside.

A tall man stood in the yard next door massaging his lower back with his right hand. The fingers of his left hand tangled in his curly light-brown hair. I didn't mean to stare but his entire body pulsed with tension. Muscular arms charged out of his rumpled white shirt's short sleeves, and his broad back rippled with energy. As he turned toward me, anguish flooded dark eyes set deep in a large square face, his bottom lip quivered and tears threatened to spill down his ruddy cheeks.

Their front door crashed open and Pamela ran to the man who enfolded her, clutching her, swallowing her in his arms. His massive chest muffled her wretched sobs.

My phone emitted a buzz and pinged a text message. *An Amber Alert has been issued for Columbia, Minnesota. Text 'INFO' for details.*

The distant claxon of police sirens preceded the roar of four blue-and-white cars as they caromed around the corner and pulled to a stop in front of the house next door, lights flashing. The doors of the cruiser thunked closed. Officer Ronnie Christianson stood, straightened his bolo, and hitched his uniform pants over his bulging belly before entering the yard. The neighborhood came alive as people erupted from every household and were drawn next door. The rush dragged me in its wake.

The crowd hummed as an officer stood with a stack of clipboards and Officer Christianson called out, "Listen up." Everyone quieted. "We'll make teams of two or three, and each team will be given an area to search. Make sure you work the area in your grid, first in one direction, and then again in a direction ninety degrees from the original. If you see anything unusual or something warrants checking out, stick one of these markers in the ground next to it." He held up a wire stem with a yellow flag on top. "Be thorough, but the more ground we cover the better. Time is of the essence." Small groups lined up to accept clipboards and markers.

My insides churned. I was drawn toward the front of the line.

"Katie," Pete called as he jogged into the yard. He wrapped his arms around me, pinning my arms to my sides. He released me from his bear hug, took my hand and pulled me with him to the head of the line. Officer Christianson nodded at Pete. "How's the chief? We could sure use him."

"Getting better all the time. Where do you want us, Ronnie?"

My heart thudded in my chest when I glanced at the map clamped to the clipboard. Highlighted in pink, our area included the south side of the wetlands slough and the walking path around the pond Maverick and I tended to bypass for fear of what we might find again. The folks in line pressed forward to receive their instructions and we stepped away.

"Give me a sec." I dashed inside and changed shoes, grabbed a flashlight, and, with the chill encroaching earlier on our evenings as of late, I lifted a jacket off the hook by the door. Shrugging off a strange feeling, I raced outside.

"Pete?" I began. We set off at a quick pace.

Breaking through his single-minded concentration, he said, "Hmmm."

Afraid of the answer, I swallowed and asked, "What happened?"

Not breaking stride, he answered, "You hadn't heard? Emma has disappeared."

CHAPTER NINE

My cheerful neighbor, Maverick's tiny friend, the beautiful little girl with the sparkling personality, had vanished.

We confirmed our strategy before beginning the search and followed the path closest to the water first. We walked three feet apart, taking small steps. We crushed through the brush, probing, sliding the curtain of cattails to one side, scrutinizing any aberration in the terrain: a line of broken branches, tattered fabric, footprints, trash, anything that shouldn't be there.

We paused when we caught sight of a lone shovel tied with a yellow ribbon, standing upright, anchored deep in the black dirt. The grave marker loomed in the lessening daylight and brought back powerful memories of the body

Maverick had found here a month before. Pete took my hand and squeezed it.

We walked and called Emma's name, hoping if she was within earshot, she'd answer, and then we waited for what seemed an eternity for no response. Other voices echoed around us. When we reached the water's edge, we turned around and repeated the process. It wasn't a long path, maybe half a mile. We cleared the area as we walked back and forth along the south side of the slough. The last traces of reddish-gold slipped down in the west and the sky turned black. A few dazzling stars glinted, and then flashlights blinked on. I shivered.

Pete and I combed through tall grasses, raked the area near the water, and pushed plants aside. A whoosh of flapping startled me when we flushed a ring-necked pheasant.

My mind reached back two years, to another time and place, to images of Michael Gregory, Jr.—a bright, handsome eight-year-old boy with curly brown hair and magical blue eyes. He'd waited patiently for a rescue that came just in time.

Charles had planned a trip around Lake Superior for our honeymoon. We'd just finished lunch at an Italian restaurant in Wisconsin Dells when Charles received a text.

"What?" I smiled and jostled his arm with what I thought was a light, loving touch. He looked right through me to some far-distant frightening place, and I asked again, more seriously, "What?"

"We need to call your father."

A stickler for records, Charles usually examined receipts and verified the amounts of his purchases. An ace with numbers and quite frugal, he invariably left an eighteen percent tip, but this time he dumped an abundant amount of cash on the table, grabbed my arm, and led me out of the restaurant. I called Dad.

He answered on the first ring, his voice quavering as he struggled to say, "They took him!"

We packed our things, praying for the safe return of sweet Mickey.

My dad's sister, Marissa, had undergone surgery and IVF and had waited sixteen years to get pregnant. And then she did everything suggested by her obstetrician, but she died giving birth to Michael Gregory, Jr. His dad retreated from life and buried himself in work, leaving Mickey in the hands of a very capable nanny. But someone targeted him because Michael Sr. was loaded.

Michael received a message and arrived home to find Mickey's nanny gagged and tied to a chair, a note pinned to her chest demanding a ransom for his son. He was ordered to stay away from law enforcement. He paid the ransom and received unintelligible instructions to find Mickey within a forty-eight-hour deadline. After that, all bets were off, and they couldn't ensure Mickey's safety. Ten hours later, when Michael couldn't make heads or tails of the message, he went to my dad. My dad would do anything for his sister.

Hunched over at the kitchen table, with his head in his hands, his bloodshot eyes brimmed with unwept tears, Michael tried every way he knew to decipher the message. "Katie," he cried when we walked through the door, "they're going to let him die if I can't figure this out! This person wants to absolve himself of Mickey's death, but the answer has to be here." I knelt next to him and peeled his fingers away from the scrap of paper. "I thought if I kept Mickey at a distance, he'd be safe. I thought I'd be shielded from feeling, but I was wrong on both counts. What am I going to do?" he wailed.

"Sir," Charles said, with the authority of an uncommon Brit; candor, and confidence he later admitted to having none of, "what type of people have you pissed off?"

Michael gulped air and looked up at Charles. He fixed his gaze on an unknown man asking extremely personal questions. "Who the hell do you think you're talking to?"

Charles stood his ground. "Mickey's dad."

Michael's stoic façade crumbled. "I'm sorry. I'm so sorry."

"Uncle Michael, who would do this?" I asked again, throwing a lifeline into his quicksand of misery. Dad silently laid pencils and paper on the table and walked back to stand in front of the sink, gazing out the window, clutching the countertop.

"I did this," Michael said. "It's my fault."

"Uncle Michael." I wanted to shake him. "Think."

He sat back in the chair and closed his eyes. We could see his brain cells firing as he concentrated. "I've been most successful at IT takeovers, small companies with potential but no capital to fund research and development, just independent idea men with no means to make their dreams come true. I bought them out, a lot of them."

"What did they do?" Charles asked.

"They designed apps for smartphones or formulated ideas for increasing the ease of computer use for non-techno people." A smile almost reached his eyes as he added, "Like your dad."

We heard a 'harrumph' and waited for Michael to continue. "I bought the ideas, lock, stock, and barrel."

"What happened to those people?" Charles asked.

"I don't know. I didn't care."

I had studied cryptanalysis and information systems with Charles and we'd encoded and decoded communications for Scotland Yard. We set to work, bouncing ideas around, rattling off possible ideas for the solution. The message on the scrap of paper read, "yoeewofivxsfcsfczxobqyzy fucnzuojzuovbcnukkexgbeewoqfjovjtxfudvjnzfkdffib jqsbjtybpvz %2C %20 %202 / %5D %24 %138."

"This person provided the means for Mickey to be found," I said. One way or another.

Charles wrote the first six characters and tapped his pencil on the paper. "What does this look like to you?" he asked, underlining the first four letters.

"It could be *itll*—it'll, or maybe *hell*—he'll, but *pull* or *settle* might work." I exhaled, frustrated.

The cryptogram omitted the spaces usually used to divide the sentences into distinct words. Charles and I worked through the text, using a substitution cipher, and translated until the appearance of the percent sign.

"It reads, 'He'll be okay for forty-eight hours then the air supply will be gone and you can stop looking. Find him at %2C %20 %202 / %5D %24 %138,'" I said.

"Mr. Gregory, please tell us again what these people did, the people most upset by your takeovers?" Charles asked with gentleness and understanding.

Michael thought carefully and said, "Some of these programmers were top-notch techies I could blend into my company. Some were first-rate nerds, geeks of the highest order, gamers with the least sophistication. I usually bought their software outright. They probably had the most to lose, not monetarily, but pride in ownership. I knew their ideas were great, but without me, or someone like me, those concepts would die on the vine. Maybe they felt I stole their property."

Programmers. Programming languages. Numbers. "It reads, 'Find him at…' It's a place. A location," Charles said.

I pulled up the calculator on my phone and began crunching numbers. "In hexadecimal, it translates into a local latitude and longitude. Mickey has to be here."

Charles entered the coordinates on the app and handed me his phone to read and deliver directions. Then he grabbed keys, and we were out the door, Michael and my dad hot on our heels. He spun our wheels, but I had to remind Charles only once to drive on the right side of the road.

We followed the directions to a wooded area. We brushed back the foliage that crawled up the sides of a large metal storage bin dug deep into the side of a hill in a small wooded development next to a stream. A plastic tube tethered three oxygen tanks together and led to a door. My ever-prepared husband pulled a pair of bolt cutters out of his backpack and hacked off the padlock.

Flashlight beams found Mickey sitting alone in the dark. When the light focused on his face, I saw streaks where fallen tears had cleaned a curvy path down his dirty cheeks, but he glowed when he said, "Katie, I'm hungry. Where's Daddy?"

Michael said, "Right here, buddy." Mickey took a huge leap into his father's waiting arms and, after a long embrace, rode out piggyback.

"They said you didn't care, but I knew you'd come, Daddy. Can I have ice cream?"

We fed Mickey and when he nestled in Michael's strong, protective arms sound asleep, Charles asked, "Sir, can you think of anyone capable of doing this?"

"No." But, as I later discovered, Charles wasn't convinced.

With Mickey safely home, and permission from Michael, Charles delivered the case and its ultimate denouement to the authorities, who were angered to be out of the loop for so long. Although satisfied with the outcome, they ultimately asked for documentation and our references and begrudgingly granted us credentials to enable us to work in Minnesota. Our contact was Agent Thomas Blaise.

Now, searching for Emma brought it all back. We had to find her. But this time there were no puzzles to unlock, no contact from kidnappers, no clues to decipher.

CHAPTER TEN

A dense fog swelled and swallowed the stars one-by-one, obscuring what could be five feet in front of us. A disembodied voice from a loudspeaker called off the search. We were likely to overlook a clue if we continued. Pete and I returned to Pamela's yard, artificially on fire under multiple trouble lights, a beacon for the searchers.

"Anything?" Officer Christianson asked Pete.

"Nothing," Pete said, returning the clipboard.

My phone pinged with a school alert. Columbia Public Schools suspended tomorrow's activities at the high school, allowing students and faculty the opportunity to assist in the search for Emma. Many hands would make lighter work.

A scratchy voice hailed, "Pet-er!"

Pete looked around, hunting for the source. His eyes caught a birdlike woman standing across the street, supported by an aluminum walker with yellow tennis balls attached to the base. She stood still, a blue knitted shawl sliding off her bony shoulders. Her piercing eyes lit up in a face creased like onionskin paper folded and unfolded into tiny squares. Deep grooves formed parentheses at the corners of her asymmetric mouth. One side frowned a great deal more than the other. Scraggly wisps of silver hair framed her pinched face.

Pete and I bounded to her side. "Miss Grace," he said gently. "What are you doing out here? Let me help you." He lifted her shawl and draped it around her shoulders then turned her walker toward the red-brick colonial.

"He. Flew." She forced the words through her lips, syllables carefully formed, articulated with extreme difficulty.

"Miss Grace, it's cold out here. You're going to catch your death." She brought him up short with a surprising snort.

One word at a time, she struggled. "That. Dog. Vaulted."

Then I remembered what I'd seen when I'd grabbed my jacket from the hook. The leash was hanging there, but I didn't see Maverick.

Pete matched his steps to those of Miss Grace, supporting her, guiding her toward her home as he calmed her and helped interpret her words. I followed, waiting for her to help me with my Maverick dilemma. He could be with Ida, but I'd never known her to walk him without his leash.

It took tremendous effort for Miss Grace to mount

the three steps, grunting while heaving her walker in front of her. I couldn't imagine how she'd descended the steps alone.

"Take it easy," Pete said. "Let me help you."

Once inside, Pete flicked on the lights, and I blinked. Three curio cabinets were populated with what looked like Christmas ornaments, snow globes, music boxes, and glass figurines. Her collection would rival Ida's. I took shallow breaths, protecting my sense of smell from the cloying odors of mothballs and peppermint.

Pete walked her past the chaotic accumulation into a spotless room cut right out of a style magazine illuminated by a soft lamp standing in one corner. A white grand piano rested on the polished parquet floor. Books and folders lined one wall of the built-in shelving. An antiquated reel-to-reel recording system filled another. Large gleaming trophies stood atop two wooden filing cabinets, and an art light hung above a pencil drawing titled, A MUSICIAN'S TOWER BUILT BY A DREAMER. The drawing morphed from a piano's construction blueprint to a glistening keyboard, the dimensions melting into musical notation that floated from beneath an open lid.

Miss Grace dropped into a royal blue wingback chair and faced Pete, who had pulled a straight-backed chair in front of her. He reached for her, his long fingers dwarfing her weathered hands. "Miss Grace? You said the dog flew?" She nodded. I knelt at her feet, waiting for more information.

"Black. Dog. Delivery. Van."

"The black dog? The black dog went after a delivery van?" Pete asked.

With a tremendous effort, she said, "Yes."

I couldn't believe what I heard. Since we'd finally decided we were meant for each other, we'd been training together, and I'd taken care of him. Why would he take off?

"Miss Grace, this is Katie."

"Pleased to meet you," I said. I took one of her very soft hands in mine and rubbed my thumb over the paper-thin skin of her forefinger. "Maverick, the black dog from across the street, is my dog."

"Good. Dog." She closed her eyes as she struggled to form the words.

"Where was the van, Miss Grace?"

"Farley's."

"The van was at Farley's house?" Another nod. "And Maverick followed it when it drove away?" Another nod. "Do you know the little girl, Emma?" A smile. "She's disappeared. Everyone's looking for her."

Miss Grace's eyes flew open. She tightened her grip on our hands and she moaned, "Noooo."

Pete laid a hand on my shoulder. "I'll see if I can find out anything about Maverick when I talk to Ronnie. I hadn't heard anyone mention a delivery van. He needs to know. Katie, can you stay with Miss Grace?" He stood and I moved onto the chair, still holding her hand.

A silent silver tear found its way down the crevices in the wrinkles of Miss Grace's face. "It'll be all right," I volunteered with as much positivity as I could muster. She closed her eyes and appeared to doze, and my eyes wandered about the room. Candid photos of her playing piano or accepting an award lined every wall. I was drawn to a small table next to the piano. The gooseneck lamp from the music stand illuminated the photo of a tall teenager, stooping to drape a protective arm around Miss Grace, and in the second photo, I recognized the bright eyes and wry smile on the face of a captivating young woman with chopped black hair and a glistening nose ring. I'd have known that face anywhere. I'd replaced Elaine Cartwright as the high school math teacher, but after she died, Ida and I proved she'd been dismissed without cause.

A half hour later, the front door squeaked open, and Pete returned with Susie. "Miss Grace, Susie's going to stay with you tonight." I thought Miss Grace might protest, but she'd resigned herself to Pete's plan. Assuming her compassionate caretaker role, Susie inclined her head toward me, and Pete and I headed toward the door.

Once outside, he said, "Ida's been out knocking on doors. She thought Maverick was with you. Ronnie said searching for a dog was way down on the priority list today and,"—he put up his hand in defense—"no one in the neighborhood has had a delivery. I don't know what to think, Katie."

I didn't know what to think either. My tether to normality was nowhere to be found.

Ida waited on her porch, rocking, ashen, her usual joviality gone. Not knowing Emma's whereabouts sat heavily on her shoulders. And now Maverick was missing as well.

"Can they link the delivery van to Emma's disappearance?" I whispered.

"They have to explore the possibility, but Ronnie hasn't had much experience being in charge." I felt a surge of intent storm through Pete, and he added, "I'm going to see what Dad has to say." He put his hands on my shoulders, leaned over me, and kissed my forehead. "Goodnight,

Ida," he said.

Filled with worry, I got in my car and went looking for Maverick, but when I almost hit a parked car because of the dense fog, I turned around and waited all night at my kitchen table. My mind wouldn't turn off.

CHAPTER ELEVEN

Pete rapped at the door. He peeked in and said, "They have to wait to begin the search until the fog lifts. Let's see how Miss Grace is doing."

We crossed the street and Susie yawned as she answered the door. "I think she had a peaceful night. She's been up for about an hour. I'll get her. For such a little thing, she has a voracious appetite. Have you heard anything?" Pete and I shook our heads. "Do you want to come in and wait for Monica Parks, Grace's caretaker? She should be here soon."

"Katie, wait here and I'll try to get an update."

With uncharacteristic patience befitting a saint, Susie escorted Miss Grace into the music room and eased her into the blue chair. Miss Grace's color had improved and she looked stronger.

Rather than labor over a conversation with someone who might or might not be a rival for the affection of someone with whom a person might or might not have a romantic interest, Susie and I hovered over Miss Grace until a spitfire burst through the door, demanding, "Who the hell are you and what are you doing here?"

Not one to back down, Susie answered with equal assertiveness, "I spent the night with Miss Grace. There's been some difficulty in the neighborho—"

The fireball interrupted, "Why didn't someone call me? I'm responsible for Miss Grace. What's she doing up already? She can't get herself out of bed."

Smiling at Miss Grace, Susie answered confidently, "We did it together."

Eyeing the multiple locks that secured the front door, Monica asked, "Who let you in? She's not even supposed to stand." I inhaled, surprised; Miss Grace had performed solo well.

Susie ignored the question. "The police went door to door last night looking for the little girl across the street. She's missing."

There was no immediate response. I offered my hand. "I'm Katie Wilk."

Monica glared at it "I know who you are. You have my daughter in a class or something."

I retracted my hand. "Yes, that's right."

"You both need to leave now." She ran her finger under her watch, scratched, and added, "It's time for Miss Grace's medication." Miss Grace sighed.

Susie insisted we stay until Pete returned. "Dr. Erickson will be back shortly. He wants to check out Miss Grace. It was a long night."

"He's not her regular physician," Monica said, glowering.

"Nonetheless, she's temporarily under his care," Susie said, equally intimidating.

Monica brushed the gold chain around her neck. "Fine. I just want what's best for Miss Grace." She sighed and turned to Miss Grace. She raised her voice a bit and said, "Are you doing all right, dear?"

Susie gritted her teeth but relaxed when the front door burst open. "Look who the cat dragged in."

"How're you doing today, Miss Grace?" Pete asked. He knelt in front of her. She smiled. Monica backed away, arms crossed protectively. He glanced in her direction. "Ms. Parks, you're doing a great job with Miss Grace. She's looking well. How long have you been with her? Last time I checked in, her caretaker was Frannie Yates."

"Frannie bugged out last spring after her daughter took off. And no one has visited Miss Grace in quite a while," she answered, her message clear.

"You're right and I plan to rectify my neglect." Pete stood and he said, "I'll be back this afternoon." He turned to Monica. "Officer Christianson will be over shortly to interview Miss Grace." Before Monica's sputtering became words, we stepped out.

The sun hid behind weighty clouds ready to burst. I wore jeans, a long-sleeved T-shirt, and a sweatshirt under my orange rain jacket, but the cold, damp air penetrated my layers and I shivered, waiting in line for our clipboard. Pamela's husband stood stoically next to Officer Christianson, thanking each searcher. When Pete stepped to the front of the line, he reached out, but the powerful man deflected his hand, and instead, pulled Pete into a bear hug, tears rimming his swollen eyes. Pete slapped his back and turned to introduce me. "Katie Wilk, this is Adam Farley."

"Mr. Farley," I said, "we're going to find your daughter."

Susie gave Adam a big hug, and Officer Christianson handed us our clipboards. Maple Street swarmed with young and old. Trucks, cars, and SUVs lined the streets again; friends and family converged, wearing camouflage hunting gear, raincoats, waterproof Gore-Tex, and carrying umbrellas, all on a mission to locate Emma. Groups of high school students congregated, quietly following the directions of a supervising adult. A sobering buzz of conversation surrounded us.

Behind the crackle of a megaphone, Officer Christianson announced, "We'll be searching throughout the daylight hours." He stopped speaking as a Crown Victoria and an ambulance rolled down the street.

The car pulled into the driveway, and when the door opened, Chief Erickson unfolded his six-something frame from the passenger side. "Go ahead, Ronnie," he encouraged.

"Agent Rutherford from the state Bureau of Criminal Apprehension has a few words."

A tall man stepped forward. "The first twenty-four hours are critical. If you see anything, give us a call. Use 911. The dispatcher will forward your call to the command post. Okay, folks. Let's find Emma!"

The small groups scattered, whispering. Then the timbre of the buzz changed. The hush was contagious, and movement stilled from one end of the street to the other, like dominoes falling. Pete took my hand and held me in place, as a black dog and a little girl came into focus through the haze, the hulking figure of a man trailing them.

CHAPTER TWELVE

Emma's fingers gripped Maverick's collar. Adam got to her first and knelt in front of her. "Hi, Daddy. This is Maverick. I'm tired."

The precocious child released Maverick and wrapped her arms around her father's neck. He swept her up, and they walked slowly toward Pamela, who madly swiped tears from her face. Maverick limped next to them. Then Emma twisted around and said to the retreating figure, "Aren't you coming too, CJ?" He stopped, and all eyes turned toward the giant leaning heavily on a cane. He removed a black felt hat and fingered the turquoise beads around the brim, looked down at his feet, looked back up, and nodded to Emma.

I wiped my face too but kept my feet firmly planted as

congratulatory embraces and celebratory whoops swirled through the crowd. Emma had returned, and Maverick was with her. A picture-perfect ray of sunshine sliced through the mist, alighting on Emma's curls.

"Move back. Give them room." Officer Christianson took the lead on mob control, parting the crowd. Chief Erickson's dark eyes twinkled as he spoke a few words to a bubbling Ida. The warm sunshine quickly dissipated the miasma, cheering the crowd.

When Adam and Emma reached Pamela, Emma said, "Thanks, Maverick."

Maverick made a beeline to me.

"Pete?" Adam strained. Pete donned his doctor face as ever-prepared Susie pulled a black bag from the cab of his truck and placed it in his outstretched hand. Pete acknowledged Adam with a wave, and then he and Susie joined the Farleys, entering the rear of the ambulance. The doors clanged shut, and the ambulance turned on its flashing lights.

I knelt to welcome kisses and hugged Maverick. I nuzzled head-to-head, burying my fingers deep in the fur of his neck, and came away with a sticky residue. I signaled him to sit.

"That dog has a great spirit," said the Native American man who'd walked out of the fog. He was broad across the chest with biceps straining against his windbreaker sleeves, and he leaned heavily on a brass cane topped with a finely sculpted scrimshaw dog carved into a gray-and-black resin. He continued, his face in shadow, "May I see to his injury?"

"W-what?" I stammered.

When he attempted to kneel, a hand restrained him.

"Who are you?" demanded Agent Rutherford. "And

what were you doing with the girl?"

The man closed his eyes and lifted his face to the warming morning. The sunlight poured through what remained of the clouds and glinted off his long blue-black hair, which was pulled into a ponytail. When he opened his eyes, icy gray quickly darkened to a challenging black in a wave of sadness. "On my way to work, I heard a radio request for assistance in searching for a little girl." Looking down at Maverick, he went on. "I saw those two walking through the fog against traffic on the highway and stopped to see if they needed help. This spirit would not let me near the little one. He has a mean growl. The little girl told me her friend Maverick was taking her home." He snorted.

When the stranger reached into his back pocket, Officer Christianson rushed forward, fumbling for his sidearm. If there had been an altercation, the officer would have lost. "Whoa, Officer!" He held up his left hand, and with his right, he pulled out a billfold pinched between his thumb and forefinger. After waiting for permission, he shuffled through the contents, handing a business card to Officer Christianson. "I wanted to make sure they arrived home safely, so I followed them. We have been walking for more than forty minutes. Emma must be tired and hungry. I know I am." He looked back at Maverick and me. "And this one needs care too."

Officer Christianson saw the blood on Maverick's shoulder, glanced at the card, and remarked, "You're the new vet in town?" After an almost imperceptible nod, he asked, "Why didn't you call 911?"

"I didn't have a phone with me."

"Make sure you keep yourself available," Officer Christianson said gruffly.

The man nodded again. Officer Christianson and Agent Rutherford stepped back into the crowd. After handing me a business card too, the man knelt in front of Maverick and asked, "May I?" I nodded and his huge hands tenderly probed Maverick's long gash. Maverick sat motionless, aware of safe hands, healing hands, helpful hands. "We need to clean the wound and stitch it up. Can you bring him to my clinic?"

"Are you really a vet? A veterinarian?"

"Yes," he chuckled. "I really am a veterinarian. CJ Bluestone at your service," he said with a tiny bow. "My clinic address—"

Knowing an address might not help me locate the clinic, I interrupted. "You don't have a car here. Why don't I give you a ride to your vehicle and we can follow you to the clinic?" I held out my hand. "Katie Wilk, and you've met Maverick."

The small smile flickered across his broad face. The worry lines softened, and I thought I saw a few more crinkles at the corners of his eyes; I couldn't really tell.

On our walk to my car, I said, "How long have you been here?"

"About four months," he answered. "It is a nice little town."

He left something unsaid, so I prompted, "But?"

"But it's a very tight community." Dr. Bluestone spoke formally, and chose his words carefully. "I have found easy acceptance lacking."

"That's true of many small towns," I said. "It's like being a new in-law, an interloper in a close-knit family."

"Yes."

"I haven't been here long, but I've been lucky. I've met

some great people."

With one-word instructions, he directed me to his truck—a long walking distance for a little girl and an injured dog—and from there, Maverick and I followed him a mile out of town to the clinic. A white rambler set back from the highway served as the pet hospital. A black chain-link fence surrounded a large manicured yard. Maverick hobbled through the grass and into the building.

An hour later, after placing nine neat stitches that crisscrossed a small shaved area of Maverick's shoulder, Dr. Bluestone said, "It looks like he was struck with a sharp metal edge. I believe Maverick was protecting the little girl. He would not allow me near her. He bared lots of sharp teeth, snarling and barking with his entire being."

I looked at my dog with newfound reverence. If someone had taken Emma, it looked as if Maverick might've been the one who'd saved her and brought her home.

"You should really think about SARTECH. He is a natural."

Having no idea what he was suggesting, I waited for wound-care instructions. "I am serious," he continued. "He is a born search-and-rescue canine. I have worked with quite a number of K-9 teams. Maverick operates on instinct."

Understanding and pride seeped into my brain. I totally agreed. Maverick had an uncanny ability to find. He had found Emma. And when I needed him most, he was there for me as well. I thought I was lost forever, but he'd made his way through the woods, dragging Pete behind. He'd been my protector. He'd also proven his aptitude for finding dead bodies, but I wasn't about to share those morbid details with Dr. Bluestone.

We sat in the waiting area, Maverick still a little groggy from the sedation, and Dr. Bluestone manipulated Maverick's shoulders. He stroked his legs and aligned his hips.

"What are you doing?" I asked.

"Animal chiropractic." Before I could process his words, he added, "I have information on training and evaluation for search-and-rescue K-9 teams. Excuse me." When he reappeared, he carried a few brochures that described SARTECH and a DVD titled *K-9 QUEST*. "Take a look at this material. Maybe we can get together over a cup of coffee sometime and discuss it."

"How do you know so much about SARTECH? Do you have a search-and-rescue canine?"

Dr. Bluestone looked down and shook his head. "Not anymore."

CHAPTER THIRTEEN

The little hairs on the back of my neck stood on end. "What happened?" I asked.

Dr. Bluestone pulled two paper cups from a tube next to a water cooler. He filled them and handed one to me. "Outlaw was a Belgian Malinois Navy SEAL. I trained with him and was his handler for three years." His voice cracked.

"You don't have to talk about it."

"But I do." He looked down at his hands and interlocked his long slender fingers. "We were clearing a building in a distant unnamed land." He glanced at me, assessing the effect of his slight attempt at humor. I forced a smile, encouraging him to go on.

"Outlaw did his job, ferreting out hostile humans and explosives, but it had been quiet on our turf for over a week, a relatively long time. We thought we had taken everyone out, and I let my guard down. Outlaw outranked me. I should have listened. Heedless of his general agitation, three of us stepped into a crumbling structure and found ourselves encircled by a ragtag paramilitary group. I signaled Outlaw to wait until I was hidden and to find me later. No one noticed as he faded into the landscape. It had been an accidental encounter, and they had not predetermined our fate. Outlaw did not wait for them to figure it out. He crawled in through a window of the warehouse where we were being held. I didn't even know he had found me until he was chewing the ties on my hands. Our captors were not very vigilant, but during our escape, one of the men took a few shots at us. Outlaw threw himself in front of me and took a bullet for his trouble. I took one in the hip." He gestured to his right side and offered his cane as proof of his story.

The intensity of my own parallel images of gunshots momentarily assailed me. I swayed and grabbed the armrest. Tears threatened to spill over as snapshots emerged of Charles racing in front of me just after Dad had yelled, "Gun!" I heard our bikes collide and felt, again, the warm pool of sticky blood.

Dr. Bluestone tentatively reached out a hand to steady me. "Katie?"

Maverick nudged my side and then laid his head in my lap.

"I'm sorry," I said and struggled to gain control. Dr. Bluestone read my face and knew I understood his pain.

"The bullet did not kill Outlaw. He was wearing body armor and the bullet only creased his rump." He sighed. "They loaded us into separate medivac units. The last I saw of him, he was looking out the rear of the vehicle, his head on crossed paws, his ears forward, as he lay quietly before the metal doors clanged shut. It appears our K-9 partners caused more trouble than their human counterparts, so the opposition targeted the veterinary ambulance, and the IED aimed at Outlaw took out two medics and the driver." Dr. Bluestone breathed deeply. "All four earned a Purple Heart. Outlaw's second, and he died a hero." His voice hitched. "And I had to bury him over there. He is remembered well."

A phone ringing somewhere deep in the building remained unanswered. Dr. Bluestone took another deep breath. "That brings me to Maverick." He raised an eyebrow. "He could do well."

I smoothed the wrinkles on Maverick's worried forehead. *No problem, friend,* I thought. "What would we need to do?"

"I guess it depends on you. If you have what it takes to be a search-and-rescue technician, if you like to work with others, if you are willing to learn…" I urged him to go on. "You also need reliable transportation and physical stamina."

Thinking of my winded bicycle workouts, I said, "I can work on that." As I skimmed the fifty-page manual he handed me, which included an assessment tool, I became aware of my many areas of deficiency.

He continued to highlight the characteristics we needed to be good candidates. "There are quite a number of study guides." He pulled one from a shelf behind me.

I surprised him when I said, "I've already read that one. May I?" I reached for the book, opened to a familiar page and continued. "In fact, here's a picture of Maverick's mother." Dr. Bluestone leaned in for a better look.

I nearly swooned. I caught the slightest scent of English Leather, Charles' cologne, on Dr. Bluestone.

"There is good blood in Maverick," he said.

"I think his training had begun before they left him with me and I almost messed up." I grunted. "I couldn't even get him to sit then."

Dr. Bluestone chuckled, and said, "You need a mental toughness because you cannot always predict a favorable outcome." That might require a bit more work on my part. "Do you like being outdoors?"

"I like biking and walking."

"You have to pass a criminal background check."

"I passed a background check to teach in Columbia." He didn't need to know what else I was enabled to do.

"And," Dr. Bluestone said slyly, almost fishing for information, "you have to have an understanding family."

That would be easy. "I'm single."

My phone jangled in my pocket. We both started and laughed. "Excuse me," I said. My brow crinkled. Reading "Unknown Caller" on the screen, I answered guardedly. "Hello?"

"Where are you?" It took me a moment to identify the voice. "Dr. Erickson has been trying to reach you." It was Susie.

"I had Maverick's wound looked at," I answered. "Do you know what Pete wants?"

She took a beat too long and said, "I suppose he wants to talk to you. He plans to visit Miss Grace, but he'll be waiting for you at Ida's."

I covered the mouthpiece. "Is Maverick ready to go home?"

Dr. Bluestone said, "Yes."

"I'll be there shortly."

His lumbering gait was more pronounced without the assistance of his cane, but he insisted on carrying my big guy out to my car. I reached into my purse, but before I could even ask the cost of his services, he put a gentle hand over mine and shook his head. "Consider this my small attempt to honor another hero." Tears pricked my eyes. "Could you bring him back for a checkup on Thursday?"

"Absolutely. Thank you," I croaked.

* * *

Pete's pacing stopped when I rolled into the driveway. When he saw the bandage on Maverick's shoulder, he carried him into the house. Maverick squirmed, but Pete held him close, soothing him with nearly inaudible murmurs of, "Good boy" and "It'll be okay" while massaging his back. Maverick relaxed. Pete lowered him to his cushion. Maverick looked up for a moment, then flopped onto the pillow, exhaling heavily. He closed his eyes as if to say, *You are dismissed.*

Pete and I crossed the street to Miss Grace's. Monica met us at the front door and reluctantly led us to the music room, where Miss Grace sat listening to a piano recording. "Don't upset her and don't keep her too long," Monica said, then withdrew.

"Peter," Miss Grace announced happily, reaching out to take his hand.

"Miss Grace," he answered. "Thank you for all of your help. With what Emma and you have told us, I think we've put together some of what happened."

"Who was it?" she said slowly.

"We don't know yet, but the description of the truck and your timeline will be of immense help." He looked at me, took my hand, and drew me into the mix. "You remember my friend, Katie. She lives with Ida."

Miss Grace reached a hand out. Her skin felt fragile, but her firmer grip telegraphed a message in there somewhere. "Tell Ida I'm sorry," she said carefully, "for everything. How is the little girl?"

Pete said, "Emma is good, aside from being hungry, thirsty, and tired. I think Maverick jumped his fence because he sensed trouble and he chased after the truck. Emma said when the man slid open the door, Maverick was right there barking and making funny faces with his teeth, but when she made the faces for us, she looked like a little lioness. He jumped at the man, who hit him with a stick of some kind." Pete turned to me. "That's probably how Maverick was injured. We asked if he bit the man, and Emma said, 'No. Maverick's a good dog.' She didn't remember much more except that Maverick kept pushing her like her mother does when they're at the store. She doesn't recall much about the man or his vehicle, but she sure loves your dog, Katie. He's her champion."

I beamed, and Miss Grace smiled with me.

"Miss Grace, is there anything else you can think of?" Pete asked. "Anything at all?"

She closed her eyes to concentrate. When she opened them, she said her words slow and deliberate, "The vehicle was a yellowish-green."

"I'll let Ronnie know."

A knock came at the front door. A moment later, it blasted open with Susie striding inside. "Hey, everybody!

You too, Monica," Susie said. I wondered when Monica had crept into the room and how long she'd been standing in the shadow of the doorway. "The Farleys are celebrating Emma's safe return with a barbecue Thursday, and we're all invited."

Thursday would be a busy day.

My phone pinged with another school alert. Classes would resume at noon.

CHAPTER FOURTEEN

The *Columbia Sentinel* published a convoluted state of affairs in Wednesday's edition. Although the perpetrators of Emma's abduction had yet to be found, she was home, carefully guarded by her doting parents and the neighbors kept watch for the delivery van. The murder of Lorelei Fiorillo of Center Valley remained unsolved. Law enforcement had interviewed the friends last seen with her, but they were still seeking witnesses and questioning anyone with a motive. A short article detailed the theft of some electric tools and equipment from detached garages and sheds in the area, but there were no witnesses and no suspects to those crimes either.

The open house at school crept in quickly. I distributed grade reports for my students to share with their parents before attending the evening conferences, and required a signature from a parent unable to attend to make sure the information wouldn't be a surprise at the end of the quarter.

I thought it was a perfect day for a mathematical history lesson and a puzzle, so I shared the story of one of the greatest accomplishments in the history of cryptography. In 1940, Arne Beurling, a moody and secretive Swedish mathematician who had inherited Einstein's Princeton office, broke the German code used for strategic military communications. In an attempt to investigate the concept of true problem solving, I gave each student a mixed-up miniature magic cube with seemingly incomprehensible but perfectly workable instructions and told them to use their imaginations and give it a try.

Although they weren't scheduled to meet, my science club students appeared after school again.

"We'll be just a minute. We wanted to check our terrariums," Brock said as he pulled a chair to the bookcase and liberated the box from the top shelf. "Oh, geez, Ms. Wilk. Look."

The students huddled around my desk as Brock removed the clear plastic lid. "Gross," he said. "What happened?"

I examined the white splotches that covered each of the clear glass balls and laughed.

"What's so funny?" Galen asked. "They look awful."

The white residue affixed to each of the ornamental terrariums was replete with whorls, arches, and loops. "Fingerprints," I blurted. "Each of these terrariums is covered with your fingerprints. The sealed box locked in the superglue fumes, and they chemically reacted with the oils on your skin from latent fingerprints. This is the result. Look up there." My students focused on the shelf that held the box. "That vent must have provided enough heat to create cyanoacrylate fumes," I explained. "These are very personalized gifts. However, if you'd like to make another, I have the materials."

"Really?" asked Ashley. "My fingerprints?" I nodded as each student pulled out a terrarium and compared the visible markings with the pads of their fingers.

Galen laughed. "My mom is going to love this."

Brenna already had shifted gears and complained, manipulating the magic cube I'd handed out earlier in the day. "I can't follow these directions. Can you give me a hint?"

I recited the iterations as described in the step-by-step instructions found in Margaret Sullivan's *Tool or Toy* and steadily rotated the sides and edges back and forth for four minutes and twenty-four seconds, turning each of the mixed faces one color. Then I held up the solved cube. The algorithms eventually would re-create the unscrambled cube, but I never had confidence until the final square slid into place.

"You repeat something, don't you?" asked Brock.

Each of the students grabbed a cube.

"Every phase of the solution has a formula, usually performed over and over to complete the cube. Sometimes it requires one manipulation, sometimes more. I repeat each algorithm until I achieve the result I'm looking for." I remixed the cube and handed it back to Brenna. "Your turn."

"Oh," she moaned.

"It's very visual. The first phase is a plus symbol on the top face. See if you can get that," I suggested. "The letters and numbers indicate a coded instruction to follow. What do you think *U* and *D* mean?"

"Up and down?" Carlee volunteered.

"How about *R* and *L*?"

"Right and left?"

"The apostrophe?"

It took a few more guesses before Galen offered, "Is it a way to tell whether you should rotate the face counterclockwise?"

"Yes. And if you try to perform the algorithm knowing some of the terminology, it's much easier."

Brenna waved her cube, the plus sign facing forward. "I got it."

All the science club students decided to bring their parents to my room that evening to meet me, even those who weren't taking any of my classes. That's when they'd pick up their terrariums.

Staying back, Carlee asked, "Do you know how to solve a larger magic cube? My sister gave me a cube with four squares on a side. Can I use the same directions?"

"The process is similar, but I don't have those algorithms memorized. I have printed instructions I can bring tomorrow, and we can give it a shot." I glanced at the clock, quickly ticking away the minutes I had to walk and feed Maverick and get something to eat before returning to school. "Right now, I have to get home. Will you be stopping by tonight with your parents?"

"My mother and I are coming," she said as she headed through the doorway. "See you later, Ms. Wilk."

* * *

As Maverick and I passed the Farley house, Pamela waved. I returned the gesture. Miss Grace pulled the curtain aside and acknowledged us with a nod. Then she let the curtain drop back into place. Maybe Ida was right. Our neighbors needed to get to know us.

After our walk, Maverick and I gobbled our food, and I raced back to school to meet my students' parents, carrying a bundle of nerves with me.

Vehicles of all kinds filled the parking lot. Early parents wandered around the building, getting their bearings, fortifying themselves for their teacher talks. I straightened desks, organized my space, turned on the SMART Board with a PowerPoint depicting our science club activities, and readied my classroom to accept guests.

I watched the clock for the first ten minutes and thought maybe I wouldn't have any visitors until I heard a sharp rap on the doorjamb.

Monica Parks swept around the corner with Carlee in tow. She trounced up to my desk and stuck out a cold, chapped hand. "Ms. Wilk." Her shake was short and curt. "What does my daughter gain by taking part in the science club?"

I offered them seats in front of my desk. "Would you sign in, please?" Monica ignored the clipboard I placed in front of her. Carlee scribbled her name. "If you want to take a look at what we've done, I have a PowerPoint—"

"I don't have time to watch a silly slide show. Give me the highlights and I'll decide if this is worth her while."

She threw me for a loop. I handed her Carlee's glass terrarium, and Monica rolled it upside down, dislodging the moss. She jabbed her forefinger at me, drawing my attention to her misshapen pinkie, and demanded, "What is this?" With a sour look, she tossed it to Carlee.

Clearly embarrassed, Carlee explained, "It's a science experiment, Mother. The club is great." Ms. Parks slowly turned her head and glared at her daughter.

To discharge some of the tension, I said, "We meet after school a few times a week and do experiments. Some of our students think science club will look good on their résumés. My students—"

"What do they learn?"

"We ask questions, pose hypotheses, and perform—"

"Pose hypotheses," Monica huffed, irritated.

"The students share research on the topics of their choice. There are no grades, but we appreciate participation." I couldn't tell if my explanation was acceptable, so I changed the subject. "Congratulations to Ana for being crowned Homecoming Princess. I haven't seen her to give her my good wishes in person."

Monica stood to take her leave, and said, "She wasn't particularly happy with second place and she's gone to visit her father."

Carlee bobbled her terrarium, which crashed to the floor, splintering into tiny glass shards.

CHAPTER FIFTEEN

I'm so sorry, Ms. Wilk." She stooped to pick up the pieces, her hands shaking.

"Don't worry, Carlee. I can clean this up, and you can make another."

Abruptly, her mother turned to her daughter and said, "It's a good thing you're so smart. It makes up for your being such a klutz. Let's go. You have a performance piece to prepare for Columbia Days. I'll think about whether your continued attendance in the science club will amount to anything."

Carlee looked back apologetically, and Monica shot me a withering glance, almost colliding with Lorelei and her parents at the doorway. Lorelei made her introductions with efficiency and charm, and I grabbed the dustpan and broom from the math office and swept away all traces of the visit by Carlee and her mother. I hoped I could salvage the moss and Carlee's attendance with our group.

By the end of the evening, parents' names and contact information filled my clipboard. At least half the students who needed encouragement attended with their parents and promised to work harder. Some of the parents had been on the front lines of the search for Emma and had seen Maverick bring her home, and they wanted to meet the new teacher who had a dog with a reputation for finding people, dead or alive. All night I accepted congratulatory handshakes in honor of Maverick. He was the star.

All my science club students stopped by to visit and take home their terrariums. The positives far outweighed any negatives.

I went home feeling the evening was a success, where I found Maverick relaxed on a new bed, chewing a new toy next to a new ceramic water dish. Someone had come bearing gifts. I sat on the floor. He flopped his head into my lap, closed his eyes, and heaved a contented sigh.

The door slammed when Ida returned from her evening dance class, and I made my way next door.

"Come in," she sang in answer to my knock.

"Hi, Mrs. Clemashevski."

"Ida."

"Hi, Ida. Thanks for all the new doggy stuff."

"It wasn't from me."

"Do you know who sent it?"

"It all came from Pamela and Adam, but Emma spent the most time with Maverick. I hope it's okay that I let them in. They've really come around."

"I'll have to get over to thank them."

Maverick raised his head and smiled a satisfied doggy smile.

* * *

After the open house, with gentle persuasion, marginal students had completed their homework. Several students had deduced part of the magic-cube solution so they could help others by decoding more of the instructions: right, left, front, back, top, and bottom.

Thursday was on its way to becoming one of the best days so far this school year.

During my break, I opened an email from Jane. She'd regained much of her strength after nearly succumbing to a bleeding ulcer exacerbated by a blood thinner, and she couldn't wait to come back. I replied, wishing her good health and outlining everything that had happened since she went home. I felt as if I were writing the lyrics to a country song, with so much dramatic cliché. I decided not to tell her how much I missed her nagging, her smile, and her snappy attitude, but I hoped her return was imminent.

* * *

On my way to the vet clinic, I cautiously navigated Columbia's streets, my eyes on the lookout for a yellowish-green delivery van carrying the thug who had both kidnapped Emma and struck Maverick. No luck.

After Dr. Bluestone examined Maverick's wound and checked the stitches, he requested one more checkup to make certain the wound continued to heal.

"Have you thought any more about SARTECH?" he asked.

"You gave me an awful lot of material. I haven't quite finished it. Can you tell me more about Outlaw?" I asked.

His eyes lit up as he sat down in the chair behind his desk. "I initially trained him to do a few tricks to alleviate some of the tension and distract from some of the ennui my compatriots experienced, but before long it seemed Outlaw could read the mood of most of my team and used his tricks to improve morale as well. I taught him to stretch out over his front paws, which we called 'bowing to royalty.' We used 'Who is the king?' as his cue."

"Maverick does something like that too."

"It is a great trick. Our commanding officer brought a local dignitary and his small entourage to visit our camp. The K-9 units were introduced, and the leader was quaking in his boots. I thought we could put the man at ease with a little canine humor. When I asked 'Who is the king?' Outlaw immediately bowed before one of the other men in the contingent. Embarrassed, I apologized. I held my breath until the man before whom Outlaw bowed smiled.

"Fearing for their lives among the Americans, the man and his bodyguard had switched places, but Outlaw revealed their sham, and the real bigwig knelt in front of Outlaw and told him he was brilliant. Following that, I accepted his acuity every time." He looked wistful. "Except for the last time."

"Are you going to the barbecue celebration the Farleys are having?" I said.

"I am not yet sure I'm out of the woods with Officer Christianson."

"Maverick has to go, but he'll be busy. Come with me." He still looked unconvinced, so I added, "You could tell me more about SARTECH."

Dr. Bluestone beamed. I saw his mind whir as he weighed the pros and cons.

"It's Emma's party, and hers is the only opinion that matters." I hoped to give more weight to the pros.

He followed me in his truck. Because of the crowd of cars on Maple Street, he pulled into Ida's driveway behind me. Maverick jumped from the car. With his head and tail held high, he sauntered into the Farleys' yard, straight up to Pamela, Adam, and Emma, who pulled a new Kong toy out of a blue gift bag, scratched Maverick's ears, and presented another reward.

"Maverick!" I heard from all three as they petted him vigorously.

In good hands at the center of attention, Maverick sat. Dr. Bluestone and I jostled our way through the mob to an enormous buffet table piled with hamburgers, brats, hot dogs, and wings accompanied by potato salad, coleslaw, bowls of JELL-O, and what looked like Ida's famous peanut butter bars. Pete, Susie, Miss Grace, and Ida sat in matching chairs holding court, a serious discussion passing among them. Only Monica Parks appeared to be missing.

Their conversation came to an abrupt halt when they saw us. I smiled and waited in vain for some sort of greeting. Uncomfortable with silence, I asked Pete, "Are you going to the homecoming game?"

"We were just talking about that," he said.

"And what did you decide?"

Susie and Pete exchanged glances. Susie smiled and said, "We're beginning our fellowship training tomorrow evening, so we won't be attending many more football games this season.

Unsure I'd heard her correctly, I turned to face Susie. "We?"

CHAPTER SIXTEEN

Pete looked like he'd been caught with his hand in the proverbial cookie jar. He turned three shades of red as he stammered to pacify Ida and me. "Remember, Katie? I told you I was accepted into the fellowship program?" I remembered his telling me about improving *his* skills using highly specialized technical ER equipment, but I didn't recall any mention of a *we*, so I let him stew as I waited for an explanation.

I didn't have to wait long. Susie was itching to tell all. "We leave at three on Friday and work the evening shift in the university ER Friday night. On Saturday and Sunday, we attend advanced education classes at the university in Minneapolis, and then we're back in Columbia late Sunday afternoon."

"It's a once-in-a-lifetime opportunity," I said, with enthusiasm I didn't feel. Relief flooded Ida's features as she assumed I knew more than I did, ever hopeful Pete and I might remain an item. I couldn't read his face, but at that moment, I didn't care. "I'm going to be working with Maverick to prepare him for SARTECH certification. Dr. Bluestone thinks he'd be a great search-and-rescue candidate."

"Chantan," he said as he offered his hand to each in turn. Dr. Bluestone spoke eloquently about how well Maverick did bringing Emma home, the characteristics that made a good search-and-rescue K-9, and the time, training, and testing necessary to belong to the program. I'm not sure how, but he must have understood the social dynamics of our small group and pragmatically delineated Maverick's attributes, diffusing some of the tension.

"When do you begin?" Pete asked.

I looked for guidance. "This weekend?" I said hopefully.

Dr. Bluestone grinned with ease, hiding his surprise.

"That's great," Pete said, reassured, and then he began a thorough interrogation about where, how long, and what would be required. Each answer aroused more curiosity. The more questions Pete asked, the more information I was able to glean. After passing the SARTECH written exam, along with training Maverick, I'd participate in coursework related to the behaviors of a lost person, radio communication, and how to use the incident command system—a framework for coordinating emergency responses from multiple agencies. Fortunately, I'd already taken first aid and CPR, and when I worked with Scotland Yard, I'd taken a course in crime-scene preservation and orienteering. To find our geocaches, my students and I had been using handheld GPS units, so I was familiar with those as well.

Maverick squirmed his way into the middle of our group, gripping a new plush toy in his mouth and wagging his back half with the strength of an elephant. He planted himself front and center among his circle of admirers.

"Where do the assessments take place, Dr. Bluestone?" I asked.

"My friends call me CJ." Around bites of his dinner, he added, "And we begin right here in Columbia."

Surprised eyes were riveted on CJ Bluestone.

"I am a qualified SARTECH K-9 evaluator." He leaned back on his heels, tipped up his felt hat, and crossed his hands on his cane.

Susie asked, "How long will it take?"

"From what I have seen, Katie and Maverick already work well together and communicate with ease. There are some very important hoops to go through, but I believe we can make it happen soon. Training is ongoing."

Pete stood and shook CJ's hand. "Good luck," he said. He bussed Ida's forehead and assisted Miss Grace to a standing position behind her walker. "I'll call you, Katie."

I smiled.

Susie closed the gate and followed them across the street.

I'd just about forgotten. "Ida, Miss Grace said to tell you she's sorry ... for everything."

"I've missed her," Ida commented. "I thought she hated me. I didn't think we'd ever fix the rift, but we've taken that first big step." She breathed a sigh of relief and turned to go inside, leaving me wondering.

The barbecue crowd dwindled. Friends and neighbors

wished the Farleys a good and safe night, receiving in return a genuine thank you for a job well done.

Maverick wriggled near me. "Do you really think Maverick will make a good search-and-rescue dog?" CJ slowly nodded. "Can you really help us?"

"If you have the desire, I believe so. He has a fine, strong soul. How long have you worked with him?"

"I've had him since he was ten weeks old. After the first few frustrating months, a friend suggested I put more of my energy into training him with positive reinforcement. I bought different manuals, and we did the exercises described in the books. Maybe with your help, we can do something useful."

"We can begin tomorrow. What time works for you?"

"If my science club students check in after school, our meeting won't last long because tomorrow night is Columbia's Homecoming football game. Even so, I'd like to see part of the game. Where do you want to work, Dr. Bluestone?"

"CJ, please. And I have all of the materials at the clinic. How about meeting at four thirty? Study your manual tonight."

CHAPTER SEVENTEEN

After school, Carlee arrived ahead of the others with a great suggestion to do a blood typing test. She had researched the cost and handed me the information. I needed to order the kits.

"Could I make another terrarium?" she asked. I opened the cupboard and she took out the supplies.

Brenna walked in and said, "Ms. Wilk, do you have any suggestions for hosting a large party?"

"Why? What's up?"

"During our annual Columbia Days' celebration, the town's ambassadors provide opportunities for visitors to discover the hidden gems found in our fair city," recited Brenna.

"Spoken like a true Queen Santa Maria." Ashley

laughed, following close behind.

"Can you please explain?" I asked.

"Once a year, we have a city-wide celebration and coronation for new ambassadors," she said. "It's happening in two weeks.

"I'm in charge of hosting the social for visiting dignitaries. My friends volunteered to help." With a huge smile, Brenna nodded at Ashley.

"Lorelei and I are both candidates this year and we said we'd help too," said Carlee.

"We're thinking of hosting a *Titanic* Tea," said Brenna. "Don't you like the sound of that? Can you help us?"

"I'm not well known for my culinary expertise." A giggle erupted from the girls. "But I'd be happy to help in any other way."

They researched what they'd need for their tea. Brenna estimated costs, and divided duties. The girls found recipes, generated a grocery list, devised a timeline for baking, composed a program, chose background music, and assembled a menu to bring to the Columbia Days committee. It had been a productive forty-five minutes.

"Carlee, where's Ana?" Brenna tried to sound nonchalant as she packed up her things. "She hasn't been in school and some kids are hinting there's a royalty killer."

"She's fine. She's with her dad."

"That's good. The mayor was afraid he'd have to hire security." Brenna looked more at ease.

Everyone but Carlee left. She followed me to my office. "Ms. Wilk, I'm sorry to be so bothersome, but could I leave this cube with you to solve when you can?"

"Sure, Carlee." I'd forgotten. "I'll try to get it done before the game. Will you be there?"

"I'm planning on it. And thanks."

"What's wrong?"

Her eyes glittered with tears. "Ana's been gone for almost a week. I was so surprised when my mother said Ana went to visit *her* dad. Until she spilled the beans the other night, I didn't know we had different dads."

"Your mom probably had a very good reason to keep that from you."

She forced a smile. It sounded lame even to me.

Carlee sniffed. "And after my mother met Lorelei, she told me I shouldn't waste my time trying to be an ambassador if I can't win."

"Do you still want to do it?" She nodded emphatically. "Then do it if she'll let you. It sounds like a fun-packed week." I picked up the cube. "I've got this," I said. I slid the cube into my briefcase and promised myself I'd try to put it right. I liked Carlee's smile, but then I thought again about the tiara in the tree. Was there someone targeting royalty?

CHAPTER EIGHTEEN

Assuming Maverick demonstrated his understanding well, he'd get lots of treats, so CJ requested I hold his supper. I'd be too excited to eat anyway. I scratched behind Maverick's velvety ears, telling him over and over what a great dog he was. I reread a copy of a sample exam in the SARTECH manual, and nervously chewed on my lower lip—a bad habit I'd been trying to break—until it was time to head to the clinic.

At four twenty, Maverick hopped into the backseat of my Jetta and circled twice before sitting. He panted and made his observations, alternating between the two back windows. I concentrated on the directions, but by the time we pulled into the clinic driveway, my heart was racing.

"Okay, Maverick. Let's see what we can do," I said and

released him into the yard.

CJ lumbered our way, his limp noticeable, yet he seemed somehow lighter on his feet. His white teeth shone brilliantly in his unlined face. Wearing scruffy blue jeans, a well-worn leather vest over a blue-and-red plaid flannel shirt, and striding forward in combat boots, he erased the space between us. His straight black hair fell loose past his shoulders. As he neared, the heady scent of his cologne brought me up short again. To hide my embarrassment, and possible melting, I knelt quickly and buried my face in Maverick's neck.

"Ready?" he asked.

I looked up into patient eyes and relaxed as I answered, "Absolutely." Then I followed him into his office.

CJ rolled out a black leather chair, and seated me behind the enormous mahogany desk facing white walls decorated with framed diplomas and a huge round clock set with Roman numerals. The lights blazed. Four number two pencils with new erasers crisscrossed a stack of blank pages. A laptop computer, already primed, pulsed a welcome message and instructions.

He put on a solemn face. "I have set you up as a NASAR member, which stands for 'National Association for Search and Rescue.' This is your formal exam."

"What?" I panicked.

"After passing the test—and you will pass," he declared, "your membership number will be recorded in the NASAR database as a SARTECH III. You will receive an official certificate, and a colorful NASAR patch will be mailed directly from the headquarters in Virginia. You must allow several weeks for delivery." Pacing, with his hands clasped behind his back, he glanced at me with dancing eyes.

He recited the rules. "You can take the exam as many

times as you need to pass, but you have to pay a fee each time. Follow the prompts to begin the exam. The results will read 'pass' or 'fail.' No other feedback will be provided.

"Do you have any questions?" Not waiting for a reply, he continued. "Maverick and I will be practicing outside. You may begin." As CJ stepped out of the room, the heavy door shut out the world.

* * *

He had correctly predicted the results of my exam and explained the next phase of training. "I have witnessed Maverick's skills firsthand. Now we will work on *your* dexterity and communication."

We spent the next hour identifying my areas of weakness, along with clicking and treating successfully communicated behaviors. Maverick understood everything, exhibiting the agility and stamina necessary to search, but I lacked the confidence and decisiveness required to work in the field. I needed to be more specific with my instructions.

"You are required to pass multiple field tests," CJ said. "The first is used to evaluate the minimum knowledge and performance skills possessed by a team to locate a single subject at the end of a hot track during a half-hour period."

While he was talking, a chubby man with tortoiseshell glasses wandered up the drive. He wore a camouflage shirt and pants and carried a backpack.

"Right on time. Katie, meet my friend, Westin." We shook hands. "Your first field test will begin immediately." Westin handed CJ the bandana from around his neck and disappeared. "This test requires you to follow Westin's trail using land navigation skills, and thoroughly document your route on a map, directing Maverick with visual cues." He handed me a map and a red marker. Then he allowed Maverick to sniff the bandana. Maverick wagged his tail and his muscles rippled. I had high hopes.

When he finally released us, the woodsy terrain of the county park surrounding the animal clinic hid Westin well. We climbed over brush-filled hills, and jumped a small stream that cut through the foliage, but Maverick never veered from his course. CJ even had two other individuals stashed on the property to distract Maverick, but he didn't deviate from his path and effortlessly located the correct subject, sat and barked, then returned to lead me to Westin.

CJ commented, "You have passed the K-9 SARTECH level III beginning field test."

"Maverick was great! He did everything right. What happens now?" In my excitement, my words tumbled over one another.

"If you have the time, there is a field-exam spot open tomorrow, and we can evaluate the two of you for SARTECH II. "

"T-tomorrow. Aren't we going awfully fast?" CJ knelt in front of Maverick, touching foreheads. I surrendered. "Where do we need to be?"

CJ's features relaxed. He was quite a nice-looking man. I hadn't thought about Pete and Susie at all. Not much anyway.

* * *

I'd promised my students I'd watch the half-time show, and I arrived with seconds to spare. I hadn't solved the cube and I didn't see Carlee so when the astounding marching band finished, and with nothing else to hold me there, I gathered my things to head home.

"Is this seat taken?" a familiar voice asked. I looked into the mirth-filled eyes of my friend, Andrew—Drew—Kidd. I threw my arms around him, then backed away awkwardly.

"I finally have some free time. Are you hungry?" he asked, riffling his bright blue Cougar tie, which let out a battery-operated roar.

"Starving."

I followed him to the golf club, recalling the routine that Pete, Jane, Drew, and I began until life had gotten in the way. We even sat at the same table.

"What have you heard from Jane?" I asked.

"She's great. She and her dad have reconciled. He's seen the beautiful, independent, intelligent woman she's become, thanks to me." I gave him a tiny shove. "Well, she has."

"Has she said anything about coming back?"

Soberly, he shook his head, "Not yet."

We sat in a silent bubble as we waited for our order, the same one we'd made every time we'd eaten here: cheesy hamburger sliders, barbecue chicken wings, and crispy hand-cut fries, way too much food for two.

"I miss her." Drew sighed, and then he jolted, asking, "Where's Pete?"

It was my turn to sigh. "He was awarded a grant to purchase some new equipment for the ER." Drew waited patiently. "And to study the new equipment in its environment."

"What an opportunity for him! And?"

"He'll be working in the Twin Cities three weekends

a month studying with the university technicians and doctors, upgrading his techno-medical skills."

"That's terrific. So why the long face?"

"It's for about three months."

He waited but not too long, "And?" He took a big bite of his burger then swiped at the ketchup that dribbled down his chin.

"Susie went with him."

Drew choked on his food, and his eyebrows rose. "You know he thinks of her as a high maintenance little sister, right? You're the star in his skies, the minor in his blues."

"But he's not here."

I bit into a juicy, cheesy, perfectly done burger and lost my appetite.

"What brought you back to town?" I asked. He was originally assigned as an undercover agent by the Bureau of Criminal Apprehension, teaching psychology at Columbia, but the agency had moved him on to his next job after the drug pipeline had been closed.

"I've been assigned to a burglary task force in the five-county area. Monongalia is at the center, so it makes a brilliant base of operations. I might even take up dance lessons again." I knew his heart wasn't in it without his dance partner extraordinaire—Jane. Drew set down his burger too.

Our spirits lifted as I described Emma's safe return from an apparent kidnapping, and I bragged about Maverick's training and testing for SARTECH.

"He'll make an amazing search-and-rescue dog. If I'm ever lost," Drew said, "send him to find me."

I glanced at my watch and, flustered, said, "We have our second field test tomorrow. I need to pack a kit, and

I don't even have a backpack, let alone everything listed in the book, and we have to be on-site at ten tomorrow morning. What was I thinking? I'll have to make a Walmart run tonight." I stood, upending my plate.

"Slow down," Drew said, picking up the shattered dinnerware. "I have a ready pack in my car designed to safely keep someone out in the field … for a short time. It has a personal first aid kit, extra clothes, and basic survival gear. We can tear the bag apart and reconfigure it to fit your needs." He nabbed the bill and strode confidently out of the restaurant with me stumbling in his wake.

We?

CHAPTER NINETEEN

Morning snuck in, and I had to peel my eyelids open. Drew and I had disassembled his ready pack and matched the integral components of the SARTECH list to the items at hand. He accompanied me to our local twenty-four-hour Walmart to purchase the few items I needed to complete a rudimentary kit. And he added a few of his favorite extras. But Maverick was raring to go and we'd be prepared to test today.

My phone chirped. The message read: *Good morning sunshine.*

I chuckled. *Good morning, yourself.*

Miss you.

Ditto.

Pete had texted five more words than I'd ever received

before. I wasn't sure that was good or bad, but I enjoyed hearing from him.

How did Maverick do?

He passed the first round. Second round is today.

Good luck!

I checked off each item on the packing list one last time after reading, "Every item on this list must be present for the candidate to be evaluated at the SARTECH II level. There are no exceptions." The bulky pack held the bare essentials and minimal survival gear. CJ had warned me about a possible wait time so I grabbed extra bottles of water, dog food, and granola bars.

"We're as ready as we can be, Maverick. Let's go." His tail whumped against the door, and he circled in excitement. His exuberance replaced some of my anxiety.

We pulled into Monongalia Park Number 7, the exam site, and managed to squeeze between two full-sized trucks.

Three dogs strutted in the lot, looking professional in scarlet vests. "Sorry boy. You're going *au natural*. I don't have anything fancy for you to wear ... yet."

I clipped the leash to Maverick's collar, exited the car, and approached the registration table under the S-Z sign.

"Maverick and Katie Wilk," I announced proudly.

The cheery girl behind the table cooed, "What a beeeayoooutiful dog!" She thumbed through the manila folders. "There's nothing here. What's your dog's name again?"

"Here it is. Maverick and Katie Wilk," called a young man holding a folder under the H-R sign. As I reached for it, he snatched it back. "First time?"

"Yes."

He smiled broadly and handed me the folder. "Good luck."

From inside the folder, I pulled identification badges, a copy of the list of required equipment, a map of the park area, a schedule, a description of the exam, credentialing instructions, and an invitation to all candidates to congregate at the park shelter to celebrate their successful accomplishments.

I clipped my ID to my jacket pocket and Maverick's to his collar then went in search of CJ. He hailed us from across an open field. As we headed toward him, a hulk of a man with a monster German shepherd stepped in front of us. The dog boldly braced on his four paws, and his ears stood erect. He bared his teeth, the upper lip drawn back to show a mouthful of sharps. He stared at Maverick. Then he barked and his jaws snapped. Maverick took one look at me and sat.

"You're just a little bit of a thing. Whatcha think you're doing here?" boomed the hefty man. The man stepped closer. Maverick looked up at me. "What's your mutt's name?"

I backed up to walk around them. A dogfight couldn't have a good outcome. The man put his hand on my shoulder. "I asked you a question, missy."

I thought I caught a whiff of alcohol and looked up into an ugly leer, noticing the circle of watchers waiting for our reaction. The guy and his dog were big. He and his dog were bullies. I gently shrugged off his hand. "Heel," I cued. When the man saw CJ striding toward us, he rubbed the stubble on his chin with his knuckles, grabbed his dog's collar, and yanked him out of sight.

CJ knelt. He took Maverick's head in his gentle hands, and they touched foreheads. Maverick sat and licked CJ's face. CJ looked up at me with a face full of delight. "Maverick will do well."

A female voice, thick and raspy, bellowed, "Jimmy, get a leash on Scar." I turned to see a cherubic woman poured into a khaki uniform, sporting emblems and patches, a gorgeous tri-color border collie prancing by her side.

Jimmy pulled a leash from his pocket but struggled to snap it on the German shepherd's collar. "Just weedin' out the undesirables. Don't want anyone wastin' our time," he snarled, glaring at me. He finished fastening the leash, and I cringed when he cuffed his dog.

CJ shook his head. "There will be unexpected obstacles in your path."

Three other candidates introduced themselves and their well-trained dogs. We were all excited about the prospect of showing off our canine companions, but I had the inside scoop on Maverick and took a cleansing breath.

A bullhorn screeched.

"Welcome," the woman in the uniform began. "Greetings from our vice-president, Jimmy Hanson, and me, Hazel Sommers." Her voice was deep and gravelly, but she didn't look nearly as old as she sounded. "We're here to evaluate six candidates for SARTECH II. Your written exam will occur immediately after these announcements. During the exam, each of your backpacks will be reviewed to confirm the presence of all the required elements. Upon completion of the exam, you'll be sent out at thirty-minute intervals. Your team has ninety minutes to successfully conclude your search for the owner of the piece of clothing you will be given. Jimmy will be handing out your assignment number and an evaluation rubric. We're hearing atrocious weather predictions for later today, so let's get a move on."

After taking a deep breath, I made my way to stand in

front of Jimmy. I took hold of the edge of the cardboard, careful not to make contact when he handed me my number, but he wouldn't let go. "It's tough going, missy. Sure you're up to it?" he hissed, tipping his head to read my ID. "Katie Wilk." I gave a swift tug: number six.

When team five failed to produce an inflatable personal flotation device from the loaded pack, Jimmy gave a satisfied fist pump. "Gotcha."

"C'mon, Jimmy," said the human half of the team. "I forgot, and we ain't suppose ta be doing any water saves. And 'sides, it'd make the pack so heavy." He stumbled as his dog strained against the leash. Jimmy sneered and shook his head, his camo cap oscillating back and forth, a wicked grin on his grizzled face.

An hour and thirty minutes later, the first team headed out. A fine mist blew in from the light-gray clouds in the southwest, leaving the grasses and leaves slick. I'd pulled on my rain gear, and Maverick and I stood next to the registration table where Jimmy hovered, waiting to pounce on any misstep.

The mist thickened. Before another minute had passed, it was pouring. One of the evaluators proposed calling off the searches, but I heard Jimmy read from the rule book, "'You can't ever predict the weather or the circumstances you will encounter. Be prepared.' You was a scout, weren't ya?"

Reluctantly, I had to agree with him.

CJ hovered protectively. "Ready?"

I nodded. "Ready as we can be. I think Maverick already knows what's going on."

Three teams returned, successful in their quest, with time remaining on their clock. Hazel, her border collie trailing at her heels, approached us. "Ms. Wilk? There's only one team remaining out there. We have a mark, one hundred eighty degrees from their search area, so you shouldn't overlap, and they have to complete their rescue in the next thirty minutes. Would you be willing to head out early?"

"Happily," I said, swiping rain from my face. "Let's get going, Maverick."

CJ took my phone. I also handed over my car keys, lest they be lost on the hunt. I poured one of the bottles of water into a collapsible bowl, and Maverick lapped it dry. Hazel produced a Columbia High School chess club T-shirt for Maverick and a walkie-talkie for me.

The clock started. "Find," I said, letting Maverick sniff the T-shirt.

CJ had such high hopes for us. Maverick raced back and forth, checking out the ground as we neared the beginning of our search area. I pulled out the grid and marker to keep track of where we'd searched. When we reached the taller grasses, I brushed beads of water from Maverick's coat and unclipped the leash. He bolted.

I shouldered my pack and rushed after him. He made a beeline through the trees, on a mission, sure-footed, and heedless of the terrain, rain, and wind. I stumbled after him. Jimmy was right; we couldn't predict the weather when a real search was imminent, but as the rain continued, I could only hope for a quick find, followed by a hot cup of tea, dry clothes, and a warm fire. Maverick splashed through the puddles that had accumulated in the lower depressions; he was made for this. I initially tried to skirt the puddles in the ladylike manner my stepmother had required but promptly decided splashing wasn't all that bad.

The woodsy acreage we'd been assigned darkened quickly. Clouds roiled above as rain pelted us. I slipped. Mud sloshed down my right side and into my boot. Maverick slowed, giving me time to catch up, then pressed on, traversing back and forth, nose to the ground as I floundered behind.

I glanced at the fleeting time on my watch. How could that happen? We'd been out hunting for an hour, and Maverick didn't look like he was ready to slow down. As we made our way through the thick vegetation, I jotted notes on the map, indicating our relative position, and attempted to match the confusing topography. According to the map, we'd covered most of the assigned territory, and we'd found no trace of anyone. Nor had we come across any animal, insect, or anything out of place, nothing but water in this lousy weather.

Maverick stopped on the crest of an outcropping, the tip of his tail wagging high, signaling a find. I scoured the area but didn't see anything. A moment later he barreled down the hill to a field of trampled grass. Sunflower seed shells littered the ground, along with an empty plastic Coke bottle and a relatively clean cellophane bag containing a few dry seeds. Maverick circled and barked. Someone had been here recently.

CHAPTER TWENTY

Maverick snagged a waterlogged wallet and delivered it to my hand. "Thanks, Maverick. I wonder how long this has been out here." I clenched my teeth when I read the name on the ID—Jimmy Hanson, Jr. The photo replicated a sixteen-year-old version of his dad. I exhaled and shook my head, dreading that he was the subject we were sent to find. I zipped the wallet into the front pocket of my pack and gave it an extra pat.

According to my watch, one hour and twenty minutes had rushed by. Moisture fogged my watch crystal, and I wasn't sure how much longer my old timepiece would remain accurate. My rain gear was no match for the weather. The water-repellent boots might have been useful once upon a time, but water had seeped through my socks, and I pictured my toes wrinkling and fading to white. The cold crept up my shins. Sleet accompanied the torrential raindrops lashing my face, small pellets sending icy signals to get in out of the rain. The steel-gray clouds had settled in. After taking a few tumbles in the slippery grass, I ached. Our time was nearly up, and we'd failed.

I poured half of a bottle of water into Maverick's bowl and gulped the other half. "Let's head back," I said, disheartened. Maybe we weren't cut out for saving lives, only finding dead bodies—morbid but true.

Maverick spun away from me, up the hill and out of sight. "Maverick, this isn't the time to play games," I whined.

The walkie-talkie crackled from my pocket. I took it out but couldn't understand any of what was said, so I trotted up the hill for better reception.

The voice on the walkie-talkie could have been CJ's. I couldn't understand the words. I waited for a break in the squawking and pressed the "speak" button. "Team six responding," I said. "You are not coming through. Our time is up. All we found was a wallet. Sorry, we didn't locate the subject, but Maverick has decided he's not yet finished with today's task. We hope to return soon. Thank you for the opportunity. Out." I couldn't quite pull off sounding chipper; Maverick had disappeared.

I dashed after him across a gravel road, which, according to my map, took us out of the park. "Maverick," I called. He waited just long enough for me to spot him then took off running again. "Not funny."

Suddenly I heard cascading white water. Fear enveloped me. "Maverick," I yelled. "Maverick!"

I raced to where I'd last spotted him, a rocky promontory that overlooked a fast-moving stream. Giant oak trees arched over the water, barely hanging on to the soft black soil at their bases. Maverick had made a path through the primeval glen, definitely the road less traveled. He glanced up at me from where he stood at the water's edge. The rising water foamed at his paws. I slipped and slid down the vertical hillside, twigs and brambles scratching my face and hands, my eyes locked on Maverick. My cap was whisked off my head, nabbed by a branch. The side of the hill was crumbling, washed out by sheets of rain. The level of the water rose, flooding the bank.

"Maverick, we have to get out of here. Come!" He didn't take his eyes off the water. I grabbed for his collar, and he whirled out of reach. He bounded closer to the bank and then back, a death dance as far as I was concerned. "Maverick!" I commanded with my most imposing voice. Maverick barked.

A reply made its way through the air—a cry. I turned and squinted, my hand shielding my eyes from the burst of rainwater. About forty feet away, a figure, curled in on itself, sat on a tiny island, in the middle of the stream, being devoured inch by inch by the seething water. Maverick bounded ecstatically when he realized I'd seen what he'd brought me to see. He took a tentative step into the water, but I grabbed for him and heaved him out of the churning jaws. *Now what?*

The cry across the water became a wail. "We see you!" I called. "We're coming."

We needed help. I reached into my pocket and grabbed for the walkie-talkie, but it danced from my fingers, plunked into the swell at my feet, and disappeared. I swallowed the lump in my throat.

I rummaged through my pack, recalling what little I'd

read about a swift-water rescue. I removed my rain jacket and pulled the PFD—personal floatation device—over my head and crammed what I thought might be useful into my pockets. Rope would help us cross. I snipped off a piece of webbing and made a water knot. Then I twisted the rope to form a figure eight and slipped my legs into the loops. I added another loop of webbing around my waist and fastened it with a carabiner. I tied one end of the rope to a tree trunk and secured the other end of the line around my torso, over my shoulder, and under my arm.

"Maverick, stay." Trussed up like a Thanksgiving turkey, I took my first step into the bubbling spume.

The ice-cold water swirled at my feet, a beckoning trickster. It didn't seem dangerous at first, water only inches deep. By the fourth step, however, my feet sailed out from under me. I stood, sputtering, water inching its way up my thighs. My lumbering steps on the slippery stones required intense concentration. I slid one foot forward and brought the other next to it. My hands chafed as they slid along the nylon rope. The wailing continued as the deluge increased.

Maverick waited until I was halfway across before he sailed into the water. He plunged into the surge and labored for every foot, instinctively paddling upstream against the current only to be pulled back. Rotating to keep my eyes on Maverick, I fell again. The water whisked me downstream, but only as far as the rope could reach, which was still too far. It held. Hand over hand, I pulled myself through the water. Maverick and I reached the shrinking landmass at the same time. I dropped to the ground and hugged the earth. Maverick scrambled up the incline, shook the water from his coat, and dashed to the small figure.

The wailing stopped. I hauled my waterlogged body

over to Maverick, who sat patiently while being squeezed. The little head burrowed into the wet fur at Maverick's neck.

"We have to get out of here," I said. The skinny arms clutched Maverick who stepped from one paw to the other to keep his balance. "That's Maverick, and I'm Katie. What's your name?" I waited for an answer. "Are you alone?" I waited again. "Will you come with us?" The boy looked over the water, and his arms gripped Maverick tighter. "We'll help you."

His blond hair was plastered to his head. Gray circles outlined his huge brown eyes. An elbow jutted from a tear in his muddy Minnesota Golden Gophers sweatshirt. Blood oozed through the torn knees of his jeans, and his blue lips quivered. One Nike tennis shoe peeked out from under his leg, bent at an impossible angle. He looked about six years old.

I knelt in front of him. "Let me look at your leg." Maverick licked his face as if to say, *It's all right.* When I reached for the boy's leg, he recoiled and cried out. Maverick licked his face again, and the boy settled back against my dog.

A splint would keep the leg immobile and make it easier for me to help him cross the deafening water. I hacked off a few feet of rope. A piece of bark from a rotting tree came loose in my hands. I pried a second piece loose and found two smaller, fairly straight branches and stripped them clean. I removed my jacket and bent over the boy.

"I need to wrap your leg so we can get you over there." I nodded toward the bluff. He sidled closer to Maverick. "That's right. Hold on to Maverick. Hold on tight." He reached over and grabbed Maverick then drove his head into Maverick's side. Maverick's NASAR badge came loose and I pocketed it.

I wedged one of the pieces of bark close to the boy's leg, my jacket stretched beneath it. Maverick moved closer. "Lie against Maverick." When he did, he whimpered, and his leg rolled onto the splint. He screamed and grabbed at Maverick, then stilled, which was frightening as well. As tenderly and as hurriedly as I could, I created a splint. His eyes darted from Maverick to the water, but he remained silent.

"I'm going to put this vest over your head." I removed the PDF from my shoulders, but as I reached for him, he reeled back. Maverick nudged him forward. I gently placed it over his head. "Pull the cord. It'll blow up like a balloon." The child looked at me dazedly. When Maverick licked his hand, he looked down at the ripcord and complied.

We had to be quick if I was going to get him safely across the raging water before it eroded the small piece of ground on which we stood. The boy huddled in on himself, moaning until Maverick howled with him. The boy was taken by surprise. He stopped struggling and met Maverick's eyes. I placed him in the harness, supporting his light weight against my hip and side. I grappled with the line and locked the second carabiner between the rope loop and my belt buckle.

"Ready?" I reached my arm over the boy, who began to writhe. I raised one arm in surrender. Maverick barked. I handed Maverick's ID tag to the boy. He gripped it and quieted. I lifted the harness, one leg dangling uselessly behind him. "Is it all right if I put my arms around you? We'll all cross together." I reached around the boy again and took another step into the flood. "Come, Maverick."

We collided with floating tree limbs and I couldn't begin to count the number of times I lost my footing. Each time the boy was jostled, he mewled but never cried out. When the water became too deep to wade through, I dragged the boy onto my side and locked my arm over his chest. I yanked the rope, drew it into my right hand, made one loop, pulled at the water with my cupped left hand, and scissor kicked as mightily as I could. Grab, kick, glide, and pull—a water ballet or more likely a water polka. I repeated the process for what seemed forever, yet we made so little headway.

Maverick's head bobbed furiously with each stroke he made, and when he bumped into us, he recharged me. Though my arms and legs felt like noodles, I fixed my sights on the bank and doubled my efforts. When the boy stiffened, I latched on tighter and kicked faster. I heard a crack. An oak tree loomed above us. Another crack, and the earth gave way to the rain's superior power. The tree fell. I stopped swimming and covered the boy's head with my arms, ducking mine as well. My feet touched the bottom, and I shoved off toward the embankment as the water pummeled us from every direction.

The immense wave created by the displaced water launched us near the bank. I grasped the dirt and grass and towed the boy out of the water. Breathing hard, I unclipped the carabiners and rolled the boy onto his side. His eyes were closed. I shook him gently. He sputtered and struggled to take a breath. I watched the rise and fall of his chest, then suddenly his eyes flashed open. He grappled with the PDF, confounding his efforts to sit up. He cringed when I put my hand on his arm, so I quickly unclipped the strap and helped him shed the bulk. He finally wailed.

I searched for Maverick. I scanned the bank and across the water. Frantic, I screamed, "Maverick!"

Maverick was gone.

CHAPTER TWENTY-ONE

I called his name again. I searched as far as I could see. Maverick was nowhere to be found. He'd been swept away in the raging current. I'd failed my best friend. I closed my eyes and slumped to the ground. My heart went numb. Warm tears mixed with the cold rain on my face as I moaned.

A small hand caressed my cheek, tracing the tears. I opened my eyes to a face mirroring the sadness I felt on my own. His lips were turning purple, and his little body was shivering. "We have to make it up that hill," I said, choking on my sobs. The little boy didn't make a sound.

He wrapped his arms around my neck and I checked the carabiner. I scrabbled up the face of the bluff. When we reached the top, I crawled away from the edge and untethered us. I could smell his fear. I picked up the badge he'd dropped, Maverick's photo covering the front. "Hang on to this and don't move." The boy clutched it with both hands.

I slid back down the bluff. I hoisted my pack and glanced over my shoulder, before climbing up again. I gasped, the loss slicing my heart open, and slogged back up the hill.

Two sturdy trees stood thirty feet back from the top of the embankment in a small clearing. Pieces of mined granite, stacked in a pyramid, formed a short wall on relatively even ground. The pack dropped from my shoulders. I rummaged through it and came up with more rope, which I tied between the trunks for a frame to drape a tarp and block the torrent of rainwater.

Beneath the tarp, the boy reclined with his back to the tree stump. I heaved the pack into the shelter after him and followed. Although I knew the contents, forgetting Maverick for a moment, when I opened the pack, it felt like Christmas.

"Are you hungry?" I reached for the granola bars and gasped in agony as my hand brushed the extra dog food I'd packed. *Oh, Maverick!* My soul was gutted and there was nothing I could do.

I peeled back one corner of a nutty granola bar and offered it to the boy. He snatched it from me and finished it before I opened a second one.

Drew had stowed extra socks and a sweatshirt in my pack. "Can I put some dry clothes on you?" No answer. Hearing Lorelei's disapproving voice in my head, I corrected myself as I prepared for the screeching wail. "May I?" I pulled at the sleeves of his Gophers sweatshirt and hauled it over his head. Then I gently tugged off a drenched T-shirt.

Drew's sweatshirt dwarfed his slight frame, but it was dry. I yanked the socks off my feet, and he looked up. I drew on a pair of white crew socks and offered him another pair. I unrolled it and pulled one sock onto the foot of his good leg, the sock heel reaching halfway up his calf.

The ultra-light sleeping bag blossomed when I drew the compressed form from the drawstring bag. I wrapped it around the boy and shrugged a thermal Mylar blanket onto my shoulders.

The heavy raindrops thudded a rhythm against the tarp. The sky darkened. Shadows folded in on us. I trembled. I knew the command post had certified search-and-rescue personnel, and I drew on the hope they'd surely come looking for us.

"Are you getting warmer?" No answer. "I'm going to get some wood. Maybe we can start a fire." I rose, and the boy began to rise with me. He mimicked my actions then fell back, pain etched on his face. He huddled beneath the sleeping bag. I stretched to retrieve a few dead branches without leaving him alone in the protection of the little shelter.

The wet bark on the logs wouldn't burn. Using my pocketknife, I laid bare the inner wood. The SAR equipment list required matches and Sterno, and Drew had thrown in a disposable paper cup filled with cotton balls and fine steel wool mashed together with petroleum jelly. He swore the cotton balls and steel wool would burn. I had my worthless topological map and the papers from my file to supplement the fire starters. I snapped off some dead twigs that didn't seem to be as wet as the ground cover and peeled a few pieces of birch bark from the underside of a tree branch, trusting them to be dry enough to ignite.

I never thought I'd even open the pack during the certification examination let alone use the odd combination of components from the list. I pried open the can of Sterno and tamped down the cotton balls and steel wool next, then covered them with the tree bark and twigs. I rolled the paper and compacted what little I had to make it burn more slowly. I made a teepee, standing the stripped branches on end, leaving a gap on the upwind side. Needing all the help I could get, I prayed. I struck a match. It was blown out by a gust of wind. I cupped my hand around the next match and touched it to the cotton ball. It took long enough before it lit for me to think I'd failed, but when the tinder glowed orange and the twigs crackled, I finally took a breath. The paper sheets turned black and red and curled, ash and embers floating away from the stack. Yellow and red fingers of light encircled the sticks. If only the larger wood would ignite, we'd be in business. I blew directly into the flickering sparks. When smoke climbed from the smoldering bid for fire, my eyes watered.

"How old did you say you were?" I paused. "Not very talkative, are you? Let me know if you need anything. Are you thirsty?"

The boy looked down. I was thirsty, and we could have fresh water at any rate. As I set a cup out to catch the falling rain, the thudding turned to a light tapping, and then the rain stopped.

The tarp sagged in the middle; water hung heavily between the ropes. I pulled one edge down, funneled the water into the cup, and handed it to the boy. He took one look inside the cup and tossed it onto the fire.

Smoke billowed. I coughed. My heart sank. His aim was true. The fire sizzled and sputtered. Wisps of smoke waved a final farewell. I squelched my disappointment and put on my game face. Then the rain began again in earnest. When I fell back against the stone, a piece of granite dislodged and dropped on my left shoulder, shooting pain down the length of my arm, which fell uselessly at my side. Tears burst and clouded my vision.

A little gasp escaped, and the boy leaned back against one of the granite blocks. Through quavering blue lips, he rocked and said, "Matthew."

"Hi, Matthew," I said through teeth clenched to prevent their chattering. "We'll be okay, Matthew." He handed me Maverick's badge and turned away from me. His right leg was swollen and discolored. The left side of his face was scraped, his left eye puffy.

I snuffled. I'd have to think about Maverick later. Matthew's dry eyes drooped, and he drifted toward sleep. Purple veins pulsed on his pale face. His lips formed a thin line, but at least he'd eaten a granola bar. We could wait out the storm. Someone would come looking. Even Jimmy would want to find me, if only to gloat. I knew CJ would be on our trail and someone must be missing Matthew by now.

He crawled deeper into the blue bag, and he closed his eyes. The nylon straps had rubbed my shoulders raw, and my muscles had stiffened. A sharp pain wracked my shoulder, and the little finger of my left hand tingled. I laid my head back, listening to the rhythm of the raindrops, and a whimper escaped. *Maverick.*

CHAPTER TWENTY-TWO

A rough wet tongue slobbered all over my face. My cheeks hurt from smiling until I opened my eyes and found a gangly Goldendoodle inches from my face. Startled, I lurched and clunked my head on the jagged stone behind me. I shoved the nose away and saw CJ peeling the little boy out of the sleeping bag. He nodded at me. I nodded back and let my head drop back onto the stone. *Maverick.*

The rain had stopped, and I glanced out from under the tarp. Red, yellow, and green leaves glistened in the flashlight beams that crisscrossed the clearing. The stark black bark of the wet trees and shrubs clawed into the vivid hues of the foliage.

After a cursory examination, CJ swept Matthew up in his arms, but before he could shuffle by, Matthew flung himself at me, grabbing my neck, his head crashing into my shoulder. I hugged him with my good arm and kissed the top of his head, his damp curly hair tickling my chin. He pushed himself out of my embrace, and CJ carried him from the lean-to, nearly stumbling into the arms of a uniformed officer.

I sat still. No words came to fill the void. What was I going to do? Maverick was gone. I'd lost him.

When he returned, CJ pushed up the tarp, spilling icy water over the lip and splashing it onto my thermal blanket. I yelped. I shook the Mylar with one hand, not an easy maneuver, and crumpled it over my forearm. I'd never get this one back into the tiny pack. I'd have to buy Drew a new one.

CJ pulled me upright and handed me a red-and-white striped terrycloth bath sheet. With my good arm, I rubbed it over my wet head and my hands and arms. He then handed me a flashlight. Holding the beam made me feel safer. I searched for the source of the sounds filling the air. The clearing bustled with law enforcement, medical personnel, and searchers.

"Where did all these people come from?" I asked CJ. I blinked as trouble lights clicked on.

"Most of them made up the search party for Matt. After Emma's apparent abduction—"

"Foiled abduction," I interrupted.

The corners of CJ's lips turned up and vanished so quickly I might have imagined it, but his eyes told the naked truth. "Matt walked away from his parents' campsite this morning. They immediately called the authorities. You have done well, grasshopper." I flinched as his warm hand gently cupped my injured shoulder. "But we must see to this."

Scar barreled into the clearing, the leash so taut that Jimmy Hanson skied through the wet leaves. They stopped in front of us. "Too bad, missy," he sneered.

CJ stepped between us. "There were mitigating factors."

"Rules is rules," he taunted.

Hazel's amplified voice cut through the tension. "NASAR evaluators, please. Over to the blue tarp."

CJ and Jimmy turned and stomped into the gathering.

I searched for Matthew and found him sitting in an ATV surrounded by three adults, his arms crossed, drawn in on himself. One bandaged leg stretched out in front of him. I watched as he shied away from a curly-haired redhead who ran her hand up and down his side, inspecting him for other injuries. Her kind eyes were bright with tears, and when she finished her examination, she crushed him in an embrace, pinning his arms to his sides. He cringed. When she released him, he said, "I'm hungry." The adults scurried to find him something to eat. He saw me. I thought he almost smiled before looking away.

Missing Maverick, I turned back, tears threatening to fall, when a voice boomed through the loudspeaker, "Katie Wilk report to the…" The voice faltered, looking for an apt description. "…shelter." I swiped at my eyes and traipsed back the way I'd come. Groups of searchers congregated and whispered. Eyes surreptitiously peeked at me, wary of a call sounding too much like a command from the principal's office.

The assembly spilled out from under the tarp. Loud voices rose above the low murmuring, persuasive, vigorous, and robust. The bodies parted, and I walked through to find CJ and Jimmy nose to nose, Hazel's border collie nudging first one and then the other as if she could break up the fight brewing.

"Listen, my Na-tive-A-mer-i-can friend," Jimmy bellowed, deliberately articulating each syllable. "Rules is rules." He jabbed his forefinger into CJ's sternum. CJ's jaw clenched as his torso rose and fell in rapid succession.

"If she had not been out here, we might never have located Matthew in time. We don't know what could have happened to him. Katie and Maverick have met all the conditions for certification."

"Everyone has ninety minutes to locate their subject. That's it. No more. She failed." Jimmy slapped the rulebook in front of CJ's face and fanned the pages.

"Your son was no longer at his post when we contacted him," said Hazel.

"He heard the flash flood warnings, don't ya know," Jimmy mocked. "I can't help it if missy here ain't smart enough to come in outta the rain."

"My name's Katie," I said, closing the gap between us. Jimmy snorted.

I pulled the drenched wallet out of my pack and peeled it open. "I think we found where he should've been before our time was up. You can check the call-out log on the walkie-talkie. We couldn't understand what you were saying, but according to my watch, we were at one hour and twenty minutes. I can take you to what we found. Your son left a pile of garbage I'd like to pick up anyway." I hoped the roar of one of the ATVs meant that Matthew was on his way home.

"We'll sort everything out. Where's little Jimmy now?" Jimmy answered Hazel with a shrug.

"The rookie who took the missing-child call didn't have the protocol for contacting us right away, but we had a great number of kindhearted individuals willing to help search. Katie, however, made a remarkable save, and Maverick brought her to Matthew," she said.

"If there ain't any ex-ten-uating circumstances, and the dog knew what it was supposed to do, it would've returned to missy here and shown her the way back to the kid," said Jimmy.

A woman from the crowd interrupted. "Excuse me. I know Matthew. He's a high functioning autistic child, and his parents were immediately concerned." Everyone fell silent. "Maverick followed procedure exactly. Matthew's extenuating circumstances just weren't visible to *your* eyes."

Smiling gently, CJ said, "It's time to get everyone home, to dry clothes, hot food, and drink. Everyone is safe."

I couldn't hold it together anymore. "No, they're not. I lost Maverick!" My voice broke, and I hunched over, my arms wrapped around my empty heart. I fell to my knees and sobs were torn from me. As CJ knelt in front of me, worry clouded his face, making deep crevices in his forehead.

A bark answered my sob.

CHAPTER TWENTY-THREE

It wasn't just any bark. Maverick's scraggy form limped from the rear of the shelter. His head bobbed deeply and he struggled to lift his paws. He panted heavily but made his way through the forest of legs. He budged his bruised, battered body next to me. Blood seeped through his stitches, and he wore a wooly wet-dog odor, but he was mine. Unable to speak, I cradled his head and gave a silent prayer of thanksgiving.

CJ said, "We have more than a quorum, more in attendance here than at any other meeting. I move we take a vote now."

"Fine by me," Jimmy said with an air of superiority, exuding a feeling that the outcome of the vote was predetermined and would go his way.

Hazel nodded. "All in favor of granting credentials to Katie and Maverick as a probationary K-9 Search-and-Rescue Phase II team, please signify by a show of hands."

CJ's hand shot up as his penetrating eyes swept every square inch of the shelter. One by one, hands rose all around me, slowly at first and then in a flurry. Stunned and silent, Jimmy stalked out from under the tarp.

"Katie, you and Maverick are on your way." A smile eased onto Hazel's serious face. "Good job." She reached into a pack on the floor and pulled out a red vest. "Have Maverick wear this when you are working as a search-and-rescue team." Then she led the group out of the shelter and directed them to a variety of tasks.

CJ helped me up. "He brought us to you. I would have told you right away if I had known you thought Maverick was lost."

My good hand lingered on top of Maverick's head. He licked my fingers.

"We need to get you back," CJ said. "Mrs. Clemashevski will string me up if I keep you much longer."

He held my keys and opened the rear door for Maverick and the passenger door for me. I held out my hand to collect my phone, which he fished out of his vest pocket. I turned it on and swiped through a long list of missed calls, voicemails, and texts. It seemed everyone had heard about our escapade.

"Alrighty then," I said, and connected with Ida first.

"Katie." Her voice was calmer than I'd expected. "Dr. Bluestone called and told us you're safe."

"I just wanted you to know we're on our way back to town."

"I'll have something ready for you to eat."

"Thank you, but you don't have to do that."

"Humph. See you soon." She clicked off.

"You should have told her about your injury," CJ said.
"She will know soon enough."

"But I'm fine. My shoulder is just sore."

"You should get it checked out. It could be worse than you think."

"Or better than *you* think."

He kept his eyes forward, both hands on the wheel as he drove. Maverick licked my ear and I had to laugh. CJ looked at Maverick and me and laughed with us.

My phone rang. "Dr P" flashed on the screen. Still laughing, I answered, "Hi, Pete."

At first, I thought no one was there. Then I heard a tight voice ask, "Is that you, Katie?" Maverick kept me giggling, licking my ear and my neck while I tried to answer. "Are you all right? Ida called and said you hadn't completed your certification. Then she called and said the group had assembled a search party."

"We passed." I tried to temper my happiness; he sounded so serious.

"I was worried. But it sounds like you're doing just fine."

"We are. We found a little boy." Maverick reached a paw over the back seat, struggled to get closer, and pressed on my shoulder. My laughing stopped abruptly and I cried out in pain.

"Katie?"

"My shoulder's a little sore," I said.

"Do you want me to come home?"

In retrospect, I probably answered too flippantly. "Absolutely not. You take care of business. I'm fine. I'll see you when you get back Monday. Okay?

"Sure," he said, sounding deflated.

I heard Susie in the background. "You're being paged, Dr. Erickson."

"I've gotta go. Glad you're good. Is CJ taking care of you?"

"Yes, he is. See you soon." He hung up and I sat, looking at the photo of Maverick on my phone screen, trying to determine the tenor of our conversation. Maverick nudged me and licked my ear again. I repeated quietly, "I'm fine."

"Did you say something?" CJ asked.

I made my face bright. "We should celebrate. Could we stop and pick up a bottle of—"

"Champagne would be an appropriate libation. But I think dinner is in order first."

Before she got too involved in creating another scrumptious dish, I called Ida and invited her to join us for supper. CJ and I would drop off Maverick, and I'd clean up before heading out for a bite to eat. She declined with a grunt, her opinion of restaurant food.

By the time we arrived at Las Tapas, the line snaked out the door, and patrons crowded next to the building. Fine mist beaded on my raincoat and water dripped from the brim of CJ's felt hat. There was no waiting in the bar, so he ushered me through the throng. He ordered a margarita instead of champagne for me, and club soda with lime for himself. The celebration commenced with chips and salsa.

Five mariachi musicians strolled among the tall tables, wearing silver-and-turquoise studded *charros*, the sequins and gems on their black jackets glinting in the lights. Speedy fingers flew over the *vihuela's* strings with the opening strains of *La Malagueña*. When they finished, they took requests and played old standbys. The trumpeter, Felipe, a student in my third-hour math class, grinned widely. They sauntered to our high-top table amid strains of *Cielito Lindo*, and the entire bar joined in the refrain.

"You and Maverick did well today," CJ said. He dunked a warm tortilla chip and hurried it to his mouth.

My cheeks ached, and I could barely form words around my proud smile. "Not everyone was happy, though."

"Jimmy is a selfish blowhard. Just ignore him."

At that moment, the blowhard bulldozed his way up to the bar. He sneered in our direction, and my heart nearly stopped. "Speak of the devil," I muttered.

CJ glanced over his shoulder and lifted his chin in acknowledgment. Jimmy grabbed a tall glass filled with amber liquid and headed our way.

"Celebrating?" He snatched a stool from a nearby table and shoved it in at the end of ours. Liquid sloshed over the sides of his glass as he sat down. He elbowed the bowl of chips out of his way, hunched his huge shoulders, and squeezed his bulk between us.

CJ nodded. "They earned it."

Jimmy hollered, "Hey, kid." Felipe took it in stride and stepped up to Jimmy. "Bring me some clean chips and dip." He pointed his index finger at my nose. "You have work to do, missy, or I'll make sure the certification don't stand."

"The paperwork is already complete, Jimmy. You know we can always use the help," CJ intoned mildly.

"What's this 'we' shit? You don't have a dog and you don't do diddly."

CJ went silent. Jimmy didn't read the signs, the calm before the storm. CJ said, "Will you excuse us, please?"

CJ motioned to the server, who'd been waiting patiently to place our paella on the crowded tabletop. As CJ lifted the chips and salsa to make room, his hand deftly caught the rim of a passing tray of margaritas and upturned the icy slush. As it cascaded down Jimmy's back, the primitive howl silenced everyone around us.

"You son of a bitch!"

"Sorry, Jimmy," CJ said with exaggerated remorse. He pulled too much cash out of his wallet and placed it on the table. Felipe scooped up the bills and winked my way as waiters, waitresses, busboys, and even the host rushed to clean up the mess. CJ handed the host another twenty and said, "*Para pagar por el otro.*"

As he pressed a towel onto Jimmy's shoulder, Felipe said sincerely, "*El hombre esta un desastre.*" We then stood to take our leave.

"Whadya say, ya beaner?" Jimmy said.

"I said this is a disaster, sir." Born in Minnesota, Felipe answered in perfect English and stifled a chuckle.

By the time we reached the exit, the energy in the restaurant had reignited, and we no longer could hear Jimmy's protests. CJ chortled, and it took a beat before I laughed with him. "How about a pizza?" I asked.

The double doors in front of us opened. We stepped back to allow two uniformed officers access. A pudgy redhead swaggered in with his thumbs hitched onto his belt, thrumming the fingers of his right hand over his sidearm, itching for action, his gaze darting around the room. As the officers' eyes adjusted to the dim light, they scanned the sea of curious faces, zeroing in on CJ and me.

They both took a step closer.

"Chantan John Bluestone?" the younger of the officers inquired. CJ nodded and handed me my car keys. "Ma'am, I'll have to ask you to step aside." His hand came up between CJ and me.

I sputtered. The voices in the room quieted, again. I heard glass clinking and utensils clanging. With all eyes on the activity at the door, Officer Ronnie Christianson pulled out a well-worn note card and recited, "You have the right to remain silent." He looked up briefly for a reaction from CJ, who nodded curtly, then continued. "Anything you say can and will be used against you in a court of law."

Disbelief flooded my entire being and I quaked. "There has to be some mistake."

"No mistake, Ms. Wilk," Officer Christianson said sadly and continued. When he read the line about hiring a lawyer, CJ's jaw tightened and he threw me a lost look. Officer Christianson concluded the Miranda warning as his fellow officer spun CJ around and roughly snapped on a pair of handcuffs. CJ lifted his chin.

"What did he do?" I asked. "Why is he being arrested?"

"Murdered that girl in the state park," the young officer volunteered, much too eagerly.

Officer Christianson hissed, "Quiet!"

CJ's stoic face showed the resignation of someone who had undergone similar treatment before, a misidentified perpetrator, first on every hit list. He nearly toppled as the officer shoved him out the door.

"Yeah!" Jimmy bellowed, then pumped his fist and turned back toward the bar.

I stood frozen in the entryway, seeking a sympathetic face. One by one, the staring eyes retreated behind large plastic menus and super-sized margarita glasses—that is, all but Jimmy's. He smirked, toasting me with his tall glass.

My trance was broken when Felipe stepped in front of me. "Ms. Wilk, can I call someone for you?"

I lowered my eyes to my shaking hands and my keys tumbled to the floor. Felipe scooped them up. Flashing a dazzling smile, he said, "It's my birthday. I'm one hundred today."

"What?" He was an exceptional math student and absolutely couldn't be one hundred today or any other day in the foreseeable future.

"I'm one hundred today," he repeated, lights dancing in his dark-brown eyes. "In base four. One-zero-zero. Gotcha, didn't I?" He chuckled and offered his arm.

I took it and couldn't help but marvel at this young man's compassion. He escorted me to my car, but before he handed me my keys, in a manner much older than his newly acquired sixteen years would dictate, he asked, "Are you okay to drive?"

"I'll be fine," I said, yet again. "Thank you, Felipe." He bowed slightly, gave me a thumbs up, and made his way back to the restaurant.

I sat in my car and considered my options. I could call Pete, but he and Susie were in the middle of their weekend training. Ida would undoubtedly worry overmuch, and Drew was on assignment. Chief Erickson might take my call, but I was unsure of where he was in terms of recovering from his heart attack, and I didn't want to upset him unduly. I pulled my phone from my bag and scrolled through the short list of contacts. My finger hovered for a moment over one name, and then I pressed down firmly.

CHAPTER TWENTY-FOUR

Jane Mackey's voice sang when she answered, "Katie."

I could barely hold back my tears. The ride on the emotional rollercoaster stole my words: fear of failing the SAR exam, pride in locating Matthew, despair when I thought I lost Maverick, euphoria at his return, and utter confusion with CJ's arrest.

"I'll be on the first plane out," she said, and before I could speak, I was left contemplating the silence in my hand.

I concentrated on safe driving, hands at ten and two, steady foot on the accelerator, the officer's words circling in my head. A murderer? Not CJ. I hadn't known him long, but I knew him well enough to bet he was being railroaded. New to the community, he was a huge, powerful presence.

He'd helped bring Emma home—anyway, it *appeared* he'd brought Emma home. He was an ex-Navy SEAL with all the skills and training that came with it, but he also was a kindhearted veterinarian. He'd taken great care of Maverick. He spearheaded the search party when I didn't show up. He'd helped find Matthew. And he was my friend.

I shook my head to clear away even the shadow of a doubt. When Jane arrived, she'd know what to do.

My car rumbled up the drive to my apartment. On one side, lined up perfectly straight, the squat apple trees of Ida's small orchard guarded the grounds. The new earth that had been turned over in the garden plot smelled fresh and healthy from the composting. For a few minutes, I sat in my car, taking deep breaths and exhaling over a slow count to ten. In with the good air and out with the bad, and the headache niggling behind my eyes receded.

No sooner had I closed my back door than a bold knock rattled my porch door. Ida stood, stout and stalwart. Wisps of hair escaped from a white bandana, framing an understanding face. I'd already forgotten how quickly the gossip tree tendrils curled into the obscure corners of Columbia. Of course, she already knew everything.

Her arms reached up and I stumbled into her embrace. "There, there, *a chara*," she muttered with a faint Irish brogue as she stroked my back. She'd been cast as Caitlin, Dylan Thomas' wife, in the community-theater performance of *Dylan,* and continued to perfect her take on the role.

I reluctantly pulled away when our height difference overpowered my need for a hug. I dug a half smile from my bag of tricks. "I'm okay, but I have to do something."

"When I heard what that devious little hussy had done, I wanted to wash my hands of the both of them, but I suppose I should give him the benefit of the doubt. She thinks she can just waltz in and he'll stumble over his own feet in order to do whatever she'd like him to do."

"I'm sure he didn't do anything. He's a good man, but I guess being new in town paints a target on his back." I replayed the words she'd just spoken. "Ida, what are you talking about?"

Her eyes opened wide. She reddened—even the tips of her ears looked like they were burning with embarrassment. "Faith and *begorrah*, what are *you* talking about?"

"CJ was arrested at Las Tapas." I closed my eyes and shook my head. When I opened them again, my eyes met compassion and support.

She hustled me back into an iron embrace. "Oh, Katie, I'm so sorry." Then she held me at arm's length. "Tell me what happened."

"They hauled him away in handcuffs. I need to find an attorney, someone who can figure out how to help him. He didn't do what they said he did. I know he didn't." I knew, absolutely.

"I still have friends in my husband's law firm."

"I didn't know Casimer was an attorney."

She smiled softly, reminiscing, still missing the love of her life. "Well, he was and a darn good one at that. We can call…" She hesitated. "The best criminal defense lawyer in the firm would be Dorene Dvorak," she announced, seemingly as much for her benefit as mine. "Let me get my little black book."

When she returned, she flipped through the pages. Thick angry lines were drawn through many of the entries, even "Dvorak, Dorene," but the numbers were still legible. "I haven't had much interaction with members of the firm lately, but call her and tell her I gave you her number. I don't know whether it'll help, but it can't hurt."

I punched in the numbers. After two rings, an unexpectedly young, disembodied voice told me to leave my name, number, and a brief message. "Ms. Dvorak, my name is Katie Wilk. Ida Clemashevski told me to call you. The police arrested a friend of mine who's new to Columbia, and I'm looking for a way to help him. Please give me a call." After I left my number, I punched "end" and sat for a minute, staring at the phone in my hand.

I flinched when Ida put her hand on my shoulder and squeezed it. She pulled her hand away and asked, "What happened to you?"

"I got a little dinged up is all." My shoulder already felt better. She headed toward the door, but before she left, I asked, "Ida, who's the devious hussy?"

Guilt kept the corners of her mouth from making their way into a real smile. "Susie."

CHAPTER TWENTY-FIVE

My fists sat on my hips. "Out with it."

She looked down, trying to hide the guilt in her eyes. Then, she looked at me. "This is all hearsay, mind you."

"You're stalling, what could be so horrible?" I stepped in front of her, blocking an escape.

She took a deep breath. "I heard Pete might not be back this week. There's a conference in Las Vegas on the use of telemedical robots to extend the reach of specialists not available in our remote area, in an attempt to upgrade our hospital to a Level II Trauma Center." She rushed on; she'd clearly been rehearsing these lines. "Pete and Susie are attending."

"Well, doesn't that just beat all?"

"I'm sorry, Katie."

I could pull off nonchalance; I'd had plenty of practice. "Pete and I are just friends." But she and I both knew I secretly hoped for more.

Before she could comment, my ringtone chimed, and I read, 'Unknown Caller.' I felt Ida's anxiety mount as I continued to let it ring. "Curiosity killed the cat," I said.

"Satisfaction brought him back," she retorted in her theater voice.

I took the call. "Katie Wilk."

"This is Dorene Dvorak of Tupy, Dvorak, and Sticha. You said you're looking for legal representation. Where did you say you got this number?" Dorene spoke so rapidly I had to ask her to repeat what she said. "Never mind. Why do you need an attorney?"

"I don't need an attorney. I think my friend might need one, though, and I heard from a very good source that you're the best."

"Why do you think your friend needs an attorney?"

"I was with him when he was arrested an hour ago."

"Where was the arrest made?"

"At a restaurant, Las Tapas."

"Was he Mirandized?"

"The words about anything you say can be used against you? Yes."

She sounded disappointed. "What's your relationship with him?"

"We're friends; we're both new in town, and I thought…" Her interrogation made me uncomfortable.

"What's the charge?"

"He didn't do it."

"They never do." She raised her voice. "What's he been charged with?"

The word caught in my throat. "Murder. That teenage girl from Center Valley." I heard a gasp behind me.

The rapid-fire questions ceased. Then a low slow voice crawled over the phone, "You expect me to take the case of the son of a bitch who killed my little sister's best friend?"

I gulped. "He didn't do it!"

"That's what they all say," she repeated.

The silence grew. I heard keys clacking and labored breathing. "I'll talk to him myself. The arraignment is scheduled for Tuesday afternoon," she said.

The phone clicked off. Ida stood wringing her hands. "Murder? Katie, no."

"I'm not sure having Ms. Dvorak would be a good thing. She said the murder victim is her little sister's best friend."

Ida's brow furrowed deeply. "Lorelei Fiorillo?" Her attention shifted back to me. "Katie, you shouldn't get involved."

I felt the unspoken word—again. The last time, both of us could have died.

"CJ needs a friend. He's a good man, Ida."

The unease grew until I changed the subject and added, "Jane's coming back."

Ida let out a sigh. "When will she get here?"

"Not soon enough."

Jane had been collateral damage when a bottle of wine I'd given her had turned out to be poisoned with the blood thinner, Warfarin.

"Speaking of …" Ida began but was interrupted by the old-fashioned ring tone on her cell phone. "Hello, Grace."

With a huff, Ida hefted her body out of the chair. "She's at my front door." I accompanied Ida, concerned over why our elderly neighbor was out at such a late hour.

A flimsy sweater slipped from Miss Grace's narrow shoulders, and a cane extended from a tightly clenched gnarled hand.

"Grace," Ida ushered her inside and escorted her to the most comfortable chair in the room. "What are you doing out at this time of night?"

"Pete cut back on some of my medications, and the fogginess I've been struggling with seems to have lifted a bit." Miss Grace shivered again.

"You sound wonderful. Let me get you some hot tea."

Miss Grace sat like a queen, head up, hazel eyes clear, back erect, hands folded in her lap. She spoke so distinctly I never would have known it was the same woman.

"Monica Parks' daughter, Carlee, came to call on me." I took her cold hand in mine. She took a deep breath before continuing. "I believe she needed an ear." She pulled some well-worn papers from a pocket in her dress.

"She was curious about these letters and her mother isn't very patient. I know from personal experience." Miss Grace's hand shook slightly as she handed them to me.

I carefully unfolded the brittle paper, splitting at the folds. Faded ink covered both sides and had begun to bleed through the stationery.

"Read it aloud," she ordered.

"My dearest one and only Alice." I looked up at Grace, who nodded for me to continue.

"I know you're disappointed about your new situation, but it was necessary in order to keep the peace in the family. You've every right to be angry. Rob's comment about you being the only one not working and, as such, the only one free to attend to her needs, was way out of line. I told him as much. But now you'll be able to put your CNA training to good use.

"Becoming a concert pianist is the dream you've breathed every day, and you work harder than all of us put together, babe, but then you aren't at the beck and call of an unreasonable boss. All of us have an eight-to-five job or one of us would have taken on the ornery old bat. Besides, she likes you. Mom promised to buy you a grand piano. Pick out any one you want. She can afford it. And play lots of Brahms. She likes Brahms.

"We bundled you off to Minnesota too quickly for me to adequately thank you. After her heart attack, we needed someone on-site to look after her. Ignore her when she gets in a cantankerous mood. She has a mean streak and she's been known to drive away more than one caregiver. Underneath it all beats a heart of pure gold—or at least one worth its weight in gold. We'll laugh about it later. Remember there's a light at the end of the tunnel, and I'll be waiting there for you. All my love, Luke."

The second note was written in a black felt-tip marker on a lined sheet torn from a spiral notebook, the shredded ends worn fuzzy with time.

"Alice," I read aloud. "Sign the damn papers dissolving our crummy marriage already. Your abandonment caused me to look elsewhere for solace. Velma and I are having the child you didn't want. The settlement is more than fair. Keep the piano. Luke."

"And no one knows Alice and Luke?"

Miss Grace shook her head.

"I'll talk to Carlee on Monday," I said, and guiltily remembered I still needed to complete her magic cube too.

A moment later, Ida arrived with her silver service

tea set, three unmatched gilded china cups, and a plate of Scottish shortbread. She poured the tea and handed a cup to Miss Grace. "It's chamomile," she said gaily. "We'll all sleep well tonight."

I hoped so.

CHAPTER TWENTY-SIX

Maverick and I raced around the block before accompanying Ida to Sunday service. I found both rituals calming and sent my own silent prayers for Dad, Carlee, Ida, Miss Grace, CJ, Jane, Drew, Pete, and his dad. Susie could pray for herself.

On our way home, I asked Ida, "Do you think they'd let me see CJ?"

"I'm afraid not. You're not family. You'll just have to wait."

"He doesn't even know I talked to anyone."

"He will. If I remember correctly, nothing remained secret at the station for long. Even if Dorene chooses not to represent him, she'll have made a thorough inquiry, and she'll know everything she needs to know about CJ's truthfulness, his military service and veterinary education, any youthful indiscretions, his political idealism, his future aspirations—even the color of his favorite socks."

She gave me a rueful smile. "I'd bet she ends up taking his case. If he's guilty, she'll see him hung by his thumbs and drawn and quartered. If he's innocent, she'll find the perpetrator and do the same." She left me deep in thought.

CJ didn't kill Lorelei, but someone did: a boyfriend, a girl friend, an ex, a boss, a stranger. Maybe I could help Dorene.

I didn't hear my bell ring. Maverick padded across the floor and I looked up. "Jane!" I cried.

My friend held me tightly, long enough for my thudding heart to slow. "Can't you ever stay out of trouble?" she said.

"You look wonderful. How are you? How did you get here so quickly?" She laughed. I'd almost forgotten her father owned an airline.

"What's going on, girlfriend?" she asked. "How's Pete?"

The words tumbled out before I could think. "He and Susie are headed to Las Vegas for a conference. Together. But Maverick earned a spot as a probationary search-and-rescue dog. CJ's a great teacher."

Jane held up a hand. "Who's CJ?"

"CJ followed Emma and Maverick home when we thought she'd been kidnapped." Her brow furrowed. "CJ's the new veterinarian in town. Pete's old flame lives next door. She's Emma's mother, and she's gorgeous." Jane shook her head and raised her eyebrows. I raced ahead with more explanation. "CJ was arrested for the murder of a girl we found, and…"

Jane put up a hand. "Whoa. You need to take a breath

and start over."

"Are you here for good?" I asked.

Warm friendship ignited in her luminescent brown eyes. It was wonderful to see Jane so vibrant and healthy. "I have one more week off before it's back to the classroom."

As I swallowed her in a second embrace, my phone buzzed in my pocket. I pulled it out and looked at the screen. "One sec." My cheeks were beginning to hurt from smiling so broadly.

"Hi, Dad."

Sometimes Harry Wilk labored to form words and they might be a bit difficult to understand, but he had been diligent with his speech therapy. The obstacle course he'd navigated in his recovery often set him on his ear, and tedious exercises he knew he should be able to do frustrated him. He understood where he had been and where he wanted to be, but he simply couldn't get there by himself. Yet.

"I needed to hear your voice, Katie." I understood every word.

"I'm glad you did. How are you?"

"Slow and steady wins the race. I am one bald turtle." His humor gene was intact. "Your mother and I are looking forward to a visit."

I believed my dad wanted me to see him, but I doubted the same could be said of my stepmother. I missed him terribly, but she had asked me to back off.

She was correct. If he wanted to talk to me, he had to pick up the phone and make the call himself. He had to articulate his words and verbalize cohesive sentences. He had to strive to make things happen.

"We'll get together. Mother…" Oh, how that word

rankled. "...asked me to wait for the doctor's okay."

Jane mimed her greetings. "Jane says hi."

"Tell her hello." His tone became serious. "When will I meet her?"

"Soon."

"Good. And how's Maverick?"

"He passed his certification to be a search-and-rescue dog."

"A proud mama." He sounded tired. "I'll call again next Sunday."

"Bye, Dad." *Get well*, I prayed.

"He'd like me to visit," I said to Jane. "But I don't think Elizabeth will give her blessing yet. She has a full plate with her fancy new job at the cryogenic firm, in addition to taking care of Dad. I'd hate to disrupt the flow of progress he's making. And right now, I'm on Elizabeth's good side."

"Stay on her good side," said Jane. "Now begin again with all of your news."

I rambled on about the last few weeks with my litany of ups and downs, disappointments, and successes. If I had to judge, I'd say the good outweighed the bad, until CJ's arrest.

"You need to prioritize. What's important right now?" I began to answer, but Jane shook her head. "If you can't do anything, you can't be effective. Decide what you can do something about."

"I can't do anything about Pete and Susie, and I can't do anything about CJ. But I can teach."

"Now that I have that problem solved, what do you have to eat?" Jane asked.

"Let's go see Ida," I said, laughing.

CHAPTER TWENTY-SEVEN

Jane and Ida left me with the dishes, my sole contribution to lunch. I'd dried the last dish and refreshed the ice in my glass of Mrs. C's Long Island Iced Tea when Ida knocked and stuck her head in the door. "Dorene's taken CJ as a client," she said, tilting her head. "Seems there isn't sufficient evidence, and the district attorney won't press charges at this time. They released him but ordered him to stay in the area."

"That's good. Right?" I said, hopeful. "I can't begin to imagine why she'd represent him if she didn't believe he's innocent."

I reached for the phone many times throughout the rest of the afternoon, only to draw back. But my few endearing qualities didn't include the ability to wait patiently. I willed the phone to ring, for CJ to call and tell me he was fine.

When my phone finally chimed, I punched "accept" so quickly that I fumbled the phone without reading the number on the display. Maverick, who'd been resting quietly, rose and barked in earnest. I couldn't hear the speaker.

"Quiet, Maverick," I pleaded. He circled his mat, gave another woof, and flopped down.

"Hello? Hello?" I said. No one spoke immediately, and I thought I'd lost the connection.

"Ms. Wilk, this is Carlee Parks," the voice said softly.

"Hi, Carlee," I said, anxious to finish a conversation barely begun in case CJ should call.

"I heard Maverick's been certified as a search-and-rescue dog. Congrats."

"Thanks, Carlee." I tapped my foot impatiently.

"I'm sorry to bother you but have you had a chance to solve the cube yet?"

My face felt red and warm. "So much was going on here ... I'm sorry. I totally forgot. I have time tonight, though. I should be able to finish it."

"Thanks, Ms. Wilk."

"You bet. Ah, Carlee? Miss Grace stopped by and showed me the letters you found. Is there anything I can do?"

"No. I guess they belonged to the previous renter. They're just kind of sad, I think."

"I think so too. I'll see you in the morning. Let's say seven fifteen?"

"I'll be there," she said solidly.

Guilt is a powerful motivator. I arranged my kitchen table with my instruction sheet, a pencil and notepad, a few of Ida's snickerdoodles, and a cup of tea. I located Carlee's jumbled four-by-four-by-four cube and turned it over in my hand. Someone had printed letters on each individual square.

The steps for rearranging the faces of the cube were similar to those I'd given my classes for the smaller cube, but I repeatedly returned to my notes to confirm that I performed the algorithms correctly. After I'd completed each move, the cube should have a certain configuration so I knew immediately when I made a mistake. Frustrated, I began again and again.

Lost in the puzzle, the ringing doorbell felt like harassment. I tossed the cube aside and stretched before looking out the window. CJ gazed over Ida's small apple orchard, pulling his hat brim through his hands. I took a deep breath and opened the door.

Fine lines at the corners of his eyes dug deeply into his face. The creases chiseled at the corners of his mouth framed a slightly forced smile.

"Come in, CJ."

"I really cannot stay, but I wanted to apologize for the other evening. I also wanted to thank you. They have not filed charges because there isn't enough evidence, but they led me to believe I remain their number one suspect."

"Ms. Dvorak must believe in you." I looked down and added softly, "I believe in you too."

I hauled him into the kitchen and sat him at the table. Then I boiled water for more tea. When I couldn't stand it any longer, I asked, "Why do they think you murdered that girl?"

He breathed in through his nose and out through his mouth. "The victim was last seen at the Lost Pirate Pub, and there is a witness who claims I left with her." He lowered his head, and when he lifted it again, fire filled his eyes. "She is mistaken."

Sensing my discomfort, CJ pushed the chair back as if to stand. "Perhaps I should go."

"It's not you. Stay. I have some promises to keep before I sleep."

"But the woods are lovely, dark and deep," he added in a charming baritone. "What can I do?"

I fanned the recipe cards I'd researched for the Columbia Days tea. "I have some baking to do. And I promised to bring this completed cube to one of my students tomorrow."

CJ wrinkled his brow. "I cannot help you with the puzzle, but give me the recipes and a short course on your kitchen." His eyes circled the room. "On second thought, let me be adventurous. I will find my own way while you solve that." He pointed to the cube.

Fifteen minutes passed. I blamed my inability to concentrate on the clanging of metal utensils against bowls and the whirring of the mixer. In reality, I thought about everything but the cube: the case against CJ, my classroom, science club experiments, the high tea, and not the least little bit about Pete and Susie off together … studying. As the savory aroma of baking wafted from the oven, I closed my eyes.

I tensed when warm hands kneaded my shoulders. CJ stopped, but when he began again, I melted almost immediately. His strong hands found all the right trigger points and I relaxed, transported for a few minutes, away from my worrisome world. The oven dinged and his hands stopped.

"Thanks," I said.

I concentrated on the algorithms until each side coalesced into one color. When the final square slid into place, I felt a huge sense of accomplishment until I looked at the clock.

In the time I'd taken to complete the cube and collect my thoughts on paper, my kitchen counter offered tasty tidbits I could offer the girls for their tea. I set the cube aside and stood, astonished by the heart-shaped shortbread lightly sprinkled with yellow sugar, covering half of the counter. There were more trays of what smelled like gingerbread in the oven. What a deal!

"Look at all this. They're perfect. You're amazing, CJ. I never could have made anything that looks this good."

A smile slid into his eyes and his hands found their way back to my shoulders. When he pulled me close, my arms reached around his waist, and I held on as warm tears spilled from his cheeks to mine. When he relaxed, I stepped back and heard my door creak open.

"Emma saw your truck and…" Pamela began. "Oh." She retreated.

"Pamela, wait," I said. Her hands were bracing the doorjamb. "Please, come in." She looked at me with a mixture of contempt and confusion. "Please," I repeated. Emma peeked out from behind her mother and scampered into the room.

"Hi, CJ," she said with a bright smile. "It's past my bedtime, but I told mommy 'no sleep' until I say hi. So here I am. Hi, Katie."

CJ bowed to Emma and her yellow curls bounced as she giggled. Resignation crossed Pamela's face and she followed Emma into the room.

"Pamela, CJ made some shortbread cookies for the

ambassador high tea. Would you and Emma like to taste test them?" I insisted.

"You made them?" Pamela looked incredulous.

"Please, Mommy? Pretty please? Then I'll go right to bed. I promise."

Reluctantly, Pamela nodded, and CJ whisked Emma up onto a chair. He put two misshapen shortbread cookies on a paper plate in front of her. Then he made a big show of folding another paper plate, and with a few snips from the kitchen shears, he reverently placed a crown on Emma's head. She tittered. He passed Pamela a plate with two more cookies. I poured a glass of milk for Emma and a cup of herbal tea for Pamela. She took her seat deliberately, eyeing the cookies with distrust.

She took a small bite of shortbread and daintily raised her teacup. "When I was an ambassador, we had cucumber, dill, and cream cheese on white, egg salad on rye, and curried chicken salad on pumpernickel bread cut into triangles. Those might work out nicely for your high tea."

Of course she'd been an ambassador.

"I still have our recipes in a scrapbook. Do you think your students would like more help?" The timbre in her voice warmed.

"Absolutely." I filled her in on the details and printed a copy of the meeting schedule.

Maverick padded over to Emma and leaned close enough for her to stroke his silken ears. CJ kept Emma spellbound by making more headpieces out of the paper plates; he placed some on her head, some on his head, and some on my very tolerant dog. Emma told CJ about the puppy she'd seen but couldn't bring home. "Mommy's 'lergic." Pamela reddened, maybe caught in a little white lie. Emma went on. "She's just like Maverick. She has soft ears." Emma mimed floppy ears by flipping the blonde curls on both sides of her head. She added, "And big feet, and she gives messy kisses. And I want to call her 'Outlaw' after you, CJ." All the air was sucked out of the room, as Emma continued, oblivious to the consternation of the adults. "That's what Daddy calls you."

"He didn't mean it," Pamela said, scandalized.

After a few heartbeats, CJ let out a hearty laugh, and I took a gulp of air. "Emma, he has a point there."

Pamela relaxed, but I watched CJ's face for any sign of heartache. When he'd spoken of his own Outlaw, his heart had squatted soundly on his sleeve. I hoped Emma had conjured good memories.

Pamela clearly had a wonderful experience as an ambassador. We'd been visiting for about twenty minutes when she glanced at her watch. "I'm sorry we bothered you. Adam is so much better at putting Emma to bed, but he has a meeting. It's way past her bedtime, and we've got to go. Thanks for the snack. And Katie, I'll get back to you tomorrow. Just a thought, but Miss Grace used to judge the competition. I think I could talk her into helping too." I nodded vigorously.

"I need to be off as well. Let me help you with Emma." Emma leapt into CJ's arms, and they strolled out into the evening, laughing.

I boxed the goodies, careful to separate the layers with waxed paper so they'd keep well, and then I put them into freezer bags to protect them. When I finished cleaning up the kitchen, I searched for the cube and had to grab the slimy toy from Maverick's jaws, the letters all but washed away by his wicked tongue. Shaking my head, I tucked the cube into my briefcase.

After one last glance at a science webpage, I discovered an experiment designed to suck an egg into a bottle that required just a few items. I boiled eggs and wrapped them in fluffy terrycloth hand towels. Next, I sorted through the recycling and found a clean olive oil bottle with a slightly larger mouth and wrapped it in newspaper. Then I rearranged the interior of my briefcase to hold all the items. Magic experiment on its way.

CHAPTER TWENTY-EIGHT

Carlee dashed through the door at seven fifteen as if she'd been waiting outside until the minute hand reached three. But when I handed her the completed cube and the instructions, her shoulders slumped. She tried to hide her disappointment, absentmindedly fingering a gold-and-blue pendant. She looked at me expectantly. I shrugged. "It didn't turn out the way I thought it might," she said. "Maybe you can show me how to do it?"

"Absolutely." I brought out the completed cube and a copy of the instructions, explaining the descriptive symbols so she could try another one herself. She copied the letters too. "Are you coming to science club after school? I bought some kits to determine blood types."

As her fingers fumbled righting the cube, she laughed.

"That has to be less painful than rearranging this thing."

"Have you heard from Ana?" I immediately regretted asking. Her eyes closed and she held back tears. I covered her hand with mine.

We heard a shuffle and looked up. Felipe stood in the doorway, a grin sitting sideways, shaking his head of curly black hair. He raised his eyebrows and gave me a thumbs-up. I returned the gesture and he nodded. "Come on in," I told him.

"Naw," he said. "I had to work late last night, and I've got some homework to finish before first hour, but maybe another time." He disappeared.

"Do you know him, Ms. Wilk?" Carlee's voice sounded wary.

"Yes. He's in one of my algebra classes." *He's smart and has a very kind heart.*

"I heard some things about him."

"Don't believe everything you hear. Didn't people talk about me too? And do you still believe everything you heard?"

"Well, you really are tough." She laughed and added, "But fair."

* * *

While I arranged supplies for my latest, great idea, the science club students chatted animatedly until Felipe rounded the corner to my classroom.

Galen glowered. "What do *you* want?"

Felipe put on a toothy grin. "I want to learn more about science."

"Why?" Brock asked.

Felipe shrugged. "Maybe I want to be a doctor."

I was about to intervene when Carlee raced passed me, and, breathless, threw her books on a desktop close to the door. "There you are, Felipe," she said. "I've been looking all over for you."

"I think this is a mistake," he told her, turning to leave.

"Look." Carlee held the completed smaller cube in her hand. "You said I could do it and I did." She turned to the rest of the students and glowed. "I tried and tried and Felipe said, 'Try again.' And here it is." She turned to me, a question in her eyes. "I invited Felipe because he likes a good puzzle too, and I told him we were the future problem solvers of the world."

Galen's attitude lightened.

Ashley called the meeting to order, and Lorelei took roll.

"What are we doing today, Ms. Wilk?" asked Brock.

"Getting an egg into this bottle, handsfree." I held up the bottle I'd brought.

Brock hissed, "Very funny. Raw?" I pulled out an egg, cracked it on the desktop, and peeled it. "Oh."

"After determining your blood types." I read the disclaimer on the packet before distributing the kits. Then we followed the YouTube link to a short video. It appeared the only squeamish one was me.

Within two minutes, everyone had his or her own blood type and Rh factor.

"But what does this mean?" Felipe asked, his eyes belying his innocence.

Galen muttered under his breath, which was unusual for him.

"What did you say?"

"My mom almost died when she was younger. They

thought her brother would be a compatible donor. Turned out they were only half siblings and weren't related closely enough." Knowing nods commiserated for a moment. "It was rough on my granddad."

"Knowing your blood type can save lives," I said.

"How accurate are these results?" asked Carlee.

"The label says it's reliable."

The students had more questions than I had answers, so I wrote them down to research later.

"If there's no more discussion, we'll move on to the next agenda item," Ashley announced, assuming presidential control.

I lit a match, put it in the bottle, and settled the hardboiled egg on rim of the bottle. When the match went out, the air pressure inside the bottle decreased, sucking the egg inside. My egg experiment performed magically.

Galen projected the puzzle geocache he and Carlee had selected on the SMART board. "It's been starred thirty-seven times as a favorite."

He was interrupted by a knock on the doorjamb.

"Do you have room for one more?"

The kids surrounded Jane, pelting her with questions about where she'd been, if she'd returned for good, and if she'd help them find their next geocache. We looked at the description and laughed.

The scenario involved orders given by a Navy Admiral to several Petty Officers. It quickly became mind-boggling.

Jane barked a laugh. "What do we do?"

"This is going to take way too much time, and I've got a lot of homework tonight," Brock grumbled.

"Me, too," said Galen. "This one needs to simmer."

Ashley adjourned the meeting and the boys raced out.

The girls stayed just long enough to discuss details about the high tea for the upcoming Columbia Days festivities and taste CJ's cookies. They were a hit. And so was getting veteran help from Miss Grace and Pamela Farley.

Jane nibbled. "I think I need to meet this man," she said.

"How about tomorrow? I owe him dinner for making the goodies."

Jane said, "You're not cooking, right?"

CHAPTER TWENTY-NINE

A potluck made up of Jane's colorful spinach salad, CJ's orange amaretti cookies, and Ida's warm oat bread, *haricots verts*, and marvelous chicken Marbella took dining at a picnic table to an all new high. I didn't think she could top serving my wine in her Waterford crystal, but I was wrong.

After dinner, Ida brought out white ramekins and torched the sugared tops. There would always be room for her fantastic crème brûlée. She'd prepared enough for an army, so when the Farleys stepped out into their back yard, she invited them to join us. Adam hesitated, but Emma insisted, pulling his hand and dragging him around the gate into the yard.

CJ made the first overture. "You have a handful there."

Adam glowed. "You could say that."

Smacking her lips, Emma skipped over to Ida and crawled into her lap. "What are we having today, Mrs. C?" She leaned in and, in a stage whisper, said, "She doesn't think I can say 'Clemashevski.'" Her hands cupped her giggles, and the adults relaxed. Emma plopped down next to Maverick and brought up her dream of owning a puppy named Outlaw.

CJ seemed to have forgotten that Adam and Pamela weren't interested in owning a dog. "I can help train the puppy," he volunteered eagerly.

Adam lowered his head and twiddled his thumbs. The spoonful of creamy dessert stopped midway to Pamela's mouth. Jane wriggled in her seat. Ida cradled Emma. Suddenly aware of his faux pas, CJ tried to retract his offer, but Emma, oblivious to the turn of events, pressed on. "Daddy, I'd take care of Outlaw. She can sleep with me. I can feed her." She scratched behind Maverick's ears. He leaned closer and gently lapped at her sticky fingers.

"And who will walk her and pick up her poo?" Pamela asked wisely.

"Ew. Gross, Mommy."

"But that's what you have to do for puppies, honey," Pamela said. "That would be a big job."

Emma thought for a moment and said, "For a big girl. Maybe next year?"

Jane had been circling the rim of her wineglass with her forefinger, and it began to hum, and then ring, the tension rolling away on the oscillating waves.

"Pretty," said Emma, yawning.

Adam stood. "It's time for bed, sweetheart."

"G'night," Emma said. Her father picked her up and

slung her high on his shoulder. She wrapped one arm tightly around his neck as her thumb went into her mouth. Then her head drooped.

"Thank you," Pamela said and followed Adam home.

"I overstepped." CJ frowned, frustrated.

"It's nothing that can't be fixed," Jane said.

CJ praised Ida for her cooking and buried Jane's hand in his. "It's been a pleasure," he said, with a slight bow.

After he left, Jane jumped out of her chair. "Katie, he's so cute. I can certainly see the attraction."

"There's no attraction." And then I wondered.

She looked at me and rolled her eyes. "Whatever."

"Do you see why I don't think he murdered anyone?"

CHAPTER THIRTY

Carlee barreled around the corner of my classroom. "Ms. Wilk. They arrested him!"

My heart sank to my knees.

"It'll be okay, Carlee," I said, as much for her benefit as mine. Tears rimmed her eyes and her face contorted in an effort to hold them at bay.

"I know Felipe didn't do it," she said. I exhaled; it wasn't CJ. "It's just not fair. None of that stuff was in his locker this morning. He didn't have it with him, and he never left school. But Mr. Ganka won't listen to me. He said a student, DeAnne something, told him about the stuff in Felipe's locker and that this was a formality, and I could make my statement later, but Ms. Wilk, all the proof will be gone."

Galen breezed in. "Told you, Carlee."

When she narrowed her fierce gray eyes, he backed off. "He didn't do it, Galen. Someone else put that stuff in there." She focused her attention on me. "Can we do a fingerprint analysis on these?" She carefully pulled a blue hairbrush and a lovely gold watch from her pocket wrapped in tissue.

"Where did they come from?"

She gauged the look on my face. "They're mine. I want to see if our botched terrarium experiment will work on metal and plastic as well as it did on glass."

I couldn't contradict her.

Galen already was on it. "Put them in here and we'll see what happens." She dropped them into the plastic box he held. He poured the super glue into a bottle cap and set it between the watch and brush and closed the container. The legs of the chair screeched as he pulled it across the floor and climbed on top. He positioned the box above the cupboard near the heat vent and shoved it far enough back so we couldn't see it.

"Mr. Ganka was waiting with a police officer when Felipe opened his locker after school. The officer pulled out a backpack, but Felipe said it didn't belong to him. Inside were some items that were reported stolen Saturday night. Right then and there, they slapped handcuffs on and hauled him away. Ms. Wilk, I saw into his locker this morning. That backpack wasn't there. I even texted Brenna, telling her I needed to clean out my locker so it could look half as neat as Felipe's." Carlee pulled up a message thread and held up her phone. "And I ate lunch with him. They can tell he didn't skip classes and wouldn't have had time to put those things in his locker this afternoon."

"What's with the watch and brush?" I asked.

She carefully chose her words. "Hypothetically, these items could have been dropped in the hallway and picked up by some unsuspecting bystander. And, hypothetically, if these were evidence of a crime, they might have the fingerprints of the real thief, especially if he, or she, wasn't careful. I have Felipe's fingerprints here." Triumph glittered in her eyes and she pulled out a water bottle. "We can at least compare."

"This isn't a game, Carlee."

"No. It isn't," she said, her eyes gleaming with intensity and purpose.

She put the water bottle in another plastic container, and Galen repeated the steps. Hypothetically, all we could do was compare two sets of fingerprints. It wouldn't tell us anything for certain.

"He didn't do it, Ms. Wilk," Carlee said. Galen snorted, and she turned to him. "He didn't!"

"I'll believe it when I see it," Galen said.

Voices filled the math commons, and Carlee shot Galen and me a pleading look. She snatched the ingredients for another closed terrarium, and by the time the other club members rounded the corner, she was ready to spray the moss and seal the lid.

The air was charged with curiosity and innuendo, but no one mentioned Felipe's absence. No one had any ideas for unraveling the mystery geocache and talked about giving up. But after a chocolate chip cookie sugar rush, they decided to let the puzzle percolate for one more day. Ashley adjourned the meeting.

Reluctantly, I packed up too, and, with an uncomfortable final glance at the boxes, turned out the lights.

* * *

A flurry of what, I thought, might once have been a roll of paper towels greeted me when I stepped in the door, and I had to admit to the minor neglect of my roommate. I hoped a long walk would do us both a world of good.

When we finished walking, I decided to organize my diverse thoughts and created a map of connections to Lorelei Fiorillo. Although there were multiple threads to possible individuals, I had only one with a certain link—CJ.

My phone chimed.

"Katie, are you up for pizza?" a familiar voice said. "We just got back from our course in Vegas."

"Absolutely, Pete. Where are you?"

"I just pulled into the hospital parking lot, and if you order now, I'll get there while it's still hot."

"Done."

My smiling cheeks ached by the time the doorbell rang thirty minutes later, but it was just the pizza guy. I tipped him well, and looked in both directions before closing the door. My mouth watered, and Maverick drooled as the aroma of goat cheese, eggplant, roasted red pepper, and caramelized onion blossomed from the cardboard box. I set it in the oven on warm.

We waited.

And waited.

I opened a bottle of Cabernet Sauvignon. It had plenty of time to breathe, the instruction Drew had given me as an oenophile.

And waited.

I folded napkins into abstract origami shapes.

I splashed kibble into Maverick's dish, and when he'd finished eating, he barked. I opened the door to let him out in time to catch CJ stepping onto the landing.

Cradled in his arms squirmed a yellow puppy. "Oooh,

CJ. She?" He smiled. "She's adorable. What's her name?"
He lowered his head and mumbled.

"Did you say 'Renegade'? Come on in," I said.

"She needs to get down for a few moments before we come in." Maverick chased the adorable puppy down the steps. They sniffed private parts and not-so-private parts, romped around the yard, ears flapping, tails wagging, and marked everything stationary before galumphing up the stairs, tripping over every other riser. Renegade leapt into CJ's open arms and, after an inquisitive head tilt, Maverick bounded inside.

"Is she yours?" He nodded. "How old is she?"

"Eight weeks and a handful. I let her out every hour last night, and she eats like there is no tomorrow and soon is going to get too big for this." Nuzzling in his arms, she wriggled beneath his gentle ministrations. "She could get to be fifty-five pounds. I don't know if this is a good idea but the Humane Society has so many to rescue." His face was full of smiles.

"Are you hungry? I ordered pizza, and it's going to dry out if it sits any longer. I have a very nice cab if you're interested."

He looked strangely at the table. "You were expecting company."

"I'm thinking something came up. Sit down. And Renegade will be fine if you put her down. I think my apartment is pretty puppy proof." She hit the floor and attacked a paper-towel scrap. CJ's warm laugh came from somewhere deep inside. She scampered to Maverick's dishes and slopped water over the rim.

"Another potty break soon, I'm afraid."

Renegade and Maverick circled the living room and

chased through the kitchen. Curious when the action stopped, I peeked around the corner and found them playing tug-of-war with a bra. Mortified, I snatched it and stuffed it far under a couch cushion.

I murmured, "Breathe." I pasted on a happy face and returned to the kitchen.

CJ pulled out my chair and poured me a glass of wine. He retrieved a glass of water for himself and sat. "For what we are about to eat, let us be truly thankful."

"Amen. Dig in."

When the meal was a memory, we found both dogs lying near the fireplace, Renegade snuggled into Maverick's side. Maverick's eyes blinked with the admonition, *Don't bother her*, then slammed shut. Thunder rumbled in the distance, and rain pattered lightly on the windows. CJ knelt in front of the dogs, placing kindling and small logs on the grate before lighting it, a cozy glow flickering on Maverick's black coat.

While we sat on the couch, CJ picked up the geocache puzzle description. "What is this?"

"It's a mystery geocache, but my students and I haven't been able to decipher the coordinates from the clue."

"Can you explain what a geocache is?"

"It's a high-tech scavenger hunt. The information should direct us with latitude and longitude to wherever this…" My fingers indicated the size of a pea, then ballooned to encompass some imaginary container the size of a triple popcorn tin. "…cache might be. Sometimes there's a log to sign. Sometimes there's trinket to exchange or a travel tchotchke to move along. But this solution has eluded us."

CJ picked up the printout of the geocache and the

pencil, and moments later he had filled in all the blanks. "Could this work for you?"

I grabbed one of the GPS units and entered the possible solution. "How did you do that?"

"I substituted each military rank with a pay grade, which, by the way, is identified by a number."

"Are you busy tomorrow? Would you like to go with us to look for the geocache? You can tell the students how you solved the puzzle. I think they'd like that."

"I'm not sure everyone would be amenable to my help."

"I am, and Jane will be there too. Besides, I told the girls I didn't make the goodies for their tea. They should meet their baker. They were in awe of your culinary expertise."

I must have frowned. CJ tilted his head and said, "Is there something bothering you?"

"Have they told you any more about Lorelei Fiorillo's murder?"

He shook his head. "I have a favor to ask. If something should happen—" The doorbell rang.

"Don't worry," I said. CJ rose and followed me into the kitchen. Renegade trotted after him. Maverick brought up the rear.

Pete stood in the doorway, dripping, extending a bouquet of flowers. "Looks like I'm interrupting."

"I came to show off my new pup and am on my way out." CJ slapped his hand against his chest, and Renegade flew into his arms. She was a fast learner. He sidled past Pete out into the rain. "Goodnight, Katie, Pete." He and Renegade disappeared.

"I'm sorry. We finished the pizza," I said.

At the same time, Pete said, "I'm sorry. We had an emergency." He delivered a stilted laugh.

"Can you come in?"

He waited a beat then said, "Sure. Just for a bit." He gave me a hug and kissed my cheek. "Susie and I have to head back to Minneapolis tomorrow afternoon." He added, softly, "I've missed you, Katie."

He talked about the courses he and Susie were taking, but after repeatedly yawning, he cut short our reunion.

CHAPTER THIRTY-ONE

Worrying about Felipe and CJ exhausted me. I had a burst of energy, however, when, at the end of the day, Jane showed up at my classroom with CJ in tow, proudly displaying his plastic visitor badge clipped to the lapel of his soft blue denim shirt.

"Welcome to my domain," I announced, arms wide. His cowboy boots clomped around the room as he investigated the displays, pulled out books, tapped manipulatives, and hesitated in front of the puzzle of the week.

Each of the science club students, in turn, stopped abruptly when they reached the doorway. They couldn't miss the imposing figure. After getting a nod from Jane and me, they entered stiffly, unsure, heaving backpacks onto desktops, and dropping into their chairs. Their eyes never left the huge man attempting to make himself invisible by reading the minuscule historical biographies on the mathematician posters I had plastered on the walls.

"I'd like you to meet Dr. Bluestone, Maverick's veterinarian, and my sous chef," I said when everyone had settled into their desks. "I think he might have figured out the solution to the puzzle for our mystery cache and I was hoping you might invite him along to see if it's correct."

"How'd you do it?" asked Brock. "What did you get?"

"Are we going to try to find the geocache today?" asked Ashley.

"You made some great pastries for our tea," Brenna said, grinning widely.

"Give him a chance." I beckoned CJ to the front of the room and said, "Dr. Bluestone, you're on."

He pulled a notecard and flash drive from his pocket and asked me to load a file named "Flummoxed." While it whirred into action, I took a seat at the rear of the classroom. He brushed the edge of the notecard. He coughed. He shuffled his feet. Then he recited a story, using his own name and rank, a story about a Navy SEAL, his dog Outlaw, and their friends and colleagues. The narrative reappeared on the screen behind him, with words similar to our original puzzle, and below it was a list of naval ranks with corresponding pay grades. He never said another word. The students worked together and they could barely contain themselves as they volunteered their solutions.

"That is correct," CJ said.

When they finished substituting numbers for paygrades in our original scenario, they raced out the door. Jane, CJ, and I plodded along behind.

The coordinates were spot on, and they found a pinkie-size, magenta-colored bison tube hanging from the branch of a fir tree

"Brock and I get to choose the next one," Lorelei insisted. "These can be…" I think she almost smiled, but she finished her sentence with, "…challenging."

For our snack, I passed around a plastic box with more baked goods. "These are the rejected samples of what Dr. Bluestone made for the Columbia ambassador tea."

Heads bobbed and Brenna mumbled her appreciation around a mouthful of gingerbread. By the time the students left, even the crumbs had vanished.

Jane said, "You were a Navy SEAL. You bake. You're a veterinarian. You're a K-9 search-and-rescue team trainer. You teach. Do you dance too?"

CJ's cheeks took on a healthy, slightly-more-than-pink hue. "Not if I can help it."

* * *

Carlee and Galen waited in my classroom, anxious to compare the fingerprints on the items Carlee had collected.

"We don't even know if it'll work," I said.

"Okay if I get the box down?" Galen asked, his foot poised above the seat of the chair. I nodded.

"What's going on?" asked Jane.

"We're conducting a fingerprint experiment," Carlee said. Galen delivered the box and Carlee took a deep breath before she opened it. She tugged on purple nitrile gloves then carefully arranged the contents on the tabletop in front of her.

The watch case and crystal were clean, polished, with no fingerprints. Carlee's shoulders slumped. However, finding fingerprints covering the watch fob and the handle of the brush, her eyes gleamed.

Galen also had donned gloves and extracted the water

bottle, which sported a full set of dusty white prints. He pushed two of the items together and demonstrated how he might have held them. "It makes sense that one of these prints could be a thumb. Let's get to it." He'd come prepared, producing a magnifying glass from his back pocket, and began to compare the prints, his head bouncing back and forth as if he were watching a tennis match.

He looked up triumphantly and Carlee paled.

"They aren't the same," he announced, and not unhappily. Carlee exhaled. We huddled closer and after careful scrutiny, confirmed the judgment.

"Although they do appear to come from different sources, how do you propose to prove your friend's innocence?" CJ scowled.

"This validates our theory," Galen said. "Someone else is the burglar, so now we have to figure out who that is. We have to determine who has it in for Felipe. Who'd benefit from his arrest? Who had access to his locker? Who had motive, means, and opportunity?"

Carlee cringed but didn't back down. "Looks like we have another kind of puzzle to solve.

"I'm going to the restaurant to talk to Felipe's grandmother." Carlee bolted from the room. Galen shrugged and followed her.

"What's wrong CJ?" I asked.

"They are too young to be playing with fire and there are embers surely smoldering." He hung his head. "But I owe the young lady an apology. Who is she?"

Jane was quick on the draw. "Carlee Parks." After noting my displeasure at her disclosure, she added guiltily, "What?"

CHAPTER THIRTY-TWO

Unable to decipher the dim red numerals on the digital clock, I repeatedly pressed the alarm button but couldn't get the noise to stop. I caught a flashing light in my peripheral vision and threw my hand in the general direction, groping for my phone. I pressed "answer" and I tried to formulate an acceptable greeting, but before I could utter a single word, a voice said clearly, "I don't like being blindsided. What's wrong with him? We have to do something about his naïveté."

I sat up, rubbing my eyes. "Who is this?" It came out more irritated than inquisitive. I read the time. "It's four fifteen!"

"This is Dorene Dvorak. I just finished having a long heart to heart with your friend. I don't know what Parks' agenda is, but she wants to slap a restraining order on him and any more shenanigans will dig his hole that much deeper, more fuel for the prosecutorial fire." Speaking of being on fire, she was steaming, but I didn't understand and when she didn't get the response she was looking for she started over. "Dr. Bluestone and I met last evening to talk. He explained the misunderstanding at school yesterday. He'd made the young lady a dream catcher, and he wanted to apologize."

I sat up, fully awake. "What happened?"

In a much more even tone, Dorene said, "We stopped at Carlee's home so he could give her the gift and tell her he was sorry. I stayed in the car. Her mother answered the door. I don't think she knew I was there at first. I couldn't hear what was being said, but I watched long enough to see she was goading him, jabbing her finger into his chest. When she saw me get out of the car, she slammed the door in his face. The next thing I knew, I received a call from Ronnie Christianson. Carlee's mother had called and made a complaint. If he ever bothers them again, she'll file a restraining order. I gave Officer Christianson my version of the events. He said he understood but also said I need to convey to Dr. Bluestone the magnitude of his actions and the possible repercussions. Carlee is Monica Parks' daughter and Parks is the primary witness claiming CJ was the last person to see Lorelei Fiorilla alive. My God, Katie! He doesn't seem to have a clue." After a long silence, she asked, "Katie, are you still there?"

"I'm still here."

"Talk to him. Tell him how important it is to stay away from her. From them. Everything he does will be scrutinized. He has to play by their rules. They're looking for any reason to throw the book at him."

"How are you so sure he isn't the one who…" I couldn't finish the sentence.

"I've talked to him. He's not her type. I believe him, and I've never been wrong."

She hung up. An unfounded traitorous retort slipped from my lips. "There's always a first time."

I crashed back onto my pile of pillows and squeezed my eyes closed for what felt like an eternity. When I finally opened my eyes and read the numbers on the clock, only ten minutes had elapsed. I decided to put the time to better use and prepare lesson plans. When my phone rang again, two hours had passed.

I took the call from CJ. "What?" I said acidly.

"Did I wake you?"

"No. I've been up for hours," I huffed.

"Ms. Dvorak has spoken to you. I would like to explain."

"You don't have to."

"Renegade would like to go for a walk with Maverick. Would you allow me to escort her?"

He hit me where my heart was. Narrow streaks of pink stretched across the sky and peeked between the dark-gray clouds that hovered outside my living-room window. I probably needed to give CJ a chance. "Can you and Renegade meet us here?" I asked.

"Yes." I could just about hear the smile on his face. It wouldn't be there long if I had anything to say about it.

Fifteen minutes later, Maverick and I were playing fetch in the yard when CJ's truck rolled to a stop. Little Renegade had matured by the hour it seemed. She sat in the front seat while CJ clipped on her leash and waited until he curled his forefinger, indicating she could join him. She sat again while I opened the gate, regarding CJ for instructions, and only when Maverick showed signs of exuberance did she drop the Miss Perfect façade and yank her leash away from CJ in favor of chasing Maverick around the yard. Her sharp teeth tugged at his ear, and he yelped.

CJ whistled. Renegade stopped immediately and dropped her rump to the ground. Maverick did the same. "How did you get them to do that?" I asked with envy.

"Practice and patience." He looked at me sheepishly, and added, patting a small black pouch attached to the belt at his waist, "And I bribe with homemade dried sweet potatoes." He tossed a small treat to both. "Down." Renegade and Maverick dropped flat. My mouth fell open.

After I clipped on Maverick's leash, CJ snapped his fingers and the four of us headed toward the wetlands preserve, a tree-lined walking path surrounded by drying shrubs and riddled with wildlife scent. I exerted a tremendous amount of self-restraint and CJ had to walk fast to keep up.

Eventually I blurted, "What on earth were you thinking? Why did you visit the Parks family?"

"The students don't know what trouble they can get into. I have a strong premonition of danger."

"Perhaps your own?" My ears burned and my face warmed.

I immediately regretted the smart remark, but CJ ignored it. The lines on his face deepened.

"Monica Parks is lying," he said with such conviction I could see how Dorene Dvorak would be swayed. "I did see the girl at the Lost Pirate. I had stopped in for a bite to eat. She and her friends were difficult to miss. They were giggling and whispering, heads bent together.

"I recognized Parks. I believe she was trying to attract my attention at the bar that night, but I must not have reacted with adequate enthusiasm. I was not interested in any female companionship...then." The word hung in the air.

Me? Did he think we could be a couple? Did I think we could be a couple? Did I want to be a couple? What about Pete? What about Susie? It was too much to think about.

He knelt on one knee. Renegade stopped romping and returned to his waiting arms. He lifted her and buried his head in her fur. Maverick sauntered over to me. I knelt and he cleaned my face.

When CJ released Renegade, we finished trudging through the preserve. The sky had faded entirely to gray, threatening rain.

"Will you and Renegade become a search-and-rescue team?" I asked.

CJ snorted. "That remains to be seen."

Raindrops sprinkled, and we hurried down the path, racing to beat the storm. By the time we splashed onto Maple Street, my hair was plastered to my head. I shivered. "Would you like to come in for a cup of tea?"

"If it's not an inconvenience."

When I opened the gate, two figures, wearing yellow rain slickers and standing beneath a cartoon-character umbrella, leaned against the jamb. A sleeve rose in greeting. CJ froze. I shielded my eyes from the downpour, squinting through the torrent. Carlee and Galen waved from the top step. "I'll leave it to you" CJ said. He glanced at Carlee, and heeding Dorene's instructions, he limped down the sidewalk, threw himself into his truck, and roared down Maple Street.

"What's up?" I asked, breathless as I reached to unlock the door.

"We have some more hypothetical questions for you," Carlee responded, her eyes shining.

I unlocked the door, and the three of us traipsed into the kitchen, puddles forming at our feet. Carlee squealed in delight as Maverick shook cold droplets of water all over. We removed our squishy shoes and our rain gear dripped from the hooks by the door.

"We're pretty sure we know who framed Felipe," Carlee said.

"Jimmy and his gang of thugs are bullies," Galen stated matter-of-factly. "Why would Lorelei have ever dated him?"

"Jimmy?"

"Jimmy Hanson, Jr."

Like father, like son.

"They choose a victim and pick on him mercilessly. They never let up. Felipe laughed it off at first, but he's been in their sights for a long time. His grandmother taught him the importance of turning the other cheek, but he only has two," Carlee sighed.

"Four," Galen teased.

"What?" Carlee said. "Ugh," she grumbled.

"You do realize none of this evidence would be admissible. There is a protocol to follow, and we're doing a lousy job." I understood the depth of CJ's frustration. We could all get into serious trouble.

"This won't be absolute proof, but if we talk to the right people, maybe they can get legal confirmation that will hold up," Carlee said.

"Let's get Mr. Ganka to place a live-feed camera in

Felipe's locker and suggest to Jimmy that law enforcement isn't convinced of Felipe's guilt," said Carlee. "If someone else can get into the locker, Mr. Ganka would find out, and if not, Felipe would be in no worse shape. It's a win-win, isn't it?"

"The locker's already been searched, hasn't it?"

"We can hint that they are coming back for a more thorough search. Looking for something they might have missed."

School officials had the right to examine lockers. But we could make things worse for Felipe. "I don't know. We need to be careful and keep quiet about all of this."

Carlee mimed turning a key in front of her lips and tossing it over her right shoulder. Galen crossed his heart.

Maverick's nails clicked across the floor. He dropped two dripping shoes and sat at Carlee's feet. Carlee knelt by his side and scratched his head.

Three heads tilted with pleading eyes. I caved. "I'll talk to Mr. Ganka tomorrow and see if we can find the hardware," I said.

Galen pulled a wireless webcam from his pocket with an instruction booklet and passed it to me.

CHAPTER THIRTY-THREE

I ain't done nothing. I'm tellin' ya, my dad's gonna beat ya silly. It's all Felipe's shit. He did it." Jimmy Hanson's words permeated the walls, leaking out to the executive secretary's desk. Mrs. McEntee continued making rapid keystrokes to drown out the vitriol spewing from the young man.

Drew Kidd, in his capacity with the Burglary Task Force, had already requested Felipe's attendance record, but had found no unexplained absences. Drew stood rooted outside the door, verifying Jimmy Hanson's attendance record. Two burglaries had occurred during school hours and Jimmy wasn't where he was supposed to be. If I squinted, I could just make out the form of Jimmy Hanson, Jr. through the thick opaque glass windows outlining the door, crossing his arms and twisting in one of the chairs next to Mr. Ganka's desk, waiting for his dad to show up.

And show up he did, in full regalia, work boots clomping down the hall, heralding his approach. I guess the boots could have pounded louder, but the sound was muffled by dirty blue boot covers. Jimmy Hanson, Sr. was poured into a long white coat sporting a mélange of red and brown, his long arms dangling below the cuffs. The coat flapped open, and underneath he wore green scrubs. His scraggly facial hair was stuffed into a white beard catcher, and the hair on his head was pulled back into a man bun. It turned out Jimmy Hanson, Sr. was a butcher.

When he saw me, anger flashed. "What're you doing to my boy?"

Mrs. McEntee rose, a barrier between us. "This way please, Mr. Hanson." She had a commanding voice. I wanted to stay, but it was apparent by Jimmy's murderous glances over his shoulder that I wouldn't be welcome. I stacked the plastic bin with cans my students had remembered to bring for the Columbia Days' food shelf collection and made my escape.

I thought the students had all gone home so I didn't expect the hum of activity coming from my classroom.

"Just wish she'd lighten up," said Brock.

"She's so good at intense," another voice answered. "But it works for her."

"I'll talk to her," said Jane.

I flew around the corner and planned to tell them that I thought Lorelei was perfect the way she was, and that we all have our idiosyncrasies.

Talking stopped.

Carlee and Galen stood next to the whiteboard, markers

in hand. Ashley and Brenna worked at the counter. Brock sat at a desk, writing furiously. Jane observed from the chair behind my desk and her eyes grew to saucers when she saw me. She mouthed the word "later." But Lorelei was directing the group so they weren't talking about her. Oh my!

"Did I forget a meeting?" I asked.

Not missing a beat, Brenna said, "We have an update."

"Felipe's family couldn't afford his bail," Carlee said, "so he's been sitting in juvie, awaiting his release. Felipe was safely locked up and was out of the picture. Your goading—"

"What?" I tried to sound incredulous.

"—gently prodding Mr. Ganka into being politically correct worked. He placed the camera in Felipe's locker. Galen discussed the lack of evidence in Felipe's case and made certain Jimmy overheard him. Jimmy took the bait and tried to plant more evidence.

"They caught Jimmy trying to slip some stolen tools into Felipe's locker. Felipe hasn't been exonerated, but Mr. Ganka is more inclined to believe him now. We hope Felipe will be released later today. Jimmy, on the other hand, is in big trouble. They aren't sure they can charge him, because he continues to deny any involvement other than returning Felipe's things. If we could put him on-site at just one of the burglaries, it would be so much easier."

"Why did he ever decide to pick on Felipe?" asked Brenna, shaking her head.

"Jealousy. Boredom. The inability to deal with someone else's success," I offered.

Jane said, "Unfortunately, Jimmy's alibis for all but two of the burglaries are almost as good as Felipe's."

My students made their way out the door, and I left a voicemail on Drew's phone. "Can you stop in when you're finished? I have something to show you." I thought he should see the pieces Carlee had fingerprinted, hypothetically.

Jane and I sat at a table in the commons area.

"Have you seen Drew since you came back to town?" I asked.

She shook her head. Her eyes grew large, and her face turned pink. This was going to be good. We didn't have long to wait.

Drew marched through the door, slipping a notebook into his inside jacket pocket with one hand while pressing buttons on his phone with the other. He glanced up and stopped midstride. A puff of air escaped. He froze. Jane had been gone a couple of weeks. I wondered if their ardor had cooled.

Nope. Drew rushed Jane, picked her up, and swung her around in a circle, reenacting a slow-motion boy-gets-girl-back love scene. Jane wrapped her arms around his neck and planted a wet one on him. As they came to a stop, he eased her to the floor, and when her toes landed, they both stepped back as if they'd touched a flame, which was my cue.

I retrieved the plastic boxes and shoved them across the table. "Jane will tell you about the pieces the kids found. They might be helpful," I said, and reached for my briefcase.

"Wait," Jane said in a high-pitched voice then covered her mouth with her hand.

Neither Jane nor Drew appeared eager for me to leave, so I stayed and listened to Jane's description of the contents.

"Felipe should be released as soon as I can get all the information to the prosecutor." Drew glanced at his watch. "I've got to hurry to get it done yet today."

He was torn; duty clearly battled with his desire to stay with Jane.

"I'll be at Katie's house," Jane said. "Call me when you finish."

Drew nodded and rushed out the door.

For the next ninety minutes, Jane and I played cribbage on the picnic table in my back yard for a penny a point. She won every game; I was glad to see her leave when Drew arrived. She took me for $3.17.

CHAPTER THIRTY-FOUR

Good morning, Ms. Wilk," said Felipe, grinning, a bright and cheery beginning to a new day.

"It is, isn't it?" I replied in kind.

"I can't thank you enough."

"Your friends did it all."

"Yes, but they needed someone to believe them, to believe me, and that was you." He beamed. "I'm not out of the woods yet, but I have a riddle for you." I groaned. "The rules are easy. You're walking in a maze with two guides. You come to a juncture where there are two paths and only one leads to the exit. You can ask one question to one guide to help you decide which path is correct. There's a catch, though: one guide always lies, and one always tells the truth, but you don't know which is which. Which one question will you ask?" His dark eyes sparkled with mischief before he disappeared.

After school, I still was trying to wrap my head around the riddle when my science club students poured into the classroom for an impromptu meeting. All talk centered around Jimmy Hanson's arrest and how this person or that person had known about it all the time. As gossip swirled, Ashley resisted calling the meeting to order. After they finally settled into their routine, roll call was taken, noting the absence of Carlee and Felipe. Galen shrugged at the questioning looks.

"The puzzle caches are great, but they take a lot of time to figure out so could we table our geocache until next week?" asked Brock.

"I so move," said Lorelei. All hands raised in affirmation.

"Do you have anything quick we can do, Ms. Wilk?" asked Brenna.

From my stash of paper magic, I pulled out a blue folder that contained identical strips of paper, one inch wide. I retrieved a small box of scissors and a few rolls of tape. "Everyone, take two strips. Tape the ends together to make one ring and interlock a second ring made the same way. Without creasing the circles, can you make a square?"

A soft rap at the door drew our attention to Felipe grinning gloriously. "May I join you?"

Galen said, "Park it here, buddy."

I had them tape one circle to the other so they wouldn't move. "Cut through one circle lengthwise," I instructed. A circle remained at each end of one of the strips.

"Handcuffs," said Felipe, the light in his eyes dimming a smidge.

I continued. "Cut through the middle of the linear paper strip lengthwise. And voilà." I held a square.

"Do you have any more of these tricks?" asked Brenna. "We could offer some entertainment with easy paper projects at our *Titanic* Tea."

Their heads bobbed. They combed through my notecards, gauging the difficulty and time involved with each exercise. The group surprised Brenna and Ashley even more by volunteering to partner up and attend the tea to assist with more paper magic. "This sure beats a word find as a way to pass the time. Thanks," said Brenna.

Each pair planned to collect the necessary supplies, retaining the receipts for reimbursement, of course, and promised to practice their paper tricks: an impossible illusion, a perpetual spinner, a tri-hexaflexagon, and an eight-and-a-half-by-eleven sheet of paper cut with an aperture large enough for an adult to step through. I added my supplies to the mix, and Ashley adjourned the meeting.

Felipe and Galen remained. I busied myself at my desk, reorganizing my files and keeping an eye on the duo. While I checked my supplies and looked for my stash of blood typing kits, I almost missed the interaction between the two boys. Felipe extended his hand and I worried when Galen hesitated, but he shoved away the hand offered and pulled Felipe into a bear hug, knocking the wind out of him.

"Glad it all worked out, man," Galen said, slapping his back.

"I wanted to thank you and Carlee," said Felipe, "but I haven't seen her. Have you?"

Galen shook his head. "She'll show up." Galen wrapped an arm around Felipe's shoulder and waved to me with the other.

I wondered what had become of Carlee too. Through

her diligence, the evidence implicated Jimmy, and she should have been here to celebrate.

I checked with the main office. "Mrs. McEntee, have you seen Carlee Parks today?"

Without glancing at her notes or discontinuing what she was doing, she said, "Nope." She glanced up. "She's never missed before, so I didn't call her mom this time."

"Thanks," I said, but I wasn't sure I meant it. Maybe today was the only day the absence mattered. I walked back to my room. Carlee's replacement terrarium would be my calling card. I removed it from the cupboard. This time her fingerprints had been placed deliberately. I secured the glass ball in plastic bubble wrap to deliver after Tuesday's in-service.

* * *

Without students, the school felt like a mausoleum, the air still. The schedule for the day included a time to work in our classrooms, followed by an all-faculty meeting in the auditorium.

With the free time, I tackled my briefcase, removing notes, copying contact information, recording grades, and sorting files. Under the last folder, I found Carlee's cube jammed in tightly. After I'd yanked it free, I examined each side. There didn't seem to be any rhyme or reason for the letters, but I twisted and turned the cube until it was time for the faculty meeting to begin in the auditorium.

Jane collapsed into the chair next to me, a welcome slice of cheerfulness. She expected to return to work soon, and she wanted to keep in the know. And I appreciated her attendance. Already one month into the school year, and I still didn't recognize many faculty members outside of the math department. Jane handed me an ice-cold water bottle and cracked one open for herself.

The in-service topic "Human Trafficking 101" began with a quiz to gauge our understanding of the local problem, its existence in our community, and what we thought we could do about it. Trafficking occurred much more often and closer to home than I realized.

Our school guidance counselor recited from an index card, "Sex trafficking is defined as the recruiting, harboring, transporting, or obtaining of a person for the purpose of a commercial sex act, induced by force, fraud, or coercion, or in which the person induced to perform such act has not attained eighteen years of age, the age of consent." Her voice rose. "These acts include pornography, prostitution, sex tourism, strip clubs, escort services, brothels, massage-parlor work, truck-stop 'companions,' and web and social-media sex. It's the most common form of modern-day slavery."

Most of her audience shifted in their seats and averted their eyes. "According to the Institute of Medicine and National Research Council," she went on, "schools in the United States are emerging as potentially promising environments for trafficking prevention and intervention. You…" She slammed her script onto the podium, her vehemence startling. She slowly surveyed her audience, and continued, "…are in a unique position to recognize changes in behavior and appearance and help put an end to the victimization of our students, both girls and boys."

After viewing a short staggering video of indescribable images, small groups were herded outside toward the tennis courts. Jane and I pulled together two picnic tables and were joined by several others. We sat for a few minutes, gathering the courage to tackle our assignment—how our school might address our local trafficking issue.

Jane finally said, "Body language is a vital component to reading what might be going on in a kid's life."

The floodgates opened and we discussed ways we might be able to identify possible victims: unexplained absences, change in attire or behavior, unexpected or expensive possessions, trauma, new body art, or the use of drugs. Given the formidable task to generate an appropriate, safe response to the perceived warning signs, we proposed adopting a formal school protocol. We organized a checklist, a timeline that included observing potential victims, deciding who to involve and when, consulting with the proper authorities, and referrals to appropriate services.

By the time we'd finished our assignment, the tantalizing aroma of freshly baked cheddar olive bread and vegetable soup lured us to the cafeteria. Jane slurped the thick hearty broth. "I'm so lucky, Katie. I've never had to worry about having enough to eat or a place to sleep. I have a good job, and my dad is finally getting me." Her dad had to witness her admirable success in her own element to support her teaching career, although I believed he still wished she was back working in his company, a very successful airline for jet setters based in Atlanta. "I have the best friends. And I have the love of my life at my beck and call." A huge smile lit up her face.

I felt the same. Except for the "love of my life" part.

"Do you want to go to the Columbia Days' block party? After all, we know royalty." I pointed to the button I'd pinned to my chest with Brenna's photo front and center. "Brenna is Queen Santa Maria. Ashley is Princess Niña, and Lorelei and Carlee are candidates for next year. I'd like to be there to support them." Jane nodded. "I have a delivery to make, and then I'll meet you there."

CHAPTER THIRTY-FIVE

I pulled in front of a split-level that might once have been blue, and rechecked the address. Paint peeled from the window casings of the 1960s rambler. A panel van slumped in the driveway, flat tires girded with yellow steel wheel chocks. Faded maroon paint chips had fallen like dandruff onto the pavement. Persistent weeds had broken through the sidewalk, and I stumbled on a chunk of crumbling concrete. A crippled light fixture dangled near the front door, its splayed black wires and empty socket emitted "Do Not Disturb" vibes.

I tightened my grip on Carlee's glass ball.

Before I knocked, Monica Parks ripped the door open. She peered out from the gap, her foot blocking it from opening fully.

"What do you want?" she asked. Piano notes floated past her.

"I brought Carlee's replacement terrarium. She wasn't in school today. Is she all right?"

"She's fine."

"Is she playing the piano?"

Monica snorted. "That's a recording I made." She added wistfully, "Almost twenty years ago."

"You're very talented. Does Carlee take lessons from you?" I wasn't getting an invitation. "Could you give this to her, please?"

Monica plucked the offering out of my hand. "She wasn't in school because…" There was just a hint of hesitation. "She found *her* dad."

"That's great! Will she still make the Columbia Days' candidate adjudication tomorrow?"

"It all depends on her, doesn't it? Now if you'll excuse me…"

She followed my gaze, which was locked on her twisted pinkie. I reddened as she tugged the sleeves of her shirt down to hide the deformity.

"Could we talk for a moment?" I pressed my palm against the rough surface of the closing door. Monica caught her shoe on the rug and stumbled. The door creaked ajar ever so slightly. Over her shoulder, I glimpsed red-and-white flocked wallpaper above white wainscoting and two lime-green suitcases standing next to the wall like sentries. She redoubled her efforts on the door, and the lock clicked.

When I finally found parking downtown and entered the pavilion, I ran into Lorelei and her face lit up. "I'm not too good with sales," she said.

"What are you selling?"

"We need to sell a hundred raffle tickets, at a dollar each or twelve for ten dollars."

"I'll take twenty-four."

She brightened and added shyly, "Would you like to buy a button too? They're ten dollars each and get you into the coronation on Saturday and onto the beach for the fireworks on Saturday night."

"Sold. How did you ever end up dating a weasel like Jimmy?" I asked.

"Like who?"

"Jimmy Hanson?"

"Ugh. I never dated Jimmy Hanson." She looked affectionately at Brock who was hawking buttons and selling more raffle tickets at the end of another line. I must have misunderstood.

The festival transformed downtown. I met Jane at the artists' tent, which overflowed with imaginative photographs; place settings arranged with ceramic plates, cups, and goblets; pastel watercolors hanging from tent poles; tactile fabric art draped strategically over tables and hangers; and oil paintings on easels.

We picked up a beverage, and Jane and I sauntered through the crowd to the metal bleachers facing a stage where the local dance studio had just finished high-kicking, clapping, and quick-stepping to Pharrell William's "Happy."

Standing next to the stage, Pamela and Miss Grace directed the parade of performers and introduced the senior royalty, who strolled hand in hand across the stage against the river of young dancers flitting by in flimsy tutus and tights.

Second-grade students had thrown their names in a hat

and clambered onto the stage, hoping to have their names drawn as junior royalty. The newly appointed junior prince feigned a collapse on stage and dropped with a thud. The emcee raced to his side, only to be startled when the boy jumped up and scrambled next to the junior princess, who glared down at him from her six-inch superior perch, not at all patient with his antics. The audience found him hilarious.

After they cleared the stage, the ambassador candidates mounted the steps. One by one, the emcee carefully pronounced each girl's name, her parents' names, and her favorite school subject. Wearing identical little black dresses, each girl paraded across the stage in taupe kitten heels, her hair pulled back in a tight ponytail. Each stopped on the center circle, caught her right hand in her left behind her back, placed her right heel next to the left instep, smiled on cue as she looked right and left, and then proceeded across the stage to raucous applause from her personal fans.

Lorelei was a natural, or at least I thought so. A smile burst from her lips as soon as her shoe hit the stage floor, and when the introduction was complete, she waved at Brock, her parents, and then Jane and me.

At the conclusion, we stood, clapping for all the girls, but Carlee hadn't been among them.

Jane and I joined Galen and Brock at the edge of the stage. Galen shook his head. "It's weird. She isn't answering her cell."

It was unusual for any teenager to ignore a phone call, particularly one from a boyfriend. Maybe she was busy getting acquainted with her dad. They had a lifetime to share.

"What?" Galen asked, scrutinizing my face, trying to

read my mind.

"Have you talked to her mother?"

"That old bitch." He gave me an apologetic glance. "She wouldn't give me the time of day. I was there twice yesterday, and she yelled at me through the door, told me to go away. She said Carlee probably decided to join Ana for the long weekend, but Carlee would have told me. Today *Mother* won't even answer her door. You know she makes Carlee call her mother, not mom, because it's *so much more civilized.*" I almost laughed at his attempt at imitating Carlee's mom.

Curious. "Ms. Parks told me Carlee went to see her dad."

Galen's eyebrows shot up. "I didn't even know she'd found him."

He lowered his voice. "You know about those letters, right?" I nodded. "At first, she thought they might be a clue to finding her dad, but they were dated before she was born. Carlee can be fierce when she wants to get her way, but she couldn't get any information from her mom without letting her know she'd seen the letters. Her mom plays that single-parent sympathy card to the hilt. It'd be all about her."

"You'll hear from Carlee soon," I said, but he didn't look like he believed me.

The kids were drawn to the flashing lights of the midway rides and disappeared from sight.

I turned to Jane. "Would you like to…" Before I could finish my question, a tall, blond grabbed her from behind and swung her around. She squealed. I could only shake my head at Drew. "Nice tie," I said, shaking my head at the length of neon-green fabric reaching to his knees. "I have to get going. I take it you have a ride home, Jane?"

They waved and were swept away by the crowd. I chuckled all the way back to my car, and there the chuckles ceased.

CHAPTER THIRTY-SIX

I'd heard eggs could damage the finish on a car. I poured the dregs of my slush over the windshield and flicked on the wipers. White bits of shell clung to the rubber, smearing slimy egg in symmetric arcs.

I rolled out of my parking space and drove straight into the nearest car wash. It took three cycles to clean my Jetta.

A walk with Maverick was in order. He strutted around the neighborhood, a four-legged king surveying his domain. Emma met him at the edge of her yard and slid her hand down his back, taking three small steps from his head to his tail. Adam waved from their deck, never letting her out of his sight.

Miss Grace's house stood dark. I assumed she and Pamela were completing final plans for the week's festivities somewhere. Ida said it had been good for both of them to have another purpose.

I needed a purpose too. In my kitchen, I balanced Carlee's cube in my hand, as if its heft might provide enlightenment. What was the reason for all the letters? I wrote the letters out in a grid, trying to spell words, but there were way too many *X*s and *Y*s and *Q*s. Then a thought came to me. Using the cube-solving axioms, I put all the *X*s on one side, *Y*s on one side, and *Q*s on another. It turned out there were sixteen *J*s as well. Four sides were solved, but the last two sides were still a disarray of letters.

I toyed with matching square *A* to the letter square on the opposite side; it mapped with a *K*. *B* mapped with an *A*. By the time I had finished, I'd written the letters "KADNDLOHTREBTROF." *Gibberish.*

Soft notes chimed. I checked my phone and the refrigerator door. It sounded again and I listened for the source. The third time was a charm, and I stepped around the deck to Mrs. Clemashevski's front door.

"I'm ready to come home," Samantha McCoy said nervously. Not too long after I'd worked with Samantha at the convention center (as part of the wait staff for a photo session at the last *Titanic* dinner to be used in the history exhibit and for marketing), she'd disappeared under a cloud of innuendo. They caught those responsible for providing drugs, and Ida always believed in Samantha's innocence. I trusted Ida. But our conversation was difficult.

I told her I didn't know where Ida was, but I invited her to wait with me on the porch. Maverick nuzzled Samantha's hand as she sat in the chair, and he coaxed her into petting him. I'd come to believe he was a fair judge of character.

"I haven't gone back to using, you know," she said, pulling at the end of her salt-and-pepper braid. "I've been clean for almost three years. They started letting me visit my kid, and I wouldn't jeopardize that gift." She'd lost her husband and the custody of her child, a job, and the trust of everyone who knew her. She had served forty-eight months for possession with intent to sell. When released from the Minnesota Correctional Facility in Shakopee, she'd moved to Columbia to continue her studies part-time. Everyone hoped she'd make it, but when the anonymous tip came in, it was all too easy to believe she'd slipped. As it turned out, she'd been framed.

A hedge shielded the street from view. We heard low voices, followed by the splat of eggs and the glug of heavy liquid. Maverick barked. We followed the sounds down the walk. Figures darted in and out of the shadows. The streetlight illuminated one familiar face. I started for the street, my ears burning, but Samantha grabbed my arm.

"It's what Jimmy wants. Never stoop to his level." Samantha tugged out a phone and punched in 911. "I'm reporting vandalism in progress at…" She glanced above the doorjamb, "…3141 North Maple Street."

The boys fled at the first sound of a siren, but Samantha stayed. Flour, syrup, ketchup, and eggs clung to the hood of her car, a mush illuminated by the harsh glare of the streetlight. As Officer Ronnie Christianson pulled in, I retrieved a bucket full of warm soapy water, and two sponges.

He circled the car.

"Samantha," he tipped his hat. "Could you come by the station on Monday?"

"Yes, Officer Christianson," she answered in a small voice, looking at her feet.

"They sure did a number on this car. Yours, Ms. Wilk?"

Samantha said, "Mine."

"Know any of them?" Officer Christianson said.

Samantha said, a touch of vehemence in her voice, "Jimmy Hanson."

Officer Christianson's eyebrows flew up.

"Junior," she added sourly. "He's a little—"

"Yes, he is. Are you certain of the identification?" Officer Christianson shook his head, as if he already knew the answer, taking photos from different angles for the record.

"No doubt," she said.

"No doubt," I repeated.

When Officer Christianson pulled away from the curb on his way to the Hanson's to have a chat, Samantha drove her dented red Ford Taurus up the driveway under the yard light, and we set to work scrubbing. Samantha's throaty chortle played like a set of timpani. She shook her head. Then her laugh stuck in her throat, and an abrupt change settled on her face. "I don't know what Lorelei ever saw in him."

"She told me she never went out with him," I said.

Disbelief washed over Samantha. "Oh, yes, she did. He dumped his old girlfriend when he turned eighteen and struck up an overly friendly acquaintance with Lorelei. She and I took classes together at the community college. If he weren't two eggs short of a dozen, I'd say he killed her."

"I have it all wrong." My heart pounded in my chest, struggling to get out, to right itself, realizing that Jimmy's Lorelei was Miss Fiorillo, not Lorelei Calder. Maverick nudged me.

"He's a little shit," Samantha said, putting all her weight onto the sponge.

He certainly is.

But could he have killed Lorelei?

When we finished scrubbing and rinsing, I said, "Come in for a cup of tea."

As she turned to follow me inside, Maverick barked.

Renegade's agile body slipped past me through the open door, and Maverick trailed her, nearly toppling Samantha. With every puppy action, there's an equal and opposite reaction. I fell on my rear.

CJ wasn't far behind her. He rushed to lift me from the floor. It was difficult; I convulsed with embarrassed laughter.

"Are you all right?" he fretted.

"It's not like that hasn't happened before," I said, but continued to brush invisible dust from my bruised ego and behind.

Once inside, Samantha tentatively thrust her hand out to CJ. "Samantha McCoy," she said.

He did likewise. "CJ Bluestone." He looked at me apologetically. "We were walking through the slough, and Renegade ran off, looking for her friend." It was clear they'd found each other. Maverick sprawled on the linoleum in the corner, and Renegade huddled under his foreleg.

"Tea?" I asked.

CJ pulled out a chair for Samantha before seating himself. I filled the kettle.

"This again?" he said. He lifted the mixed cube from the table and eyed me with suspicion. "I thought you completed it. Did I do all your baking for nothing?"

"I did finish it, but Carlee said it didn't make any sense."

CJ's brow furrowed and the corners of his mouth turned down. "What are you doing?" he asked again, his voice husky with emotion.

"What?" I asked innocently.

Samantha picked up my notes. Her eyes widened in surprise.

"What?" I repeated.

Samantha whispered, "Fort Berthold." She picked up a pencil and wrote the letters in reverse order: "FORTBERTHOLDNDAK."

"What is that?"

"It's where I grew up," CJ said. He held the cube aloft.

"Carlee got the cube from her sister," I said quietly.

A shadow passed between Samantha and CJ.

"You're scaring me!" I said.

"Call Carlee," he said.

I pulled up my student contact information and punched in the number for her cell. It rang and rang.

I tried Galen.

"H'lo," he yelled over the noise of the midway.

"Galen, have you heard from Carlee yet?"

"No. Hey, can I call you back? I can't hear very well."

"Never mind. That's okay." I punched *End*.

A sharp whistle signaled "Come." CJ pulled a leash from his rear pocket and snapped it onto Renegade's collar. Maverick padded alongside. They aimed for the door.

"Where are you going?" I yelled. When he didn't stop, I said. "I'm coming." I grabbed a jacket and my keys.

CJ, his face implacable, went to the driver's door. I tossed him my keys and he snatched them out of the air. As I rounded the rear bumper, I opened the door for the dogs.

Samantha stood in the doorway and nodded once.

"What's happening?" I asked. "You can't leave Columbia."

"If Carlee or Ana is in North Dakota, she is in trouble."

My VW shuddered under his lead foot. I yanked the seatbelt in front of me and clicked it into place. I pressed my hands against the dash, and we sped out of town. I knew he was under strict orders not to leave the area, and I started to articulate the consequences, but his glare stopped me.

We plowed through Minnesota. When we got to Fargo, the night lights reflected off the clouds reminiscent of a New Year's party. Then we passed through more dark fields and widely spaced farm sites each lit by a single yard lamp.

When we stopped for gas, the dogs and I stretched and took a quick romp around the parking lot. I cracked open one of the bottles of water I'd bought at the convenience store, took a swig, and poured the rest into the large plastic bowl I kept in the car. The dogs lapped it up. I kept one eye on the dogs and one eye on CJ, rejoining him before he could leave us stranded.

The tires screamed on the pavement. CJ's large frame crammed into the small space, hugging the steering wheel, pulling it toward his chest like a life ring.

According to the map on my phone, the distance to Fort Berthold, North Dakota, was over three hundred miles. At the rate we were going, if we didn't crash and we weren't stopped for speeding, we'd arrive in about four and a half hours. We'd be following the Lewis and Clark Trail in record time.

I tried again. "What is Fort Berthold?"

The flames sparking behind CJ's brooding eyes silenced me. The dogs flopped down onto the backseat.

The night swallowed us whole and I felt as if the sun would never rise again.

CHAPTER THIRTY-SEVEN

A battered black truck blocked the driveway of the long white bungalow, so CJ parked on the street. He trudged through the yard, onto the porch, and banged on the door. When it finally opened, a balding man peered at CJ through thick wire-rimmed glasses. He pulled his red plaid robe tighter and straightened slightly before slamming the door in CJ's face.

CJ crawled back into the car, and he pounded his fists on the steering wheel. Then his head dropped to his knuckles and he sucked the oxygen out of the air in huge gulps. I felt the dogs' heads bob back and forth. Renegade reacted first, plunging into the front seat, her tongue washing CJ's face.

"Who was that?" I asked. The words invaded every nook and cranny of the small space, as if I'd screamed in a cavern.

Before CJ could answer, his phone chimed. He signed for Renegade to sit then lifted the phone to his ear and said, "Kahula." He listened for a while, his face blank. "Thank you," he said then hung up.

His head swiveled, surveying all directions quickly, and he put the car into gear. We headed north, following the sign to New Town, passing rows of identical Cracker Jack houses, hazy in an eerie glow from the intermittent streetlights. I bade a silent good luck to a lone trucker pumping fuel under the artificial sunlight of the last convenience store in town.

"Please tell me what's going on," I said.

"The oil boom inundated Fort Berthold with many people and fast money, too much too soon. The economy has since arrested, and much of the area lies deserted. We need to talk to someone who can tell us where to look. It is an enormous area, but if Carlee is there, we will find her.

"Kahula said there are no girls here, but she is sending us to the tribal office in New Town."

"What's there?"

"Help."

CJ pulled himself nearer the steering wheel, his eyes riveted to the desolate pavement rolling out in front of us only as far as the headlight beams could reach, until a faint halo encircling a town led us to an oasis.

He pulled up in front of the gray agency building, where a young woman with dancing brown eyes waited. Leather ties, decorated with fringe and beads, held her raven-black hair in two long plaits. Her forest-green polo shirt sported a patch I couldn't identify through my tired eyes, but she wasn't what I'd expected to see in the middle of the night.

CJ exited the car. Giant steps took him right in front

of the woman, and he poured every ounce of energy that remained into the embrace he gave. "*Dosha*, sister." When they'd energized each other, CJ gestured for me to come near. "This is my friend, Katie." I stretched out my hand.

"Agent Dakota," the young woman said. She shook my hand then dragged me into a bear hug.

The dogs loped out of the open door after me and nudged between us, either trying to save me or racing to meet their new friend. They sat simultaneously, and for the first time in hours, CJ relaxed. "Renegade and Maverick." One after the other they raised their right paws, tails brushing the dust off the sidewalk. The woman knelt, took each paw in turn, and touched her forehead to theirs. "*Dosha*."

Over her shoulder, Dakota called out to a small man who appeared to be lurking on the street corner. "Go home, *Dokidáhi*. There is nothing for you to see. Go home, Shadow." The skinny man hitched up his pants and faded into the night.

Although said kindly, the words were nonetheless jarring. "Why are you here, Chantan?"

CJ turned the magic cube over in his hand before presenting it to Dakota, along with the solution. She scrutinized all six sides. "*Isiáksa juju*," she said. "This could be very bad. What do you expect of me? You know I'm only a trainee." CJ gazed into her eyes. She inclined her head and we followed. I didn't know what the devil was going on, but I felt absolutely certain the devil was involved.

Dakota led us into the deserted building. She buzzed us through heavy glass doors to a steel gray desk covered with papers and maps. Names printed on yellow sticky notes were affixed to most of the black-and-white photos that covered a corkboard leaning against the desk. Red Post-its displayed question marks on those awaiting identification. I scoured the photos for signs of Carlee or Ana.

CJ and Dakota spoke in soft tones as I looked for any recognizable features, when one struck me. Maverick barked, and Renegade yipped in response. "What about this girl?" I asked, my finger tapping the white border around the picture. She reminded me of someone.

Both of them looked at me with something like pity in their eyes. Dakota spoke. "Her body was found smashed up against Garrison Dam last May." She pointed out the date on the yellow square. "She'd been in the water a long time, and we haven't been able to identify her."

The photo tugged at my heartstrings as if I should have known her. "Do you have access to records of missing persons from Monongalia County, Minnesota?" I asked. CJ's back stiffened.

Dakota dropped into the leather swivel chair in front of the computer console. It took its sweet time waking up. She pulled up the Monongalia archives of missing persons and scrolled through the short list of names and photos. Disbelief dropped over her features. It seemed Molly Yates, the daughter of Miss Grace's former caretaker, had been in North Dakota all along. The photo on the wall didn't do Molly justice. Miss Grace cherished her photo. Molly had once been very pretty and now in shades of gray, she was simply dead.

"We can do little to dissuade transient youth from selling their wares," Dakota said. She sounded so coldhearted.

"She might not have come here voluntarily," CJ said.

"This could definitely be her. I'll verify the records in the morning," Dakota said, more gently.

"Where does that leave us?" CJ asked.

After a huge intake of breath and a long sigh, Dakota said, "Reno."

Recognition settled boldly on CJ's face. "Where is he?"

"Reno's fingers are in everything. He was first to complain when the economy slagged, but he takes care of his own. His women are with him of their own accord."

"Where is he?" CJ asked, with more intensity.

After Dakota rattled off directions, she followed us out to the car. "Good luck," she said.

The dogs jumped in and settled in the back seat. CJ drove, a man with a purpose. "Reno knows everything that goes on here. If he does not have the girl, he may know who does."

The first rays of dawn cracked open behind us in time to shed light on a buck bounding across the road in front of us. CJ slammed on the brakes, but we were too close and the body splintered the windshield before rolling over the top of the car and falling to the asphalt. The dogs careened into the seat in front of them and were only a little less shaken than I was as the car spun to a stop. CJ slammed the shift into park. "This cannot be happening now."

He walked around the car, assessing the damage, stepping toward the carcass spread across the road. As he neared it, the royal antlers rose, and the deer dragged itself to its feet. It slowly limped away from the accident. I hoped we could do the same.

The passenger door creaked open. The dented right front fender sat heavily on the tire. The bumper hung on by a thread. One headlight winked off and on. The windshield held together by sheer willpower. CJ returned to the driver's seat and turned the key. It clicked. He tried again. I heard a buzz. On the third try, the engine sputtered and died. My car and I had a history but probably not much of a future.

From the north, pinpricks of light crawled toward us. When it stopped in front of us, sunlight reflected off a Mercedes-Benz star. Blue-and-green braided bungee cords held two red fiberglass canoes in place on the roof. Shrouded behind tinted windows, the driver sent a message by revving his engine. Gravel ricocheted in the wheel wells, and the canoes rocked back and forth. CJ approached the vehicle, miming turning down a window. The deliberate, slow window slide revealed a hard face with a craggy scar running down the left cheek. Short cropped black hair hung over close-set black eyes. He might have been good-looking, but chills ran up my spine. The dogs sat still, ears flat, tails unmoving, sensing the tension in the air.

"What have we here? The prodigal son returns." The voice from the SUV sniggered. "Need a lift?"

"Reno."

The man snorted. "Mr. Reno to you, asshole. Did you come back here to make my life miserable again? Get outta here. You aren't welcome."

The door opened. Thighs as big as tree trunks unfolded, the seams of his suit straining. Fists the size of frying pans smashed together. Reno swaggered up to CJ, nose to nose. CJ didn't back down, didn't move, and said, "I'm sure Shadow told you why we are here. I do not want any trouble, but I think you can help. Do you know where they are?"

Reno grunted.

"We're looking for a girl."

"Aren't we all."

"She has family and friends who want her back."

"You think you're too good for us, and then you show up acting like we should kiss your ass." He stepped close enough for them to breathe the same air, then snatched CJ's vest. "Why should I tell you?" His spittle landed on CJ's face. "What's in it for me?"

CJ paused. "Nothing."

"Hah. Then there's no reason to help you." He shoved CJ.

"Do it for *her*." A private message passed between them.

Looking as if he'd been slapped, Reno fell back. "You've got nerve." He stepped forward again. "You take her away. You lose her. And now you want me to help you?" His palms landed hard against CJ's heaving chest. He shoved again. CJ fought to maintain his balance but kept his hands relaxed, his eyes aware. Reno crouched, reached back under his jacket, and came up brandishing a murderous knife. "I've been wanting to do this for a very long time."

CJ stood calmly, laying himself open. The weapon levitated from hand to hand. CJ seemed ready to take it all, ready to give in, but not on my time.

"Mr. Reno." As if I'd magically appeared, he altered his behavior. He lowered the knife in his left hand, stood taller, and straightened his rainbow tie with his right. I took a few steps closer, attempting to intercede. "There's a girl who's lost."

"There's always a girl who is lost." He brandished the knife.

I understood CJ, wanting this man to take away painful memories, but that would be the easy way out. There had to be great memories too. "We need your help," I said.

"You need *my* help?" he repeated, dripping sarcasm. "Chantan has never needed anyone's help."

"But I do. I need to find this child. Please," I pleaded. "Do you know where we might look?"

"Who is she to you?"

"She's my friend."

Reno closed his eyes, mulling over my words, a torrent of air streaming in and out of his chest, the vast expanse of his experience shedding its protective scales. Then he took a huge breath and opened his eyes. He threw me a set of keys, saying, "Lewiston Run." He pointed a finger at CJ and pulled an imaginary trigger as he pulled out his phone.

CHAPTER THIRTY-EIGHT

We rumbled over a bridge that spanned a body of water, dwarfing Lake Monongalia. The Mercedes SUV navigated the irregular terrain, chewing up the hills and spitting out the miles. The sky was on fire, bright red-orange melting into an iridescent yellow by the time we'd negotiated the twisty roads and arrived in front of a barbed-wire fence—a gated, desolate man-camp. The faded letters—Lewiston Run—clung to the wooden sign hanging by an eyehook, swaying. Hardy brown grasses held up rows of identical sagging dull-metal shells. We skirted a pile of rocks propping open the chain-link access, and followed the well-worn track to one of the few inhabited trailers. Parked haphazardly, a half-dozen rigs decked out for hauling blocked the walkway.

"How are we going to do this?" I asked.

"You should not be seen," CJ said, and he began shedding his Columbia persona, soft buckskin vest first, followed by shoes, socks, and belt. I gasped when he pulled his shirt over his head. Muscles rippled beneath a smooth bronze skin on his right side, but angry tears traveled up and down the length of his left side. He shoved his arms back into the vest, barely covering a cross-hatching of scars and stitches partially obliterating a tattoo of a skeletal frog carrying a trident. He removed the laces before pulling on his shoes. He tugged loose his leather tie and shook his head of hair. "Badass enough for you?" he growled with a sneer.

I clambered into the backseat between the dogs, and CJ exited the SUV.

A little man with dirty blond hair wearing a grungy T-shirt and worn blue jeans answered CJ's pounding. The man pointed at the SUV, and I crouched lower, peering from behind the headrest through the tinted windows. He shook his head, hitched up his jeans, and shoved his way past CJ, stomping toward us. I hit the floor. When he wrenched open the driver's door, angry barks and deep snarls greeted him, and as the two dogs lunged, the door slammed. I scratched both chests vigorously in gratitude, and my face received a thorough cleansing.

I ventured another peek. It appeared they'd finished haggling, and while the man bent his head over a handful of bills, a greedy grin on his face, CJ pocketed something and returned. Showing off, just a little, he whistled when he opened the door. Both rumps went down, tongues rolled out, ears fell forward, and tails wagged. CJ poured himself into the driver's seat, put the car in gear, and petted all three of us.

"We are looking for L14," he said.

When we were out of sight, I crawled back into the passenger seat. "What did you pay for?"

His usual stoic face melted in a wash of red. "A blond escort," he stammered. "For Reno."

My words rushed out in a panic. "Carlee isn't blond!"

CJ's lips turned up, cognizant of his request.

"But Ana is." I understood. Her coloring might be easier to locate. "You think they might both be here?"

"And you do not? Ana wanted Carlee to solve the cube with the location answer. If Ana knew where she might be going, she would have left just such an obscure message for her sister. Carlee is an intelligent young lady. It might have been Ana's way to keep her sister informed and Carlee must have worked it out."

We bumped along down the next row. "There it is." I pointed. "L14."

We pulled up to the vacant carport. The steel canopy rocked on its base. Pieces of broken siding curled and littered the lawn. Iron grilles barred the windows and the door. Incongruously, delicate deep purple Russian sage, bright yellow goldenrod, and seven-foot-tall sunflowers stood guard near the front door.

My seatbelt snapped back when I released it, but CJ signaled me to stay. "I do not know what I will find," he said.

He flipped the key he had taken from his pocket—the exchange for his currency, and his eyes searched for signs of life. He removed more bills, shoved them in his pocket, and handed his wallet to me. Led by a strong exhalation, he pushed open the door. The lock clicked behind him. He followed the dry dirt path to the stairs, took two steps up, and inserted the key—the magic entry to a derelict shack. I heard the door groan from where I sat.

A rotund woman, wearing a scarlet muumuu and matching lipstick, rolled her heft into the doorway, shielding everything within. One hand went to where I thought her hip might be, while the other lounged against the jamb; she looked like she was offering, but her face hardened when CJ shook his head, declining. She railed and ranted. Unfazed, CJ handed her a roll of bills. She stepped aside and let him pass as she counted the cash.

The minutes ticked by. I was sure nothing would come of it; we had interpreted the cube incorrectly. At a loss, I picked it up and turned and twisted the faces, imagining Carlee at a safe location, having a quiet conversation with a nice man.

I looked up to find CJ carrying a bundle out the door to the consternation of the red-clad doorkeeper, only slightly sidetracked by the money in her hand. She slammed the door on the trailer.

I jumped out and opened the back door. A blond head peeked out from beneath a musty green army blanket, unmoving. The muscles in CJ's arms rippled as he swung her up into the rear seat. The dogs jumped to the front to make room. He'd do better for her than I could, so I slid into the driver's seat and pressed the ignition button.

"Is it her? Is it Ana?"

"I don't know if it is Ana," said CJ softly. "But I could not leave her. Her handler suggested her newest protégé might not yet be ready, but Reno's name goes far."

Gravel spat and the backend fishtailed as we picked up speed. A few miles down the road, I pulled over, my heart hammering in my chest. My sweaty hands slid off the steering wheel. I stopped the rocket ship of a vehicle and turned, fully prepared for the worst.

Her lips were painted coral pink, her cheeks gently rouged, her blue eyes narrowly lined in black. Her hair curled in ringlets, a tangled half ponytail caught in a pink ribbon. She looked very young. Makeup muted the yellow-green bruise healing on her cheek. She wore a wrinkled white shift, bearing unidentifiable stains. The radiance in her eyes had dulled. And yet it was Ana.

The air in the vehicle became heavy with mildew and dust billowing off the blanket like Pigpen in a Charlie Brown cartoon strip. I opened the windows, allowing cool fresh air to blow the denseness into the countryside.

Ana murmured, "Carlee."

CJ gently lifted errant strands of hair away from her face. "Carlee?" he repeated.

She struggled to string words together. "Carlee," she cried and thrashed, rapping her head against the door. CJ stroked her hands. I couldn't imagine what she'd been through, but I was impatient.

"Where is Carlee?" I asked.

CJ put his arm around Ana's shoulders and rocked her, crooning in a voice, rich and low, with calming words that had no meaning to me. Her eyes drifted closed. I put the SUV into gear and drove on, putting as much geography behind us as possible.

I whispered loudly, hoping to wheedle something out of Ana. "We need to find Carlee."

CJ continued his crooning, eyes closed, rocking back and forth. In the rearview mirror, I caught him nodding ever so slightly.

I picked up my phone to call for help, but there was no

service on the empty road. I tossed it onto the seat beside me. Ana stirred.

"Carlee," she repeated.

"Ana, where is Carlee?" CJ asked. His soft voice pulled her from a long way off.

"...heard Lewiston," she breathed.

We were racing away from Lewiston. I slammed on the brakes.

"No," said CJ, this time with less volume but more authority. "We must first take Ana to Dakota."

CHAPTER THIRTY-NINE

They'll try to take her back when they figure out Reno isn't really involved," Dakota said. "He's never gone down that path before. I can't imagine why they believed you."

"I can be very persuasive. You must make sure they do not succeed."

"She's safe in the hospital for now. I have an officer outside her room, but she'll need professional help. The grooming process had just begun and you got to her in time, but she's still paralyzed with fear."

CJ stood still.

He'd taxed my patience beyond endurance. "We have to go back. We have to find Carlee."

"Carlee is not at Lewiston Run," said CJ.

"Ana said Lewiston."

"The handler said her newest protégé might not yet be ready." He had said that before. "Her newest protégé was Ana. Carlee was not there."

"Then how do we find Carlee?" I was exasperated.

Dakota turned her head as if deep in thought, looking for answers. "Lewiston Cavern, Lewiston Camp, Lewiston Stream, Lewiston Bay." Her eyes lit up. "Someone could haul a boat into Lewiston Bay. I'll alert the Three Affiliated Tribes Police."

CJ, Maverick, Renegade, and I bolted for the SUV. Once inside, CJ wiped his palms against his pants and reached for the ignition. Shadow skulked on the corner, and CJ raised his hand as we stormed past. We cleared the edge of town. CJ squinted at the horizon and out into the hills.

The asphalt gave way to a gravel access road, pebbles peppering the undercarriage of the vehicle. We bumped along the dry rocky route, kicking up a cloud of dust that, along with enough noise to wake the dead, surely would signal our arrival. When we came within sight of the water carved into the hills, CJ eased up on the accelerator and rolled to a stop.

At the primitive boat landing, we found no restrooms, no security lights or cameras, no shelter, no concessions, no courtesy docks, and no trash receptacles. Worst of all, the bay looked vacant. My shoulders slumped as a frustrated whimper escaped.

CJ stood still for a moment and then pointed to the roof of a lime-green van on the point at the end of the hook, nearly hidden beneath a rocky bluff, sheathed in dry brush. My mind went back to the description of the delivery van suspected in little Emma's abduction. Could it be?

I blinked rapidly. The look CJ gave me could have stopped an elephant. "We have no time for tears," he admonished. I brushed my cheeks with the back of my hand. He nodded at the canoes on our SUV's roof while removing his shoes.

I followed suit.

As CJ released the fasteners, the bungee cords snapped over the top and out of sight. He slid one canoe down the guide rails and onto his shoulders. I detached the two tan wooden paddles and toted them to the shore. Maverick and Renegade splashed ahead. CJ stepped onto the perforated steel planking, and water sloshed over his feet.

"Get in." The dogs hit the centerline, and I scooted around them to get to the bow. CJ shoved off.

The wind picked up. As we glided through the waves, cold water doused my knees. Renegade gave an excited yip, and CJ reprimanded, "Hush." Her frenetic activity made Maverick step back and forth. CJ reached out a calming hand, and they settled. We continued around the hook.

Two football fields away, across open water, a double-decked boat rocked back and forth. A royal-blue awning covered an empty wheelhouse. Twinkling mini lights were strung along the tinted glass that enclosed the living quarters. The name *Nautibuoy*, painted in bold red letters, advertised the boat's purpose. Its bobbing sent out a pattern of concentric circles, small waves we sliced through on our way toward the neon-orange lifebuoys tied to the boat's stern. CJ's powerful strokes sent us sailing across the water until we reached the yacht. He snared the yellow nylon rope with his paddle and hastily looped it under his seat, securing the canoe, but before he could finish, the dogs jumped out.

Maverick parked himself on the dive platform, waiting for me. Renegade tripped on the canoe gunwale. She slipped and her hind legs dangled in the water until she righted herself. She shook droplets of water, and her tags rattled. She loved to play and she bolted, staying just out of CJ's reach.

We heard a crash and a splash.

Renegade's ears perked up to listen and, energized by the new sounds, she tore down the narrow walkway around the port side toward the noise. CJ limped after her. Maverick and I moved to the opposite wall, crawling below the window line at a snail's pace. When Renegade began to bark, followed shortly by growling, Maverick picked up his pace.

As we neared the front, we heard, "How'd you get here, my leetle target practeece?"

I peered around the corner. Renegade probably thought she had the man trapped against the boat, but he was marking time, slapping a handgun against his right leg. Slowly he raised the barrel, tilting his head from side to side as he took measured aim. He wouldn't miss. I searched for anything to beat the bullet and pulled a long-armed fishing hook from its clip, but I wasn't fast enough.

Wooden chairs slid toward the man and clattered against the deck. CJ had wrenched a fender from the railing and lunged in front of Renegade as the roar of the gun filled the air. I thought I heard him yell, "Outlaw!" I swung the gaff as hard as I could, connecting with the gun hand. The weapon slid across the deck and plopped overboard.

Baffled, the man slurred in a voice heavy with alcohol, "Who are you?" He rubbed his shoulder as he blathered. "You can't do this. I'll have you arrested. What do you think you're doing?"

Renegade renewed her barking with increased vigor, and Maverick joined her. The man was trapped. Fear outlined his wide eyes. His jaw ballooned from a wad of tobacco chew, and spittle was caught in his dirty beard.

CJ lay on the boat deck, blood seeping from a shoulder wound, trying to push himself upright.

I knelt next to him and jammed the heel of my hand into his shoulder to staunch the flow of blood. "Why did you do that?" I murmured.

"I could not let it happen again." He *had* shouted "Outlaw." Tears pricked my eyes.

"Get away from me," the man screamed as Renegade bared her teeth and hunched her shoulders, her ears flat against her head as she crept forward.

"Hold," CJ croaked. Renegade centered herself on all fours, but continued to bark, never taking her eyes off her prey.

Through clenched teeth, I said, "I need a first-aid kit."

The man pointed a shaky finger at a red-and-white plastic box shoved under a bench. I yanked it out and pried it open. I pulled out gauze and tape and wrapped CJ's wound. The man screamed again, "What do you want?"

My hands stopped. "We want the girl."

His face relaxed just a notch. His eyes slid to the open water behind me and returned with a steely glint. "I don't know nothing 'bout no girl."

Maverick leapt into the water. A huge splash hung in the air. I crawled closer to the bow and called, "Maverick, here."

He swam away from me.

"Maverick, come," I said, louder, my voice rising. Maverick dove under the water. "Maverick!" I screeched.

He surfaced, and it looked like he was paddling back to the boat. "Here, Maverick," I said as calmly as I could. He circled. I heard another splash.

CJ had launched himself into the water, heading straight for Maverick. My heart banged in my chest. CJ reached one arm far ahead but barely raised the other. I thought he would grab Maverick, but instead he dove below the surface in the middle of Maverick's rippling ring. I counted far too many seconds before he came up for air, gasped, and dove again. Maverick continued to circle where CJ had vanished. My hands clenched the railing. I could lose them both. Renegade growled and nipped, keeping the man at bay. CJ broke the surface again, gulped more air, then disappeared beneath the water again. He came up a third time, hauling something behind him. Maverick paddled alongside, both straining.

CJ swam to the rear platform, where I was able to help drag the precious bundle aboard. She lay unmoving, not breathing. Her hands were tied behind her. I picked at a corner of the duct tape and gently peeled it from her lips. I checked for a pulse. I cleared her airway then pressed on her chest to the tempo of "Staying Alive" and counted the compressions before giving her a breath. Again, and again, and again.

She gagged and sputtered. Water flew from her mouth. I turned her onto her side. She vomited. She took another breath and coughed. Carlee's eyes opened. She bolted upright and I cradled her against my shoulder. Her arms held on tight.

"She's safe, CJ."

But CJ was gone.

Maverick had disappeared too.

CHAPTER FORTY

I propped Carlee against the transom. "CJ. CJ? CJ!" I screamed, scrambling over the platform, cold water lapping at my arms and legs. Renegade had abandoned her mark and paced beside me, howling. I peered onto the lake. Renegade whined. Maverick rose to the surface amid churning water, carrying CJ's limp hand in his mouth.

"Here, Maverick," Carlee leaned forward and exerted all the energy she had remaining. Together we hauled CJ partway onto the platform and turned him onto his side. His breathing was shallow, his shoulder bleeding profusely, the crimson dissolving in the water surrounding him.

A shadow fell over CJ. My eyes trained on the man, who now carried a second firearm.

"Lower the dude back into the water, slowly," he said,

his reedy voice barely audible.

Water ran from CJ's mouth, his nose, his face, his clothes, his hair, everywhere. He wouldn't live if we put him back into the water.

"And keep the mutts away."

I grabbed the dogs' collars. They weren't difficult to contain; both dogs were concentrating on CJ's still form.

"Five minutes more and you never would've found her. She ain't worth the trouble," he said, shaking his head. "Roll him back in."

Carlee shuddered next to me.

I sat back on my haunches. "Do it yourself."

The man took a step toward the platform. Maverick's growl was particularly nasty. The man recoiled and pointed the gun. "You're history."

I pulled my dog behind me. When my eyes met Carlee's, I found a spark of resolution.

I squeezed my eyes tight, expecting fire and pain. There was a ping, just a single solitary ping, but I didn't feel a thing. I opened my eyes and heard running steps along the gunwale, out of sight, away from the roar of an approaching speedboat bearing Dakota and Reno.

An amplified voice declared, "We've got you surrounded."

I'd bet Dakota had wanted to utter those words her entire life. When another boat appeared on the shore side, we heard the lake welcome the second weapon as it splashed into the water.

"Over here," I waved at Dakota.

Two more officers pulled alongside and came aboard. As they read the man his rights, they pulled his arms behind him and snapped handcuffs in place.

Dakota pulled up next to us. She paled. "Oh, God,"

she whispered.

Reno said nothing.

Carlee came to her senses faster than any of us. "Dr. Bluestone needs help. We have to get him to a hospital."

Carlee and I dragged him across the deck. Reno and Dakota latched on to his belt and hauled him in. CJ grunted and I cringed. Balancing on Reno's outstretched palm, I stepped into the rocking boat then collapsed into a bucket seat. He reached for Carlee, but his hand halted a few inches short. I waited, and when he didn't move, I extended my hand to pull her in. The dogs sailed in after, licking her hands and face, which crinkled in mirth despite the depth of concern in her eyes.

"Ana?" she asked.

"She's safe."

Reno snapped out of whatever trance he'd been in and put the boat in gear. We thundered across the lake, cool water baptizing us in Lake Sakakawea. The wind buffeted the tears from my face as the realization of what had transpired whipped up a frenzy of emotion. Our girls were safe. It was over.

But it really wasn't. Ana had experienced who knew what trauma, and Carlee had been torn from the arms of Poseidon. What had they been doing here?

Unconscious, CJ lay in the bottom of the boat, blood blossoming through the white gauze bandage Dakota held to his wound. He looked like a wax figure with his pale face and blue lips.

* * *

I hated hospitals, but the girls needed me. CJ needed me. I took a deep cleansing breath before the doors whooshed open and I forced myself to follow the clattering gurney. Two paramedics whisked CJ into triage, and the receptionist directed us to a waiting room full of crying children, cranky senior citizens balancing behind walkers or snoozing in wheelchairs, and agitated young folks losing patience. Through the glass entry, I kept my eye on an officer trotting with Maverick and Renegade on a narrow strip of grass in front of the hospital.

Although he hadn't been detained, Reno complained, to no one in particular, about being stuck here, yet he lingered, pacing and cracking his knuckles, and muttering, "I just want to make sure that son of a bitch knows who helped save his sorry ass."

Carlee cinched tight the waist of the pants Dakota had provided for her. She wore a man's blue dress shirt and she'd scrounged a pair of lavender pedicure sandals. Her damp hair hung straight down her back. After a cursory examination, and with her assurance she was all right, I handed her my phone.

"Call your mom," I said, but before she took my phone the triage doors opened.

"Bluestone?" came a high-pitched voice from a middle-aged woman in bloodstained green scrubs partially obscured by a long white coat, a stethoscope draped over her tired shoulders. She brushed back jet-black hair streaked with silver as she surveyed the room. Reno rudely whistled and waved his forefinger. She introduced herself as the admitting physician, Anna White Eagle. "We have to dig out that bullet, and he's lost a lot of blood. He needs a transfusion, but our supply is low and we don't have any in his blood type. Are any of you family?" she asked.

My heart sank to my toes.

"What does he need?" Carlee's small voice didn't carry very far.

"Excuse me?" the doctor asked, waiting for her to repeat what she'd said.

Carlee said more forcefully, "I'm type O negative."

"Kid, you can't give him blood," Reno began at the same time I said, "Carlee, I don't think that's a good idea." I think we were coming at it from different perspectives; however, the look Carlee gave us could have staunched a lava flow. Reno shrugged and put both hands up in surrender.

I said, "Carlee, after what you've been through—"

"I haven't been through as much as Dr. Bluestone. I'm a universal donor. It'll be perfect."

Reno snorted, "Doctor. Hah."

"You're exactly what he needs," said the physician. She cocked her head. "How old are you?"

"Seventeen," Carlee declared, lifting her haughty face in a challenge.

Was she seventeen? Before I could argue, the doctor motioned to a nurse who swept Carlee into the ER.

"Who is that kid?" Reno whispered, amazed.

I smirked. *Look. Up in the sky. It's a bird. It's a plane. It's Supergirl.* "What is it between you and CJ?"

His shoulders gave a noncommittal shrug, and he stood. "I'm outta here."

Dakota appeared at his side. "Can you wait, Reno? I'd like to get a statement before you disappear."

"You commandeered my boat, Dakota, and now my valuable time," he said indignantly.

She raised an eyebrow. "*Officer* Dakota, and all the same, I'd appreciate your sticking around." Her radio crackled.

Reno sat down and said acerbically, "Where's that blond escort I ordered?" It appears he'd heard about CJ's ruse to get a hold of Ana.

"Ana is upstairs." Dakota turned to me. "She's had quite a time. I think she could use a friendly face."

Dakota pointed her finger at Reno, who remained seated. I took the slowest-ever elevator to the second floor, my mind conjuring all manner of tragedy.

Ana was propped up in a hospital bed, her sunken blue eyes ringed in gray. Below the floral pattern on the short sleeves of her hospital gown, purple veins throbbed through the translucent skin on her arms, and the artery in her neck pulsed rapidly. She inhaled shallow breaths. Tiny wisps of limp blond hair escaped the band tying it back, softening her pale face. Her hollow eyes stared at the blank television screen secured to the wall. I took her left hand and wrapped it in both of mine. Although she turned to look at me, I didn't think she saw me.

My eyes wandered around the pastel room past thick blue canvas blackout curtains, skimmed over a gold crucifix, trailed the drip lines and red and black wires attached to Ana's arm, and stopped on a blue screen flashing numbers; blood pressure, oxygen, pulse rate. My heart raced. I looked away.

I told Ana a story I hoped she could hear. "Carlee's quite the girl," I said as animatedly as I could. "Has she always asked so many questions? And she hasn't even taken a class from me yet." No response. "I hear you both play the piano. I'll bet she hates to practice. And congratulations on being voted homecoming princess." Ana squeezed my fingers; I flinched but gently squeezed in return.

She closed her eyes and dozed off, and I headed to the coffee dispenser. While I stood in front of the vending machine, my finger hesitating to connect with "Monica

Parks", my phone buzzed. I smiled in response to the
display.

"Hi, Pete," I said. The day was already better. "I've
been thinking about you."

"Where have you been?" he sputtered.

I inhaled sharply. "I'm in New Town, North Dakota."

"North Dakota?" he wailed. "What're you doing
there?"

"Do you remember Monica Parks? Her—"

"Don't tell me she's with you. She left Miss Grace all
alone last night and some kids tried to break in again."

When he took a breath, I slid my words in. "I hope
she's all right. Monica isn't here, but we found Carlee and
Ana."

"Parks told Ronnie they'd run away."

"I don't have all the details, but they didn't just run
away. CJ got them away from their captors…?"

I couldn't hear him even breathing. "Pete, are you
there?"

"What do you think you're doing, Katie?" he asked.

"What?" I said angrily.

I glared at the screen, preparing to punch an end to the
call, and Pete said, "Wait. I'm sorry. You need to know…"

I held the phone to my ear. "What do I need to know?"
I said, my patience wearing thin.

"Ida's in the hospital," he said quietly.

CHAPTER FORTY-ONE

Ida took a tumble and hit her head. Samantha said she found her that way, but Ronnie took Samantha in for questioning."

I couldn't breathe. Ida Clemashevski was like family. Ida *was* family.

"Katie?"

"I'm here. Tell her I'm coming. As soon as we can, we'll be back in Columbia. Tell her even if you don't think she can hear you."

"Katie, Ronnie has an APB out on CJ."

"CJ didn't…" My phone went dead, the battery depleted. Heat rose from my chest and curled around my ears.

I found a nurse at the station. "Can you tell me where

I can find Dr. Bluestone and Carlee Parks?"

An odd expression passed over her face before she waved me down a long hallway. I concluded the room I wanted was the one with a policeman seated in front. As I approached, Dr. White Eagle exited the room, saw me, and firmly pulled the door closed behind her, giving me the cold shoulder.

I followed her down the hall. "Dr. White Eagle, how are they?"

She stopped and stared at me, weighing her answer. "We sedated him after he attacked Carlee."

"What?"

"I doubt he'll even remember, but, after all she did for him, he went for her throat. Although he was still very groggy, he could have hurt her," she hissed.

"Where's Carlee?" I demanded.

Gauging how much she should tell me, she finally said, "With her sister now."

Foregoing the sluggish elevator, I sprinted up the steps and rounded the corner. The officer opened the door, and I raced into Ana's room, gasping. The girls stared at me, a crooked smile on Carlee's lips, Ana's eyes alert.

"You're okay?" I asked, gulping air, pressing my hand against the pain in my side.

"You need to exercise more, Ms. Wilk," Carlee snorted. "Ana and I have been talking."

I pulled a chair next to Carlee and threw my arm over her shoulder. "Dr. White Eagle said she had to sedate CJ—I mean Dr. Bluestone."

Her collar covered most of the sharp red marks circling her neck.

"Oh, Carlee." The words slipped out, and I gathered

her in my arms. "Why would he try to hurt you?"

"That's just it. I don't think he meant to hurt me. Dr. White Eagle had him sedated as soon as he became agitated, but look…" In her palm, she held a necklace with a broken gold chain. I raised an eyebrow. "I think he was reaching for my necklace."

I paced the room.

"Can we go home?" Ana asked softly.

I parted the blackout curtains. The remains of the day had long since faded, the streetlights glaring orange against the black sky. "Soon," I said, hopeful, and left them to talk.

I found Dakota and Reno standing at the entry to the hospital, involved in a heated debate. They halted their conversation before I closed the gap.

"It's been real, Ms. Wilk," Reno said. "*Officer* Dakota." He gave her a mock salute. The sliding glass doors whooshed open and two dogs burst into view. Maverick and Renegade passed me and chased each other up the stairs, their leashes flapping just out of reach of the officer pursuing them. Dakota and I followed, taking two steps at a time. Near the top of the stairs, Dakota witnessed Maverick stand on his hind legs, draw the handle down, shove open the door, and lead his young friend down the long hall. Her eyes grew large in disbelief.

We followed Renegade, padding outside CJ's hospital room, yapping her puppy bark and circling the young officer, who stood flustered with his back against the wall, the tips of his fingers on the firearm at his hip. Dakota called out, "Stand down, officer. Let the dog in." The officer turned the knob and backed away. Renegade disappeared inside, and the officer secured the door behind her.

My sixty-five-pound dog skirted another officer at Ana's

door and snuggled in her bed. Under her petting hand, his cautious eyes followed me into the room, blinking as if to say, *I'm here to stay, right?*

Carlee curled in the chair, snoring gently, her legs pulled up under her. Ana put her finger to her lips before winking. I mouthed, "Are you okay?"

She nodded. I think she said, "Almost."

* * *

I spent the night in the waiting area outside the girls' room. When I woke, a seam in the plastic loveseat creased my cheek. I rubbed the crust from my eyes and the drool that had dried at the corner of my mouth before running my tongue over gritty teeth. Into the third day without a shower and clean clothes, the clear plastic bag at my feet containing a set of hospital scrubs, a washcloth, towel and soap, a toothbrush and toothpaste, a comb, and directions to the sleep rooms and cafeteria was a good start.

At a corner table in the cafeteria, Officer Dakota invited me to sit. "We need to talk," she said, furrowing her brow. When I flashed the dead screen on my phone, she pulled a single-use phone charger from her belt. Would wonders never cease?

With a cup of tea in one hand and a breakfast burrito wrapped in waxed paper in the other, my full weight plunked down noisily onto the bench attached to the table, popping up an unprepared Dakota on the other side of the seesaw.

"CJ's still in a lot of pain, but Ana and Carlee can be released soon. Do you have any idea how you're getting back?" she asked.

I'd forgotten about the collision, and I didn't even know where my beloved car had been towed, or if it had been towed. I shook my head dolefully. I needed a vehicle.

"I have a few repossessed automobiles in the impound lot I could let you have for a song," she said. Even a song would be more than I could hunt up. "Literally a song." Her eyes twinkled.

I took a breath. "What would you like to hear?"

"As much as you can tell me."

The more I told her, the more confused she became.

I told her about three-year-old Emma reappearing with Maverick and CJ in tow, ending with the murder accusation hanging over his head. "You know he wasn't supposed to leave the county, let alone the state."

Dakota accepted CJ's analysis of the message on the magic cube and agreed with his reasoning. "You couldn't have waited," she said dismissively.

"And I couldn't have made it here on my own. Is there anything you can do for CJ?"

She chewed her lower lip. "I contacted the Columbia chief of police. I've given him a rundown on what's been going on. He's agreed to suspend the charges of fleeing the jurisdiction until we finish sorting everything out and he gets a chance to speak to Chantan."

"Who was the guy on *Nautibuoy*?"

"I was hoping you could tell me. Carlee identified the boater as the first person to pick her up hitchhiking," she said with a sigh. "He's lawyered up, but his Iowa ID says he's Richie Sindelar from Council Bluffs. He has a rap sheet as long as my arm. Mostly transporting contraband, assault, drunk and disorderly, but this is pretty major: kidnapping with intent to traffic, and attempted murder.

"Preliminary forensics came through on the van parked at the bay. It was loaded with fingerprints and DNA, and it'll to take a while to sort out. There are three curiosities." I didn't like where the conversation was going. "We thought there might be another body someplace because we found blood on a tire iron." The burrito curdled in my gut.

Dakota lightly tapped her coffee mug on the table, droplets of precious caffeine splashed and landed on the back of her hand. "It was canine," she said, wiping the coffee with a paper napkin. I seethed.

"And dental records positively matched those of Molly Yates. She was three months pregnant."

"Oh, no." I inhaled and looked into Dakota's concerned eyes. "You said there were three curiosities. What's the other?"

Dakota rubbed her jaw, looking like she'd worked through some worst-case scenarios. "They found a rusted Tonka toy in the van. He might've had a kid in there."

"Emma," I whispered.

"What?" Dakota asked.

"Sindelar may have attempted to kidnap the little girl who lives next door to me. My God, she's only three years old." All the little hairs on the back of my neck stood up. "The canine blood might belong to my Maverick. Sindelar is a creep from the get-go, and his lime green van fits the description of a vehicle seen in the area at the time of Emma's kidnapping ."

"Everyone bolted from Lewiston Run, but our forensics team is out there now."

When it had taken enough charge, my phone pinged with several missed calls and text messages. "Sorry," I said, and nodded politely as I slipped the phone into the breast pocket of my scrubs after reading my last message.

I concluded our discussion and found the girls eager to be on their way. Ana had persuaded Dr. White Eagle to sign her release form so she could return home and she promised to seek counseling.

"I'm getting us transportation home," I said.

I left a message on Monica Park's phone while on our way to the impound lot.

Dakota said, "We might need the girls to testify, but even if we didn't have Sindelar on trafficking, we have him dead to rights on attempted murder, and there were plenty of witnesses. Here we are," she said, nodding to rows of cars squeezed onto a small lot. "What would you like?"

I needed a ride. "Two dogs, four humans. What would you recommend?"

"I've got just the thing."

CHAPTER FORTY-TWO

What do you think you're doing?" I asked in a huff. CJ's arm was caught in a navy-blue immobilizing sling secured to his side with Velcro. His face lacked color, and his eyes had a dull faraway look. Renegade ushered him down the hallway, and I darted after them. "And who am I not supposed to tell what to?" I asked, infuriated, recalling his cryptic text.

"I'm ready to return to Columbia to face the music."

"You can't just up and leave," I persisted. A victim of a gunshot and a risky surgical undertaking, yet here he was, planning to skip out.

"I can and I will. Dakota has nothing with which to hold me," he snorted.

"But Dakota said—"

"Dakota has always known where to find me."

"You've known her a long time?"

"Her entire life." He winced as he peeled the sling away from the Velcro and cinched his arm tighter across his body. "She is my little sister."

I stopped, dead in my tracks. "And I suppose Reno is your little brother."

"No." His voice grew darker and sadder. "But once my best friend," he said and continued walking.

We bypassed the elevator and anyone who might have gotten in the way of our exit. "He certainly doesn't act like a friend," I called after him.

"I suppose I did not act like a friend either."

"What happened?"

"We loved the same woman and Danica chose me," he said as we rounded the corner.

No one guarded their door. "Something is wrong," he whispered and moved more quickly.

"We need to leave. Now." CJ herded us out the door, down the stairs, and out of the hospital.

He canvassed the parking lot then remembered our collision. "We have to obtain alternate transportation quickly."

A 1991 sky-blue Ford Econoline chirped, and I held up the bill of sale, the title, registration forms with my name on the dotted line, and a fob jangling the keys. There was a small dent in the rear fender, and a deep scratch along the driver's door, but for $5.00, I could overlook one or two flaws. It would get us home.

The dogs took one last necessary stop before climbing into our chariot and clambering for the space between the girls. I slid into the driver's seat and plugged a charger into the outlet where the cigarette lighter should have been. CJ fumbled with the passenger door. He then slid into the seat and stretched his legs.

Carlee grabbed the headrest and heaved her body forward, stressing her chipper mood. "Nice wheels, Ms. Wilk."

CJ cringed as I ground the gears. It had been a long time since I'd maneuvered a vehicle with a manual transmission. Maybe never. The car started rolling as a black Suburban hurtled into the lot, screeching to a stop in front of the emergency entrance. Four suits stepped out of the SUV and marched through the hospital's front doors, dragging a large woman in a red muumuu. She clutched her stomach, doubled over in distress.

"Drive," CJ hissed as he lowered himself out of view. "Slowly." I rolled out of the lot in plain sight.

Minutes later, the hum of the tires on the pavement filled the interior. As the hills melted into plains and the sunflower fields disappeared, I glanced back to see Ana staring out the window, clutching her hospital file like a lifeline. The more miles we put between New Town and us, the paler she became, and I worried we'd left too soon. CJ rested beside me, eyes closed. The dogs watched.

After twenty quiet miles, CJ said, "They came looking for the girls at the hospital."

My heart plummeted to my stomach.

"Reno directed the search toward Montana. The girls will be safe for a while but they will not follow that wild goose for long." I felt my eyebrows reach toward the sky in disbelief.

After a few more silent miles, he spoke so softly I almost missed him talking altogether. "I loved Danica the moment I laid eyes on her. Reno loved her too.

"The last time I saw Reno, the day Danica and I married, he gave me a black eye." CJ took a deep painful breath. The dogs lay quietly, heads on paws, eyes closed. "He told me when we met next, he would kill me. We were all so young.

"The minute I turned eighteen, I enlisted and discovered an aptitude for the military. I rocked the exams and was awarded a SEAL contract with a good salary."

He tugged his billfold from his back pocket. Reverently, he removed a black-and-white photo.

I tried to sneak a quick peak. "What happened to her?"

Through clenched teeth, he said, "I don't know."

The car jerked when I brought my attention back to the road.

When we crossed over the Red River into Minnesota, my phone jangled. CJ turned it off.

We pulled off the interstate in Fergus Falls and picked up greasy burgers and Cokes. I took the dogs for a short romp around the block. When we returned, they were loaded, ready to go.

CJ's phone chirped. "Bluestone." He glanced my way with a wry smile. "I will tell her.

"Dr. Erickson is at the hospital with Mrs. Clemashevski, who is eager to speak to you."

We rumbled into Columbia and I dropped the girls at home with Monica. I made a beeline to the hospital, slammed the gear into park, and dropped out of the driver's seat. I steeled my nerves to enter the hospital and marched up to the information desk.

"Ida Clemashevski's room number, please?"

The birdlike blue-haired woman, drowning behind the huge mahogany desk, never looked up. "She's not here."

"But I thought——"

"Do a little less thinking and a little more moving. She already went home." She eyed me over thick glasses, pursed her lips in disapproval, then smoothed the front of her green volunteer apron, ignoring my protests.

We pulled out of the lot intending to speed toward home, but when the ringing on CJ's speakerphone was answered, I slowed. "Yes?" said the weary voice.

"Ida!" I cried.

"Katie, where are you?"

"Back in Columbia. I'll be right there. How're you doing? Are you okay? What happened?"

"I'm doing well—thank you—but I can't quite remember what I did to end up in the hospital." She giggled. "Would you do me a favor?"

"Of course."

"Would you please stop by the Parks' home and ask if Monica's able to check on Grace? Monica isn't answering her phone." I'd noticed. "And I want to make sure Grace is taken care of."

"Certainly."

"Good," she said and hung up.

As I glanced into the rearview mirror, my heart lurched at the sight of pulsing lights on a police cruiser. I pulled over, mentally ticking off the checklist of possible wrongdoings, but when the vehicle tore around us and zipped down Main Street, I let out a breath.

CJ chuckled. "Are you wary of all law enforcement?"

"Isn't everybody?" I said in a slightly lighthearted tone.

Chief Erickson stood on the concrete stoop in front of the Parks' house, poised to knock, unhappily appraising our coincidental arrival.

CJ ambled toward the house, scouring the area for cars that shouldn't be there.

"Evening, Ms. Wilk." The chief studied the sling and nodded. "Dr. Bluestone." Chief Erickson added, "Ronnie thought I might be up to fielding a domestic disturbance call. What are you doing here?"

"You know what happened to Carlee and Ana?" I asked.

He nodded reluctantly. "Allegedly."

The chief should be outraged. I couldn't think of a politically correct way to answer him. The chief gave three hard raps on the door.

Carlee opened the door a few inches and peeked out. When she saw me, she pulled the door wide open.

"Miss Parks, I'm Chief Erickson."

"I know who you are."

"We received a 911 call from a concerned neighbor. May I come in?"

She stepped to the side.

"Is your mother here?" Chief Erickson asked.

"No."

"Were you fighting with her?"

"No. Maybe. She accused us of causing trouble by running away. I tried to tell her that Ana had been taken and that Dr. Bluestone and Ms. Wilk brought us home, but she didn't believe me.

"Ms. Wilk, she went berserk when I asked her where the pendant came from."

She handed CJ a deep blue stone dangling from a shoestring. He said, "During my first deployment, I uncovered a piece of lapis lazuli and befriended a stonemason, who demonstrated how to carve and polish the piece. Because I had not been able to afford a ring for Danica, I fashioned a pendant for her and sent the necklace home." Carlee was right. He hadn't tried to hurt her; he'd tried to get the pendant.

"Where did you get this?" he asked, his voice breaking.

"It's Monica's."

A full range of emotions played over his face. "I'll talk to you tomorrow." He and Renegade marched out the door.

"Where's your sister?" the chief asked as the door clicked closed behind me.

"Ana's asleep."

"Just a few questions," the chief said gently. "Officer Bluestone told me you've been very brave throughout your ordeal. They want to press charges of kidnapping, false imprisonment, and attempted murder against the man who took you."

"I'm here to help. How did you end up in New Town?"

Carlee hung her head, her soft voice blanketed by the long black plait covering her face. "I wrote out the letters from the cube Ana gave me and plugged them into an anagram program. When it generated 'Fort Berthold, N DAK' I went looking for her. It was easy to hitch a ride, and the guy seemed nice enough. So stupid. That's the last thing I remember until I ended up on that boat."

The chief said, "How many times have you heard 'never to take a ride from a stranger'?"

A squeaking door brought an abrupt halt to their exchange as Ana stepped into the room. Her tired eyes held back tears. She took a deep breath. "Carlee came for me. I went looking for my father—that man who introduced himself about six months ago..." she gasped, "as the possible paternal half of a one-night stand with Monica Parks. He bought me a Hobo purse and a new phone.

"He was charming and accommodating and handsome. He attended the coronation. I was afraid he'd be disappointed when I was crowned homecoming princess instead of queen, but he just wanted to celebrate. He told me he'd like to take me out for dinner sometime, but he had to get back to Fargo. Then he asked if I'd like to go with him.

"While I packed my overnight bag," Ana said, "I overheard him say 'Fort Berthold' to someone on the other end of his phone. I printed the letters on the magic cube and mixed up the squares. I didn't want Carlee to worry and I knew she'd figure it out." The look she gave her sister was pure love. "He promised we'd return on Sunday. We stopped at the mall in Fargo, and he bought me a cool new outfit and a pair of shoes I'd been eyeing. At dinner, he was a perfect gentleman. He was kind to the waitress and funny and—"

Carlee recited the rest from memory, "After dinner, he asked if they could go just a bit farther up the road. Ana fell asleep and woke up when they arrived in New Town. He said he had a place for her to stay and dropped her at that trailer park, just for one night, but he never came back. And they kept threatening her with hurting her family."

The chief asked, "Why did you believe him?"

Ana's eyes grew round, and tears spilled over the red rims. Carlee's voice broke, barely a whisper. "He carried her baby picture in his wallet."

"I need to talk to your mother," the chief said.

"Mother," Carlee spat. "Monica's not my mother." She straightened, her eyes glittering triumphantly.

"She isn't your mother?" I asked. Carlee shook her head. "If what you told us about blood typing is correct, then no, she *can't* be my mother." I could barely hear her. "I'm probably adopted. Maybe I have a real family out there somewhere looking for me too."

Ana looked at her phone. Tears streamed down her cheeks; she was crestfallen. Carlee said gently. "No matter what, you're my sister, the only family I've ever known." Then Ana's cell phone tumbled from her hands. I retrieved it and peered at the information on the page she'd consulted. "What has Monica done?" Carlee peered over my shoulder and gasped.

Chief Erickson slipped the phone from my hand and read the text. "Sixteen years ago, the two-year-old daughter of Luke and Velma Sampson was allegedly taken from her home in the middle of the night. With no evidence of a break-in, Sampson and his wife were held on suspicion of child endangerment but eventually were released. Luke Sampson's ex-wife, Alice, was briefly considered a person of interest, but no charges were filed and no arrests were made. The child is still missing, and the case remains open."

He turned the phone screen to show the photo. Ana was the spitting image of the beautiful blond woman displayed in the photo on the screen.

Carlee said, "Ana, that's you!"

Ana collapsed. Chief Erickson swooped in and caught her as she crumpled. Then he carried her limp body to the couch.

He punched some numbers on his phone and said, "We have a situation."

CHAPTER FORTY-THREE

Chief Erickson completed the phone call and returned to the living room, where Ana was now sitting up. "I'll assign a patrol car to watch your house until we figure out what's going on. Monica has some questions to answer. Is there somewhere you can spend the night?"

"They can stay with me." I thought for a moment. "Or I'm sure Mrs. Clemashevski would love the company."

Carlee looked at Ana. Having a safe place to stay would remove one more headache from their young minds. They rose from the couch and made their way to their rooms to grab what they might need.

Chief Erickson said, "Katie, Ronnie got a call from the officer in charge of the case, Rutherford. It's a high-profile and far-reaching case and our interference might cripple an ongoing investigation. He also reprimanded us for putting too much faith in the information given by a trainee in New Town, a known criminal, and the prime suspect in our murder inquiry. We're outranked, but I'll put everything on hold until we figure this out."

"That creep held Ana captive and nearly cost Carlee her life. I'm not sure how they got there, but I do know how they got here. What do we need to do?"

"I'd like the girls to come down to the station tomorrow to make a formal statement, get it on the record. Because they're witnesses, they don't need Monica to come with them, but they can bring someone."

The girls returned, each hauling a floral tote and a small lime-green roller bag out to my new-old wheels.

When we yanked open the Ford van's rear door to load the suitcases, we found stacks of toilet paper. Chuckling eased the tension somewhat and we wedged the suitcases in around the rolls.

Ana hopped into the front seat and reached to the floor of the van. "When did you dress up like this, Carlee?" She handed a photo to Carlee.

"That's not me," she said, a bit surprised.

As we drove to Ida's, Carlee watched the scenery, Ana kept her eyes on Maverick, and I kept my eyes on the road until I parked the van. "May I see it?" The black and white photo of a stunning young woman, with dazzling light-colored eyes and long, straight black hair looked a lot like Carlee, but she wore CJ's pendant. I dialed, but CJ didn't answer my call.

A very tired Ida opened her door. Her hair stuck out in all directions. She wore a gray chenille bathrobe over a patterned pink housedress. Her face was as pale as the moon. Puffy purple pockets circled her shining eyes, but she seemed truly happy to see us.

"Come in. Come in," she said. She shuffled to the kitchen where water boiled in the teakettle. I pulled out her chair, and Ida sank into the seat. I poured the steaming water into four gilded cups arranged on a tray and carried it to the table, accompanied by a bamboo tea chest. We imitated Ida's selection of hibiscus tea, one lump of sugar and a sprig of fresh mint. Maverick flopped down on the tile and sighed contentedly.

"What happened?" I asked.

Ida exhaled, long and forcefully. "I don't recall, but Samantha found me on the floor next to the banister, so I must have tripped? Samantha's pretty shaken. They questioned her about the meth lab *and* about my falling." She sipped her tea.

"Would you be willing to have the girls stay with you tonight?"

"Chief Erickson already called. I'd love the company. You girls can sleep in the room at the top of the stairs to the right. There's clean linen in the bathroom. And Katie, if you don't want to be by yourself, you could stay on the couch." She looked at a stack of sheets, a pillow, and a blanket piled on the countertop.

"Thanks."

"Were you able to get Monica to check on Miss Grace?"

"I'll get the girls settled in, then run over to check on her myself."

Ida closed her eyes, letting the mint aroma relax her, and we all followed suit until a soft tapping on the front door brought me to my feet. "Stay with her," I ordered.

I peeked through the glass panel. Lorelei stood on

the stoop. I swung open the door. "Did you find them?" she asked. Ana and Carlee must have appeared behind me because Lorelei rushed around me and said, "You're back." She hugged them both.

"Carlee, even though you missed the first round of interviews, I'll bet they'd still let you compete."

Carlee's worried eyes watched Ana. "It just doesn't have the same appeal."

"You'll be there, though, won't you?" asked Lorelei, shoving her nerdy glasses up on her nose. She tried to lighten the mood. "You know you were my only competition."

"I'll get some snacks," I said and retreated to the kitchen. Lorelei followed me.

"Carlee looks anxious. I don't know if they'll need it, but my mom is an advocate for victims of sexual violence. She's a great champion to have in your corner and has access to all kinds of resources to help Ana and Carlee."

I bristled, then regretted I hadn't thought the same. I asked Lorelei for her mother's phone number. She helped me deliver the plate of chocolate-chocolate-chip cookies and a pitcher of lemonade. Ida distributed snack plates and her embroidered linen napkins and we watched her arduous climb up the stairs.

"Can I count on you to stay until I get back from across the street and check on Miss Grace?"

"Sure," said Lorelei, licking the crumbs off her lips.

Miss Grace didn't answer the bell, but the doorknob turned easily, and I slipped inside. I followed soft music to its source. She sat on the quilted piano bench, eyes closed, fingers drifting lazily over the keys, swaying in time to Erik Satie's "Gymnopedie No. 1." The music enveloped me, and I could hear my father quote from Congreve's *The*

Mourning Bride, "Musick hath charms to soothe a savage breast, to soften rocks or bend a knotted oak." I melted into the glorious sounds.

I remained still, but she knew I was there, and without missing a beat, in a voice barely audible over the beautiful tones, she said, "Hello, Katie."

"Ida wanted me to check on you."

"How is she? We were very good friends a long time ago. I'm glad we set aside our differences. I've missed her."

What could I say?

She opened her wise hazel eyes, and a small smile grew with each passage. "We were both musicians. She was much younger, probably prettier, much more outgoing, but I won all the competitions." She segued into another piece, more notes, longer arpeggios; her gentle words almost a lullaby. "I thought I loved Casimer, but in all honesty, I loved performing more. Ida was merely an excuse. She won the man, and I blamed her for my loss." She shook her head slowly. "I'm so glad she didn't give up on me. She's a lovely woman. I suppose we'll still have our moments, but…"

"You found our young ladies?"

"Yes."

She stopped playing, and rested her hands in her lap. "Thank you for inviting me to assist again this year. I'm better than I've been in years. Everyone needs a purpose. I'm certain we could get Miss Parks' preliminary introduction completed before the interviews begin tomorrow."

"I believe she's decided not to participate."

"That's a shame. Will the girls be all right?"

"I think so. There are resources we can tap to get them the help they need. We'll know more after their debriefing with Chief Erickson."

The grandfather clock behind her chimed. More time had elapsed than I'd thought. "Sorry, but I'd better get going."

When her fingers lowered on the keys again, she said, "An oldie but a goodie." The lyrics gave it away: "Love Me or Leave Me."

CHAPTER FORTY-FOUR

The rattle of dishes acted as the distant alarm, waking me from a deep slumber. Dust motes danced in the sunbeams that streamed through the crystalline windows. I threw off the covers and sat up, stretching the kinks out of my back, neck, and shoulders. It hadn't been all that uncomfortable, but I'd welcome a return to my own bed.

The mouthwatering aroma of frying bacon blended with apple-cinnamon and drew me into the kitchen. I opened the door. Carlee scooped shredded potatoes and dropped them into a sizzling cast-iron skillet. Ana arranged strawberries, blueberries, raspberries, and whipped topping in cut-glass sherbet dishes. Ida directed the action from her perch on the stool next to the island.

After a wonderful breakfast, we sat down on the porch,

a blazing sun over us, a breeze around us, a new day ahead of us, and we rolled out a plan of action.

Carlee said, "I'd like to attend some of the Columbia Days' festivities. I promised to help, and Ana and I can cut and tape and staple with the best of them."

Although Ana nodded, her eyes were focused elsewhere. "Chief Erickson wants to see us now," she said, gazing at the lone wispy cirrus cloud that drifted just above the tree line.

I settled Ana and Carlee into the back seat of the van, cuddling Maverick between them. Always one to share, Maverick lay with his tail across Carlee's knee and his head in Ana's lap. Tension rose the closer we drove to the police station, strangling even the promise of conversation. The window next to Carlee slid down and blustery air filled the empty space.

Maverick's abrupt stance and deafening bark alerted the entire block to our arrival. We tried to calm him, but it took a treat from each of us before he stopped making a ruckus.

"We're all good, Mav," I said.

Ana clutched Carlee's hand as they walked toward the entry. Carlee gave me a pleading look, so I gave Maverick's silky ears a rub. "Thanks, boy. I'll be back as soon as I can," I said. He stretched out on the rear seat and closed his eyes, and I accompanied the girls inside.

The police department droned with an imperative hustle. Officers stepped quickly from point A to point B. Multiple phones rang simultaneously. Angry squawks and painful howls accompanied clanging metal. Loud voices barked orders from the internal depths. Carlee and Ana shrank in front of the registration desk, looking even younger than they were.

An officer sat at the raised desk behind a glass enclosure. She flipped a microphone switch and said, "Can I help you?"

Neither Carlee nor Ana answered.

"What can I do for you?" she asked again.

I stepped up next to Ana and leaned into the speaker. "We're here to speak to Chief Erickson."

Her look was dubious, but she picked up the receiver next to her and punched in a number. "You have visitors," she said, then turned to us. "Someone will be with you shortly. Have a seat." She nodded at the parallel banks of scarred black plastic chairs welded to the floor and to one another. We took seats across from a scruffy man reeking of alcohol and sweat, wearing dingy clothes. Greasy hair hung over his dirt-smeared face. He raised a manacled hand secured to the seat before gracing us with a toothless grin.

The station was a busy place. A petite girl with curly brown hair and stylish glasses approached the desk after us. Her body had the fight-or-flight look, and she was holding back tears. "I don't want to go to jail," she mumbled.

"Wait over there," said the officer.

"DeAnne?" Carlee bolted from her chair. She took the girl by the elbow and led her across the floor. The girl sagged into the seat next to Ana, carefully setting her backpack to the floor. Carlee pulled some tissues out of her pocket and handed them to the girl. She blew her nose and dabbed at her eyes.

"My mom is going to kill me," she howled.

"DeAnne, what are you talking about?" I asked.

"Jimmy Hanson is—was—my boyfriend. And I'm

going to be in so much trouble."

"Why?" Carlee asked a little harshly.

"Jimmy got caught stealing," she said.

"Did you know about it?" I asked.

She didn't answer right away. "Not until he asked me to pick him up from Monongalia Park. He was supposed to be working but I thought he wanted to get back together."

My heart thudding, I asked, "What should he have been doing?"

"He was supposed to be a victim in some kind of test. His dad made him do it, but he didn't want to stay. It looked like rain, so when he called, I picked him up and brought him back to town."

"Do you remember the date?"

"Yeah." Tears formed anew. "It was my birthday," she moaned.

Drew's list of burglaries dates included the day little Jimmy was supposed to be playing the part of the victim Maverick and I were searching for the day of our SAR assessment. We couldn't have found him. He was never there long enough. Heat boiled over from my toes to my face. Then I remembered—if we'd found Jimmy, we might not have found Matthew.

"Weren't you Felipe's girlfriend before you were Jimmy's girlfriend?" Carlee asked.

"Yes. But Jimmy said that Felipe had been stealing." DeAnne added softly, "Then last night Jimmy told me I had to hang on to this until things cooled down or he'd tell everyone I was his accomplice all along." She sniffed. "I won't do it." She held out a clear plastic baggie containing a Tiffany silver teapot.

My jaw dropped. "That's Ida's."

Samantha is in the clear.

Felipe is off the hook too.

If only CJ could be so lucky.

An officer came for DeAnne. She brushed the tip of her nose. "Wish me luck."

Time stood still.

Finally, the door buzzed, and, after a click, a tall man with short cropped light-brown hair and icy blue eyes strode into the room. Surprise, then recognition flashed for a moment, and then the consummate professional walked over to meet us.

"Chief Erickson isn't here," Agent Thomas Blaise said. "Why did you need to see him?" The harsh sounds in the station stilled, and every eye in the room watched what was unfolding.

"Agent Blaise, may we speak to you in private?" I asked.

"Of course." He opened the door and led us down a gray hall into a small sterile room, outfitted with the same black plastic chairs, a table, and a water cooler. "Can I get you something?"

Ana shook her head furiously. Carlee lifted her head, defying her fear, and pointed to the water dispenser. "Yes, please. And one for my sister too."

Agent Blaise was with the Minnesota BCA and we had a history. He was the agent to whom Charles and I had reported my cousin's kidnapping, the agent who had thanked us for figuring out where Mickey had been taken, and the first agent with condolences upon the death of Charles. He was also the agent who had reprimanded me and made me promise to stay out of his business.

Carlee took a long drink, then set the cup on the table and inhaled deeply. "Chief Erickson asked us to come in and make a statement this morning."

Agent Blaise raised an eyebrow, and I could tell his attitude was tearing Carlee up inside. This wasn't going to be easy.

She continued, "My sister was kidnapped and taken to North Dakota." Ana trembled and Carlee took her hand. "Then the guy returned and tricked me into going with him." A look of fierce determination overtook her. "We want to make sure he gets everything he has coming to him."

Agent Blaise cocked his head. "I have no idea what you're talking about." He turned to me. "Their mother reported that they had run away and at their age they are free to come and go as they please."

I started to object. I'd known him to be a fair-minded individual, but he was angry. So was I.

"I'll take your statements." He opened the door, stepped out, and returned with a couple of legal pads and pens. Carlee crossed her arms; Ana dropped her head and she stared at her hands in her lap.

"Please tell me whatever it is you'd like me to know," he said. "Ms. Wilk, how exactly are you involved?" he added frostily.

"We thought you had the kidnapper..." I said.

"Alleged kidnapper," Agent Blaise said.

"We thought you had the *alleged* kidnapper in custody," Carlee said stiffly.

Agent Blaise locked eyes with Carlee.

"We're here to identify him."

"I can't take you to him."

Ana shuddered.

"What's the problem? Is he still in North Dakota? I

thought he waived extradition." Carlee shook with anger.

"He did, but—"

"But nothing. Where is he?"

Agent Blaise threw his shoulders back and raised his chin, as someone is wont to do when caught trying to wrestle up courage. "He's dead."

I jumped in. "You're sure. You have no doubts."

Reluctantly, he said, "Late last night, while en route with Agent Rutherford, there was a fatal accident. The prisoner was pronounced dead at the scene."

"Dr. CJ Bluestone and I had followed up on a lead." I felt the heat of Agent Blaise's gaze. "We rescued the girls from Sindelar and brought them home."

Anger snapped behind those blue eyes, and I didn't understand. "Bluestone stopped to assist at the site of the accident but he'd left this jurisdiction without authorization and is in custody, pending a hearing. You probably should be under arrest for abetting the fugitive."

"That's not right," I said, puzzled. "I talked to the chief last night. He said he'd put everything on hold until we sorted this out."

My ears rang with indignation, and my face flushed with irritation. "Agent Blaise, why don't you just let us talk to Chief Erickson? He asked the girls to come in."

Agent Blaise lifted a finger to halt my tirade. "Chief Erickson had a massive heart attack last night. He's under heavy sedation." My gut clenched. "I'm sorry, Katie. He didn't tell anyone anything. My superior ordered me to take over the investigation and keep this under wraps until we've questioned all parties involved. I'd appreciate your cooperation," and he added with distrust, "this time."

"Doesn't his stopping at the scene of the accident tell

you something about him? How could that agent arrest him?" *Unbelievable.* "Can I see CJ?"

Agent Blaise raised his left eyebrow and shook his head.

Another horrible thought occurred to me. *Where's Renegade?*

CHAPTER FORTY-FIVE

I followed the girls.

Ana held her head high; her breathing relaxed; her face flooded with relief; and she finally pieced together a beautiful mosaic of lilting words. "We need to be all decked out tonight when we help at the Royal Social, and we want it to be special. You're going, aren't you, Ms. Wilk? I know they're expecting you." It was the most I'd ever heard her say, and she glowed.

"And thank you for coming for us. If you hadn't…" She forced back tears. Carlee's arm curled around Ana's shoulder.

I made a call, then we drove downtown to meet Mrs. Calder. The girls wanted to walk through the art displays while I spoke to Mrs. Calder first.

"It'll get better." Standing next to me, Lorelei's mother delivered the understatement.

"It can't get any worse." I bowed my head. "Carlee and Ana need help. The agent in charge is keeping the investigation under wraps. Agent Blaise thinks I've overstepped my boundaries again. My only ally in the police department is in the hospital. Ida just got out of the hospital. They've locked up CJ, and his puppy is AWOL." I squeezed my eyes closed, hoping it was all just a dream. "What do I do, Mrs. Calder?"

She took my hand and sat me down at an empty picnic table overlooking the events of the day. She looked me squarely in the eye and said, "First, call me Marietta. Second, Lorelei believes the girls, and I have faith in my daughter."

"They are old enough to decide to talk to me without permission. I'll begin with Ana." Marietta held a doctoral degree in clinical psychology, assisting people in abusive relationships. Her empathy had garnered kudos from everyone who knew her, and I hoped she could help.

Marietta looked beyond the nearby bustle, and the light in her eyes dimmed a shade. "Carlee missed the interviews. She isn't going to compete, is she?"

"No. She isn't."

When her eyes met mine, they gleamed with steel. "We're going to get the girls through this." She forcefully clamped her hands on her knees and pushed herself into a standing position.

"Are you ready?" she asked. "Here they come." I nodded. "Let's take a walk."

I introduced Marietta, and funneled Carlee away from Ana. Carlee scrunched her forehead in worry, until, about thirty yards away from us, Ana melted into Marietta's arms, sobbing.

"What's she doing?" Carlee asked.

I answered, "Mrs. Calder has worked with other young women who've needed someone to talk to."

"That's lame. Ana has me," Carlee said, with the fierceness of a tiger.

We stopped walking and Maverick nudged her. "As tough as you are, my dear young friend, you both need to find a healthy way to deal with everything that happened. Agent Blaise gave you the same prerogative he gave me—keep it under your hat—but I think Mrs. Calder can help. She'd do anything for Lorelei and Lorelei would do anything for the two of you."

Carlee choked up. "I like Lorelei too, when she's not being a pain in the ass." We walked on.

"I'll do whatever Ana wants. Sometimes she wants justice, and sometimes she wants to put every minute of this ordeal behind her. But I don't ever want her to feel like she's alone," Carlee said, overflowing with love.

According to the health-managing app on my phone, we'd just completed three thousand seven steps when Ana and Marietta returned. Carlee mirrored Ana's modest smile, but it sure beat a frown.

"I'll see you all at the coronation," said Marietta.

I dropped Carlee, Ana, and Maverick off at Ida's. I had work to do. I thumbed through the contact list on my phone and pressed "connect."

"Erickson." The voice was a hoarse whisper.

"I'm so sorry, Pete. I just heard. How is he?"

"Katie." His voice cracked. "I'm powerless to do anything."

"I'll be right there."

I parked and walked the two blocks to the hospital. Standing in front of the sliding glass doors, I swiped sweat from my forehead. I took a deep breath and rode the three stories up to the ICU, reminding myself that good things happened here as well.

Pete sat in a wooden chair, leaning against the wall, pain pulsing across his face. He clenched and unclenched his jaw. He understood better than most the worst-case scenario, and I could almost see those scenes playing in his mind.

I entered the room quietly, took the chair next to him, and reached out to take his hand. He didn't open his eyes but gripped my hand solidly. "I'm not ready to let him go."

"He's not ready to go," I said, and I believed it.

The front legs of the chair thumped when he rocked forward, and Pete said. "The first attack was a skirmish. This one is an all-out war."

"What happened?"

He motioned me out into the corridor and I followed him to the waiting area. "He'd just called Ronnie Christianson, reporting in on a domestic disturbance, when he simply stopped speaking. Ronnie heard a clunk. He pinged the car and called out the cavalry. I'm absolutely certain he saved Dad's life. They found him sprawled on the asphalt next to his cruiser. Didn't wait to call 911, just carted him in."

I gripped his hand tighter. "I was at that domestic disturbance."

Pete stared at me.

"Parks and her…" I had to be careful or I might compromise the investigation. "The girls have some issues, and a neighbor complained. Your dad listened to the girls. He believed them, believed the girls, even though Monica reported them as runaways and the officer-in-charge is disinclined to do anything. The chief said there are more pieces in play."

Pete's phone chirped. "I've got a patient. Thanks, Katie. I'll keep you posted."

My next call met with a much different reaction. "What on earth is wrong with that man? And what's wrong with you? What part of 'Don't leave Monongalia County' don't you understand? And what do you mean, you rescued those girls, and you aren't allowed to talk about it? Who's the agent in charge?" barked Dorene Dvorak.

I told her what I could.

CHAPTER FORTY-SIX

G ood thing we dressed up." Brock puffed out his chest and smoothed the tuxedo printed on his T-shirt as he and Galen packed up the leftover paper magic supplies before heading downtown to the community theater production. The social was a roaring success and all that remained were the dirty dishes for Ana, Carlee, and me.

When we finished, the commons area looked at least as good as it had when we'd arrived. The girls still wanted to put a few finishing touches on stage for Saturday's coronation and headed to the auditorium. I dragged the garbage bags to the loading dock and heard strange scraping noises. I swallowed hard and threw open the door, smacking the noisemaker off the landing. One painful yelp was followed by excited yipping. Renegade bounded up the steps, vaulted into my arms, and nipped at my nose.

"Good girl, Renegade." I smoothed out the cockleburs matting her back; she rubbed a tattered ear against my chest. Her paws, worn raw from miles of running, left red stains on my shirt, but she'd found home.

I fashioned a makeshift leash from my belt, and she pranced through the dimly lit commons area toward the music coming from the auditorium.

Renegade and I crept into the sound booth from the balcony overlooking the empty performance area amid haunting tones drifting through the air around us. Carlee sat at the piano under a single spotlight, center stage, consumed by her music. Ana stood stage left in the shadows, transfixed by the sounds, eyes closed, her mouth curved in a smile. The decorations had transformed the stage into a wonderland of paper flowers, metallic streamers, and folds of rich fabric artistically arranged across the entrances.

Curious about all the flashing lights in front of me, I investigated the console and discovered the recording equipment in use.

Captivated, I settled into the comfortable seat. As I stretched out, the chair rolled back and dislodged the brown rubber stopper propping open the door, followed by a whoosh and a click. Renegade plopped into my lap. I closed my eyes and relished the sounds while rubbing her ears.

Clapping echoed in the huge auditorium. My eyes opened, grudgingly. Carlee stopped playing. She shielded her eyes with her hand and squinted into the glaring lights.

"Who is it?" Carlee asked.

"Just a fan," came a low, honeyed voice from a tall fit man walking down the aisle. "A great fan."

"Thanks," Carlee said, grinning madly.

I felt a thrum in Renegade's throat.

Ana had retreated into the folds of the curtain, but the smarmy voice snaked its way through the drapes. "Ana, come out and say hello," he purred.

Ana paled, and her blue eyes grew large. She cowered. Carlee stood and stepped next to her sister. She took her hand. "It's okay," she said, but Ana shook her head emphatically. She clutched Carlee's arm, sliding behind her.

"You're being a very naughty girl," crooned the man. "Papa doesn't like that."

Renegade snarled, but it didn't appear they could hear her. I seized the door. It wouldn't open. I thumbed through my phone contacts. Who wouldn't be at the play with their phones turned to silent? Despite the intermittent signal, I composed a quick text, hit "send," and prayed.

"You two cost me quite a bit of time and money. You'll need to make up for that," he said. An evil understanding cast a long shadow on Carlee's face. As if he could read her thoughts, he said, "Don't move." He drew a gun.

Renegade stood on the console, hackles raised, snarling. The girls needed help. I rattled the door. Nothing moved.

The man threw plastic strip ties to Carlee. "Put these on. Her first." He pointed the gun at the Ana. Grasping at knobs, I finally located the door release amid the light controls.

Carlee caught our movement and looked up. She blinked at my frantic sign language as her eyes found mine. Defiance replaced her fear. She stood taller. She grabbed Ana's hand, stepped over the apron and dragged her sister down the steps. When the gunman started to turn, I hit the kill switch.

I heard a pop and glass splintered behind me as I

dashed down the steps into Pete's strong arms. Renegade circled us.

"The girls," I gasped. I grabbed his hand, and Pete and I flew to the auditorium.

At the end of the hall, the stage door yawned opened. Ana fell into my arms. "He's got her," she cried.

Pete raced into the auditorium with Renegade barking at his side.

Pete knew every inch of the auditorium. He flipped on light switches and called out to Carlee, indifferent to his own safety, but he knew they'd gone. He made a call.

In a short time, policemen flooded the atrium. Ronnie Christianson directed them to fan out, reiterating, "Suspect is armed and dangerous and has taken a hostage."

I railed at Agent Blaise when he trekked through the double doors. "This is all your fault. If you had believed the girls, none of this would be happening."

"I'm sorry. Agent Rutherford is in charge, and he is of the opinion—"

"That's all you have to say? You have to find Carlee right now."

Ana whispered, "I thought you said he was dead."

Agent Blaise looked incredulous. "What?"

Richie Sindelar must have had a partner. Richie didn't take Ana. I was furious. "Where is this idiot in charge?"

Agent Blaise looked away, disconcerted.

Officer Christianson said, "Can you give us a description of the man? Anything?"

"I didn't see his face, but he appeared tall, with wavy dark hair." I sputtered. "And wearing a dark-colored bomber jacket."

Ana choked out, "His eyes are black."

I hugged her close. "We do have a recording of his voice."

Agent Blaise eyed me suspiciously.

"Carlee was recording her performance from the sound booth." Ana nodded.

Pete and Agent Blaise barreled up the stairs. Renegade kept pace beside them. They were oblivious to the glass shards crunching beneath their feet; I wasn't. "Renegade," I called. She joined Ana and me on the landing.

When the musical recording began, a voice called from the bottom of the staircase. "What's going on here?" Miss Grace and Pamela had returned from the theater performance to finalize preparations for the coronation, and were surprised by the intruders.

Carlee's entrancing music played while officers crawled over seats and checked behind curtains for clues. The notes soared through the auditorium and silenced even Miss Grace.

I had to listen again to the interruption, the unctuous voice following the applause, and in its amplified version, I could note the venom. "A great fan," he'd said.

Agent Blaise marched out of the little booth, not waiting to hear any more. He clenched his teeth, and the muscles in his jaw tightened. Spittle formed at the corners of his mouth.

I snatched at the buttons on his jacket sleeve. "What?"

He stopped in front of me, nostrils flaring, eyes afire. "I know that voice."

Instructions squawked through the radios. A trained operation ensued. I finally had to agree: we needed to be out of their way.

* * *

Pamela took the wheel to chauffeur Miss Grace, Ana, Renegade, and me back to Ida's.

My phone buzzed, and I answered it. "He's stolen a school van," Pete said. "Where are you?"

I slammed into the car door when Pamela pulled into an unidentified driveway. She shot a look at Miss Grace, who blanched as white as a ghost, then nodded. Pamela backed up and gunned back down the road, shimmying over the pavement, following the receding red lights on the van in front of us.

"Pete," Pamela yelled.

I turned on the speakerphone.

"East on Jordan, toward Hamilton Park," Pamela shouted.

Pete's voice roared, "Pam, get out of there!"

I heard pain and anger in Pamela's voice. "We'll keep him in our sights. If Carlee's in the van, I'm not leaving her." She'd been scared out of her wits by Emma's kidnapping, and it wasn't going to happen again under her watch.

"He turned south to Lake Monongalia. Pete, he's heading downtown, but it's cordoned off. He won't be able to get through. He'll have to head east again, back toward Hamilton Park. We're following."

"Get out of there!" he shouted again.

"Not on your life, Petey!"

The tail lights veered right. But Pamela knew all the backroads in Columbia. The van had doubled back and sped through the intersection in front of us.

"Dead End Alley, Pete," she said calmly. He dropped the connection.

Miss Grace grasped the handle above her head, pulling herself upright as Pamela sped down Suter Street with a steely glint in her eye. Like a NASCAR winner, Pamela yanked the steering wheel and twisted her white Audi A6 perpendicular to the entry.

We scrambled from the car and kept watch from behind a stand of maple trees. Ana's fingers dug into my arm, her eyes scouring the trees for any trace of her sister, my other arm stretched to its limit by Renegade's straining.

Five police cars spun in front of us. The officers hopped out, crouched behind the cars, and drew their weapons over the hoods. Renegade whined.

Brakes screeched as the van's headlights reflected off Pamela's Audi blocking the entrance. The driver revved the engine, spewing gravel in retreat. A shot rang out, flattening a tire. The driver lost control and the van slammed into a tree. The driver opened the door, hauling Carlee in front of him.

"I'll kill her," he yelled.

Ana gasped. I stared in horror and gritted my teeth. It was Rutherford, the cop who had been at the scene when Maverick brought Emma home.

"You know what they do to cops in jail." Rutherford yanked Carlee closer.

"Let her go. We'll talk," said Agent Blaise.

"She's my ticket out of here. Stay back."

"You have no place to go. You have to decide how you want this to play out."

"Get out of my way, Tommy," Rutherford raised the gun to Carlee's temple. He couldn't miss.

Agent Blaise raised a hand and motioned for everyone to hold positions. Carlee stopped fighting, not Carlee-like at all until I followed her line of sight. A football field away, with stealth and silence I didn't know he possessed, Maverick advanced at CJ's side.

Rutherford disappeared into the brush, dragging Carlee with him. Agent Blaise ordered the officers to fan out and take positions around the perimeter of the park. "Do not, I repeat, do not engage the suspect." Then he followed CJ and Maverick into the black.

Radios crackled. Every thought was on Carlee. Every sound was scrutinized, every movement choreographed, every heart beat wildly. Miss Grace wheezed. Pamela put her arm around the woman, supporting her. Ana and I stood by, barely daring to breathe.

A shot rang out, followed by silence.

Ana's scream echoed. "Carlee!"

CHAPTER FORTY-SEVEN

Everything went quiet. Not one leaf stirred. No walkie-talkies peeped. No motors droned. Ana's sobs penetrated the night. An eternity passed before a narrow beam of light burst from a Maglite, and we didn't breathe until the silhouettes cleared the trees.

Carlee's slight arms wrapped themselves around CJ's neck as he carried her out of the darkness, one careful step at a time. Maverick strutted by his side. Ana ran to them. As he released Carlee, CJ croaked, "We're just about even." He fell to the ground. Blood seeped through his shirt, and the color drained from his face. He needed medical attention, but they were alive.

Happiness bloomed in my chest, and a smile burst on my lips. *All's well that ends well*, I thought, but then the good feeling vanished when I met Agent Blaise's angry eyes. His steps pounded the earth as he approached. "Katie, I told you to stay out of this!"

As I backed away, Maverick bounded to my side and took an aggressive stance. The hair on the back of his neck was standing straight up.

Miss Grace put herself next to Maverick. She said calmly, "Young man, you won."

My phone rang. "Pete," I sighed. "We have Carlee."

"That's great, Katie. Dad would like to talk to someone in charge."

I handed my phone to Agent Blaise and he spoke to the chief. "Thomas Blaise. BCA. I'm sorry to report we believe Agent Rutherford headed a trafficking ring using his position within the state agency to subvert apprehension. He played his game three steps ahead of us. As per your instructions, we released Dr. Bluestone. He then trailed, shot, and killed the suspect, who had taken a hostage we believe he would harm. We needed Bluestone's expertise."

He nodded. "We're good here." He ended the call.

He returned my phone and took a deep breath. "I almost can't believe what I saw. Using some sign language, Bluestone directed the dog ahead of the suspect. He gave a puppet-like talking gesture, and when the suspect wheeled toward the sound of barking, he was shot. We also believe Richie Sindelar's death was no accident. At the time, the account Bluestone gave didn't coincide with Rutherford's, so we thought Bluestone was trying to cover for himself. We were wrong."

I smiled and looked around for CJ. I had a few things to tell him but I didn't see him anywhere.

"Is Rutherford the one who took my Emma?" Pamela asked.

"The probability is high it was either Rutherford or Sindelar," Agent Blaise said. "We'll check the fingerprints against those found in the van in North Dakota. Ana positively identified Rutherford as the man who posed as her father and delivered her to New Town.

"I'm sorry. We should have done better."

CHAPTER FORTY-EIGHT

CJ's phone went directly to voicemail. I had to find him, and the best way I knew to find anyone was with Maverick.

I drove home to pick up Maverick's uniform.

I clipped the sharp, new scarlet vest on my dog. "We're going to work, Maverick. For real."

Maverick jumped into the backseat of the van next to Renegade, and I rolled the windows down, hoping they could differentiate the open air better than I could. I had no idea how it worked. Maybe they'd catch CJ's scent. Maverick's head hung out the passenger side and Renegade panted, standing next to him. They were ready, but I had to come up with a plan. I pounded my hands on the steering wheel in frustration.

I shifted into reverse, but before I could back out, a truck rolled up behind me. Pete bounded out of his vehicle.

"I'm sure glad they caught that guy. Katie, care to celebrate? It's a beautiful night. I haven't seen you in forever," he said, rubbing his hands in anticipation.

I took too much time to answer and burst his delighted bubble. His hands gripped the doorframe as he leaned toward the window. "Unless you have other plans?" The dogs whimpered, and he reached in to pet them.

"I…" I stammered, "I mean, *we're* going to look for CJ."

"I saw CJ going into the Lost Pirate Pub. He looked pretty loopy already, but it's festival weekend. I guess Susie was right. I hope he's a great guy. Good night, Katie." He thunked the metal roof before shoving off the car. *Susie was right about what?*

Before I could spit out an explanation, his truck rumbled down Maple Street. My throat tightened; my sweaty hands gripped the steering wheel. I had a job to do. I couldn't let emotions get in the way. I thumbed the name of the bar into my phone's search engine and followed the map directions.

Streetlamps illuminated rows of vehicles in a packed parking lot. I pulled onto the shoulder, edging into a parcel of turf vacated by a Chevy Colorado that had seen better days. Plastic sheeting covered the passenger window, and as it roared past me, I saw a pair of Minnesota Twins bobblehead dolls jiggling on the dash. The dogs popped up and yelped. I tossed each of them a chew toy for a few minutes of good behavior.

Music spilled into the night every time the bar's door opened. The bouncer examined the IDs before admitting the short line of patrons. When my turn came up, I held onto my ID and asked, "Have you seen Dr. Bluestone?"

No answer.

"Do you know Chantan Bluestone?"

He glared at me.

"I need to find him."

He raised an eyebrow. His hand stretched out and seized my ID. He returned it, crossed his arms over his burly chest, and pointed his chin toward the entrance.

The lights pulsed with the bass line in the music. I squeezed through the sea of people settled around the U-shaped bar, checking all the faces. The bartender wiped off the counter in front of me and asked, "What can I get you?"

"Do you know CJ Bluestone?"

Eyes wary, he didn't answer.

"I need to find him. Any help would be greatly appreciated."

He braced himself against the counter. I pulled out a twenty-dollar bill.

"Is he here?"

He eyed the bill with disdain.

"Please?" I grabbed the cuff of his shirt.

"He's a good guy. Leave him in peace," he said.

I haltingly released the cuff but not before noticing his forearm, which bore the black ink of a crawling frog skeleton brandishing a trident. "You're one of them. Please," I begged. "It's important."

After he rearranged his cuff, he said, "That other chick snagged him and hauled him out of here already."

I nodded.

"He's battling his demons, but I swear I only give him

tonic and lime when he comes in," he said defensively. "For chrissakes. He's earned two Purple Hearts. Isn't that enough?"

He and Outlaw both.

"Please," I pleaded. "What can you tell me about the woman?"

"She's in here off and on. Mousy thing with a big appetite." His bushy eyebrows did a lewd dance and gave me the willies.

"Do you know her name?"

"Nope. She had him eating out of her hand, though. He followed her out like a lost puppy."

"Thanks."

As I turned to leave, he added, polishing the wooden countertop, "She drives a beat-up Chevy Colorado."

I'd just missed them.

I jammed my foot down on the gas pedal which caused the rear end to shimmy and spit gravel. I let up on the gas. Who was she? Where would they go? What demons were eating at CJ? He didn't commit murder. Was he Carlee's dad? Would he want to be? Would Carlee want him?

Demons haunted the powerless, the defenseless, not a hulking retired Navy SEAL. But what did I know?

I knew CJ to be a good man. He'd be a great father if it were true. I had to find him. I had to let him know.

I almost passed the sign pointing to Sibley State Park. I wrenched the wheel and pulled onto the paved entry, roared through the gate, and headed for familiar ground, the parking lot at the Interpretive Center.

Parked across two spaces, the truck drew me like a magnet. The dogs barked. They'd barked when we'd pulled into the parking lot at the Lost Pirate, and I'd thrown them a distraction in the shape of a chew toy. Maybe they'd sensed CJ's nearness. I wouldn't quiet them again.

I thumbed a text to Ida regarding my evening foray, but when I hit the "send" button, I received an error message. Some days, unplugging in a state park is a blessing, but I didn't need the inconsistent service tonight. I pocketed my phone until I could find a better connection.

When I opened my van door, Renegade jumped over me and raced into the woods. I released Maverick with instructions. "Find CJ." He took one last look my way and took off after Renegade.

A four-wheeler rumbled behind me. "Hey!" the young driver yelled. "You need a pass."

My state park pass had been stuck to the windshield of my Jetta, but I had no time to argue. Three long strides carried me into the trees. The thick underbrush held the young man at bay, but he shrieked, "You're in trouble! I'm calling the sheriff."

Leaves crunched beneath my feet. Brambles and limbs tugged at my shirt and tangled in my hair. Burrs scratched my hands and face. I pressed on, listening. I struggled through the terrain and crawled over a ridge where the rising moon unleashed frightening images. I fought my way through silken webs constructed by spiders I imagined to be the size of my fist. I checked my phone and found the undelivered text. I sent it again with my fingers crossed.

I ducked beneath elongated and deformed tree fingers directing evil incantations at the evening park visitors and ran headlong into Monica Parks. Her hair had taken on a life of its own, and her eyes were the size of saucers. "Monica?"

"That degenerate monster took stock of his horrible

life, and he's ended it," she cried, grabbing my arms.

"Who?" I asked. "CJ? Where is he?"

She hurled my arms out of her way, and she launched herself into the brush. My head connected with something hard. I saw stars, and then a black circle choked everything out of my sight.

CHAPTER FORTY-NINE

My eyes clamped shut to ward off the pounding in my head, yet the night sounds clawed into my consciousness. I swatted a creepy bug crawling over my cheek. The damp soil yielded as I shoved off the ground, and I couldn't find purchase, sliding forward until my forehead rested on my arm. The cool night carried smells that blasted my senses: old moss, dried leaves, damp animal fur, crisp pine, and the loamy scent of earth reclaiming its flora. I touched my forehead and it came away sticky.

I opened my eyes. *Where are you, CJ?*

My second attempt to rise met with more success. My noisy rousing canceled all other sounds in the park except an incessant barking. I took a deep breath, raked the ground for something to grab on to, and hoisted myself into a sitting position. Balancing on shaky legs, I dragged my body up a tree trunk to a quavering stance.

I launched my search with plodding steps. I targeted one tree at a time to stay on course and lumbered through the deep darkness, following the sound of yelping dogs.

As I quickened my pace, the throbbing in my head increased, and with each new bark, the crackle of internal luminaries clashed with my intentions. My head told me to turn back, but the yapping drew my heart. The barking stopped when I lurched into view and dropped next to the figure on the ground, and Renegade and Maverick circled me.

"CJ?" The contents of a pill bottle were sprawled next to his hand. I nudged him and waited. I braced myself to turn him over. Renegade licked his face, and Maverick swathed me with kisses.

"CJ?" I asked more forcefully, rolling him onto his side.

I sat back on my haunches. Blurry flashlight beams snaked through the trees, and a voice called, "Katie?"

"Here," I squawked.

Pete dropped his medical bag and cradled my face in his hands. His fingers came away stained. "You're hurt," he said.

"CJ," I croaked.

Pete reached into the canvas bag and pulled out a syringe. He raised it and flicked at the contents, but before he could make any move, CJ moaned and stirred. I bent down and wrapped my arms around his shoulder, then gently shoved Renegade far enough away to give him air.

Pete demanded, "CJ. Talk to me." He turned to me. "Narcan."

Brown eyes peeked out under heavy eyelids. CJ

answered, "I failed at this too."

"CJ," I fumed, reeling back from the waves of alcohol coming off him.

A snort escaped. "She was right. I don't have reason to be alive. I am an addict. I am *the* person of interest in a murder investigation." Tears welled in his eyes. "I lost the love of my life and I cannot even take care of a stupid dog," he said bitterly. As if on cue, Renegade inched next to CJ and began a serious tongue lashing. At first, CJ raised his arms to defend himself until he realized Renegade was still here in the present. Then he welcomed the caresses, scratching behind her ears as she leaned in for more.

Pete broke in, "CJ, did you take anything?"

CJ closed his eyes. Taking a deep breath, he shook his head. "That would have been the easy way out. I deserve everything I get. I have hurt every life I have ever touched."

"We need to get you to the hospital," Pete said and dragged him into a sitting position. "Who is *she*?"

I answered, "Monica Parks."

Pete's liquid-chocolate eyes clouded, but I couldn't begin to explain it to him. He motioned to the EMTs, who carted the gurney over the uneven terrain.

I gave Renegade the sign for "stay." She plopped down unhappily, her frisky tail still.

"Why are you here, Pete?" I asked.

Looking sheepish, he answered, "I went to see Ida for some advice when your text came through. As always, they were correct." I cringed while he cleaned my wound with a stinging solution. "You won't need stitches this time, but will you tell me what's going on?"

"I'm not entirely sure." Pete pulled me up and I reeled with an onrush of vertigo.

"What on earth were you thinking?" he asked, condescension niggling the edges of his words as he supported me.

Maverick brushed next to me, reminding me to behave. "CJ's a good man," I said. "Agent Blaise says he's no longer the only suspect in the murder of Lorelei Fiorillo." I gave Pete a rundown of what we'd learned about the girls. "And he still doesn't know about Carlee. I think she's his daughter.

"Monica Parks might have kidnapped Carlee and Ana when they were babies. But," I said carefully, "she has no reason to think anyone is onto her."

"I'll give Dad a call," Pete said.

"Is he okay? Is the chief out of danger?"

"If I keep him out of this, *I'll* be in danger."

I called Ida for the same reason.

Pete hung up his phone and didn't look too happy. "Rutherford has an alibi for the night of Lorelei's disappearance and Sindelar's phone records put him out of the area at the time in question, so CJ is still a person of interest in Lorelei Fiorillo's death. His botched suicide won't help. Dorene, however, is convinced he had no part in the murder. They don't have enough evidence to bring charges, but the ideal solution would be to find the murderer."

Pete chewed his lower lip.

"What are you thinking, Pete?"

"Someone killed Lorelei or at least contributed to her death, keeping her bound while lying in the poison ivy. Not many people would have known she'd have an anaphylactic reaction to poison ivy. What if her death was accidental?"

Accidental but not without bad intentions.

After a moment of silence, I offered, "Someone could have been envious. Her crown was tossed up in the tree, right? Or maybe someone was trying to take advantage of her." I shook my head. "But that doesn't rule out CJ."

"She had both an ex-boyfriend who wasn't happy and a new boyfriend of questionable decency, and he had an ex-girlfriend who might have been jealous," added Pete.

Jimmy Hanson couldn't be ruled out.

"Maybe one of her friends held a grudge," I said.

"Ronnie checked out her friends and they truly seemed happy for her. They were celebrating at the Lost Pirate, but aside from Lorelei, they all left together," said Pete. He opened my van doors and the dogs jumped in. "So it doesn't clear CJ."

Pete read a text. "They've brought in Monica Parks."

CHAPTER FIFTY

On our way back to town, I talked to the dogs. "Hear me out."

Maverick blinked.

"What if the murderer thought she was someone else?" I went on. "But who? For what possible reason? She didn't look like anyone we know. But the only photo I've seen is a black-and-white shot from her coronation."

Renegade perked up.

"Coronation? She looks nothing like Brenna, nor Ashley, nor anyone else at the Columbia Days' coronation. But…"

I braked hard and scrambled for my phone. In my haste, my fingerprint didn't open it immediately. I punched in the passcode and continued pressing numbers into the phone. When the call was answered, I said, "Pete, make certain they ask about *her* girls."

"I thought we'd established they weren't her girls."

"She doesn't know that."

"I'll meet you at the station."

I dropped the dogs at home, kissed the top of Maverick's head, and rustled Renegade's ears. "Good dogs." Then I clambered back aboard the tank and tossed my bag into the passenger seat.

I rushed through the entry of the police station where Pete stood tapping his fingers against the doorframe. He dragged me around the registration desk, through a doorway into an adjunct room. Startled by the scene playing out behind the glass, I backed into Pete. "She can't see you," he whispered, laying a calming hand on my shoulder. Her voice grated, and I had a bitter taste in my mouth.

Parks sat across from Agent Blaise, facing the glass, a metal table between them. "Why am I here?"

Agent Blaise ignored her and said, "Please state your name for the record."

She answered his easy question, leaning into the microphone, smiling coyly. "Monica Parks."

"Where do you work?"

"Sterling Manor."

"What do you do there?"

"I get the old folks moving, if you get my drift," she said haughtily.

"We met you as you finished your shift, is that correct?" Agent Blaise said.

She nodded. "I took the late shift, helping out." She yawned.

Hiding out, I thought.

Agent Blaise nodded thoughtfully. "Do you know why

we brought you in?"

Her face clouded with anger. "I assume it has to do with that murderer. I already gave my statement to Ronnie—Officer Christianson. That horrible man forced me to give him a ride out to Sibley. When we arrived, he took a bunch of pills saying he couldn't stand to live with what he'd done. I tried to talk him out of it, but when he decided to go ahead with his suicide," she said earnestly, "I ran for help."

Agent Blaise nodded again. "Did you get help?"

"By the time I got to my car, the sirens and lights were already flying into the park. I figured that Wilk woman called, and he'd either make it or not."

"He made it."

Her expression closed down.

"Tell me about your family."

"What?"

"Tell me about your girls."

"I'd do anything for my girls. They're all I have."

"It must be difficult raising teenagers alone."

Monica nodded. "We do fine. There always seems to be a need for someone who has my knack of caring for the elderly."

"What else would you do for your family?"

"I'm always there for them," Monica said. "Standing right behind them in whatever they want to do."

I whispered to Pete, "She's lying. She didn't want Carlee to be a part of the science club. She called her smart but ugly. She wanted Carlee to win the Columbia Days' ambassador program in the worst way and was so jealous of Lorelei Calder. And don't get me started on her reaction to Ana getting homecoming princess instead of queen."

"You said you'd do anything for your girls. Would you lie to protect your girls?" Taken aback with a question couched in doing the right thing, Monica shook her head but wasn't too convincing.

Agent Blaise nodded. "Would *they* lie?"

"Of course not."

"Carlee says you can't be her mother."

Monica's face gave away nothing. "She's a teenager. Don't all teenagers wish they had different parents at one time or another? I certainly *am* her mother."

"Is she lying?"

She squinted her eyes. "Why are you asking?" She scrutinized Agent Blaise for signs of duplicity.

"Carlee has irrefutable proof that your blood types are incompatible. You can't possibly be her mother. Science doesn't lie."

My breath caught in my throat.

"That was for a high school project," Monica spat. "She probably didn't even do it right. She's been under so much stress. You know she missed out on becoming Queen Santa Maria. She was whisked off to North Dakota and almost died." She turned three shades of purple and struggled to contain her emotions. "I *am* her mother," she sputtered.

"We can redo the test if you'd like. I'm going to ask Carlee to come in."

Monica squirmed in her seat, scratching her wrist red.

Carlee stepped into the room. "I asked you for a pinprick sample of blood for a science project—one that my chemistry teacher proposed—that could form the basis for an outstanding letter of recommendation from him. Remember?"

Carlee unfurled the pages she had clutched in her hand, smoothed them against her chest, then thrust them at Agent Blaise who put on glasses, tipped his head to align the lenses, and perused the contents of the papers as if he hadn't already memorized them.

"You hinted at my questionable ancestry when you said Ana left to visit *her* father, who obviously wasn't *my* father."

Monica's eyes searched the room.

Carlee continued, "I intended to create a genetics study. You have type AB blood and I have type O, so you can't possibly be my mother." Angry eyes lasered in on Monica, and Carlee stepped closer. "Who is my mother?"

Agent Blaise cleared his throat. "How did you get these results, Carlee?"

She took a step back and looked sheepish. "I performed the experiments from kits Ms. Wilk gave us at our science club meeting."

Agent Blaise gave a sharp rap on the tabletop and startled Monica. "Are you her mother?"

She sneered. He waited. "I saved that girl from the system. They would have put her in an orphanage or foster care, moving her from house to house. Her mother gave birth in my car. Before she died in my arms, she begged me to take care of her kid. She pleaded with me. I left Danica's body at the emergency room doors, but I kept my promise. Look where that girl is now," she said with satisfaction, trying to take credit for all the things Carlee had done.

Carlee gasped. Agent Blaise recovered quickly. "How did you know Danica?"

"I gave her piano lessons. She wanted to surprise her husband. She had lots of surprises."

"What hospital?" Agent Blaise asked. "Where did you

leave her?"

She took her time before answering. "Queen of Peace Hospital in New Prague."

"I've never ever heard her say Danica's name," I whispered.

Monica looked up as the door creaked open. Officer Christianson entered carrying a tablet. He set it in front of Agent Blaise then quietly seated himself in an empty chair.

It seemed like an eternity passed before Agent Blaise turned the screen toward Monica and asked her to identify the person in the photo. She smirked. "That's my Ana. If I'd have known what really happened, I would've done anything to get her back. I should be there for her now. She needs me."

Agent Blaise pinched the photo on the screen to zoom out, and Monica's eyes widened. She seemed to grab on to the edge of the tabletop, and she said, "She certainly looks like Ana."

"Yes, she does. Uncanny. Do you know who this is?"
Monica shook her head vehemently.

"We believe this is *her* mother."

The color drained from her face. Her chest rose and fell. Finally, she said, "I'd like to speak to Agent Rutherford." She rose.

"Agent Rutherford isn't available. Sit down," Agent Blaise ordered. Monica dropped into her seat. Crossing her arms, she sat back in the chair as far away from him as possible. "Does the name Luke Sampson mean anything to you?"

Her eyes darted around the room. "No. Should it?"

"We believe Sampson is Ana's father and Velma is her mother. Their daughter was abducted sixteen years ago.

She would be Ana's age. We've called them, and they're on their way to Columbia. They're willing to submit to a DNA test, and they're most anxious to have a word with you."

Defiance flashed in her eyes. "I only wanted to talk to Luke. I followed him and he dropped his daughter off at a horrible place. I could've taken care of her for him." She said it with such disappointment. "I saved her too." She stopped talking. "Where's Rutherford?"

Agent Blaise sighed. "Dead."

First surprise then something else flitted across Monica's face. "Thank God. He's been blackmailing me for years. Rutherford found out I'd taken her—for her own good, mind you—and accused me of kidnapping. He was pure evil. I'm glad he's gone. I'd do anything for my girls."

"What exactly did you do for them?"

Agent Blaise handed her plenty of rope.

"Look at Ana. I raised a winner." Her eyes darkened as she mumbled, "I am their mother." She raged. "They had no one else."

Quietly Officer Christianson said, "They had a real family." Monica flinched as though she'd been slapped. Tears stung my eyes.

Monica whined. "Danica was all alone." I gasped. "She gave her daughter to me. I took care of her. If she would have run, she'd be Columbia's new ambassador. That Lorelei should be careful. I think her name is jinxed."

"It doesn't look like the name is jinxed."

"Look what happened to the other Lorelei. Who would have guessed she was allergic to plants?"

"What do you mean?"

"Most people just get a rash from poison ivy, but her throat swelled up, her eyes bulged, her tongue stuck out.

She threw up all over before she suffocated," Monica said. She itched her wrist. "Didn't she?" She'd gone too far.

Pete stiffened. His jaw tightened.

Officer Christianson furrowed his bushy eyebrows. "How do you know that?"

"I heard it on the news." She scratched at her forearm, which was nearly raw.

"We withheld that bit of information from the media. I ask again, Ms. Parks, how did you know the specifics of Lorelei Fiorillo's anaphylactic reaction to the urushiol oil?"

I leaned against Pete, who put his arm around me and laid his chin on the top of my head. "He got her."

Monica's face hardened. "I'd like to speak to an attorney."

CHAPTER FIFTY-ONE

W hat do you think?" Jane modeled a blue leather cross-body bag.

"Where did you find that?" Brenna asked, appreciatively.

"Right after Lorelei's coronation, she drew my name from the raffle. It's a Rethreaded." She addressed the confused faces. "It's a company that provides hope, a supportive environment, and job training for victims of trafficking."

"Jane, we have to amend our trafficking protocol. Our reaction is too slow."

"I agree."

Carlee gave her a huge hug then turned to me. "Is he coming?"

I shrugged.

The kids flopped in desks around the room and Brock huffed, "I still don't get it all."

Galen drew a deep breath and released it impatiently. Carlee nodded a go-ahead.

"Ms. Parks felt she'd suffered plenty the years she oversaw the care of her cranky mother-in-law and figured the family owed her. Parks never told her mother-in-law about her divorce. But she helped write the woman's will, and when Mrs. Sampson passed away, Monica, or Alice, got a hefty bequest and the grand piano. Sampson seldom visited his estranged mother and didn't know what was going on, so the attorney thought the terms of the will were equitable. But even though she'd begun to show signs of dementia, the mother-in-law was no dummy. She'd locked most of the estate away in trust for any grandchildren, to be dispersed when they turned twenty-one. Parks believed she'd already earned her money saving Carlee, and when the opportunity presented itself, she took Ana to double the death benefit. Before the grandmother died, she specifically named the girls as heirs.

"Rutherford was good at his job. His investigation of Ana's disappearance led him to Parks. During one of his inquiries, he slammed the piano cover on her hand and broke her fingers, ending any possible performance career. She confessed everything to him except the future inheritance but pleaded with him to let her keep the girls. They were *safe* with her.

"As payment for his continued silence and providing birth records and social security numbers for the girls, Parks furnished new victims for Rutherford. She said every girl she'd given up needed to get out of Columbia. Her word for them was 'marginal.'"

Ashley said, "She's bat-shit crazy. Sorry, Carlee."

Carlee said, "I totally agree."

Ashley continued, "Ms. Parks liked to win. She thought Lorelei Calder had jumped the gun, wearing the crown before the Columbia Days' coronation, like she was boasting that her winning was a done deal. Parks had no idea she was talking to the wrong Lorelei, and while she was trying to explain how rude it was to wear a crown before the coronation, Rutherford sent her an urgent request for a new girl. She figured she'd clear Carlee's way. But Lorelei's allergy proved fatal, and Parks panicked. She's still itching from her exposure to the poison ivy. And when Sindelar saw Emma, he thought he'd make an easy substitution."

A warm feeling crept into my stomach. *Maverick saved Emma.*

"With Parks' consent, Rutherford took Ana," said Galen. "She couldn't stomach Ana looking so much like Velma. She figured she'd finagle the inheritance another way."

Carlee continued, "Sindelar had been watching Monica. When I went searching for Ana, it was just bad luck that he picked me up. Monica probably did save me from the system. My dad never knew about me. I could easily have become a ward of the court, and I never would have met you." She looked around at all of us, but her gaze lingered on Galen, whose smile stretched from ear to ear.

"What'll happen now?" Ashley asked.

Carlee was thoughtful. "Ana and I are staying with Miss Grace until everything's sorted out. Ana graduates this spring, and she's going to spend some time with her real family. But she's *my* sister. They charged Monica … uh, Alice with kidnapping, unlawful transportation and confinement, and with the murder of Lorelei Fiorillo."

An intercom clicked. "Ms. Wilk," a pert voice said. "Yes."

"You have a visitor."

"Thanks," I said as knuckles hammered on the doorframe. "Come in."

CJ entered and scanned the room. When he spotted Carlee, his stern face melted, and his hand rose from his side. His voice softened. "This is yours." He held the pendant. His eyes still glued to Carlee, he said, "Katie, I don't know how to thank you. How could I have not seen it before? She looks so much like her mother."

"Reno recognized you, Carlee. He said you're the spitting image of Danica. But no one knew Danica had died, and sadly, no one knew she'd ever been pregnant," I said.

Galen stuck out his hand. "Galen Tonnenson, sir." CJ shook it.

A smile just about made its way to the corners of my mouth until an imperious voice boomed from the commons area. "Katherine Jean Wilk."

I excused myself, knowing full well the repercussions of anything less than an immediate response, and greeted her enthusiastically, "Hello, Elizabeth. To what do I owe this honor?"

My stepmother wore a black pencil skirt, and a low-cut white camisole under her black power jacket. She carried a pristine leather briefcase. She wore her peroxide blond locks in a tight French roll, which, I thought uncharitably, helped iron out the wrinkles she would have had. The arterial red lips cut a slash across her pale face, completing the Snow White look. She splurged on Louboutin heels, increasing her height to a solid five-ten.

"I realize your biological clock is ticking down…"

The thought hadn't occurred to me before.

"But he has to stay with you for a while," she said, and stepped to one side. My stepbrother pushed the wheelchair in front of his mother, dragging a cart piled with two suitcases and a stuffed duffel bag. My father's sallow face gazed around the room, his arms lying limply in his lap.

"What happened?" I asked and rushed to his side.

"Hey, darlin'," Dad said. He cranked a smile onto his face and laboriously lifted his right hand.

"He's apparently too well to remain at the care facility, but too unwell to be home without help," Elizbeth said. "And I couldn't think of anything else to do. I tried calling." I thought it would look like I didn't believe her if I took my phone out. "Austin and I have to take this opportunity. They're sending us to the home office."

"In France?"

"We need this. I need this. He's your father. You can take him for a bit." With that, she planted a kiss on the top of Dad's head.

"Bye, love," he said.

She turned on her heels, and walked out.

"Sorry, Jeanie." No one else ever called me Jeanie. My stepbrother cast me an apologetic glance as he shrugged and followed his mother out of the math department.

"Dad?"

When the door clicked shut, his downcast eyes brightened, full of mischief. "They gone?" I nodded. He threw off the lap quilt, briskly rubbed his hands over his gray stubbly face, straightened his glasses, and stretched. I fell into his open arms.

"Quite an exhibition, Graybeard," said CJ from the doorway.

"Who you calling 'Graybeard!'" said my dad, involuntarily rubbing his chin, and ending our embrace, caught red-handed not nearly as feeble as he made himself out to be.

"If the shoe fits, they say," said CJ.

As spry as he tried to be, he struggled to push himself out of the chair, but stood unattended.

"Dad, this is Dr. CJ Bluestone. CJ, this is my dad, Harry Wilk."

Dad raised his hand. "May I speak?" I nodded. "I was sick and tired of living in the care facility. You didn't come to visit—"

"I'm sorry, Dad. Elizabeth and the doctor thought I was an obstacle to your getting better. Looks like they were right."

"And your mother—"

"*Stepmother.*"

"Your stepmother can't have me underfoot. She's awfully stressed by her new position. I was holding her back. Honestly, I can take care of myself." He danced the tiniest jig. "But, can I stay with you for a while?" He pouted with fake puppy-dog eyes.

"You don't ever have to ask, although I might have to talk to my landlady."

"I do need to ask. I'm coming to you with a few suitcases, fair health care coverage, my social security benefits, and not much else I'm afraid. But I can still pull a weed or two, and I cook a mean grilled cheese."

"Too bad you did not teach those skills to your daughter, Graybeard."

"Who the hell are you anyway?"

"Dad," I admonished.

"Your stepmother..." It rolled off my dad's tongue

with ease. "We pretty much gutted our savings over the last eighteen months with me in therapy. And she keeps reminding me that I had a traumatic brain injury from which I might never fully recover."

He needed the therapy because he'd taken a bullet meant for me. "You're always welcome. I have a few things to tie up, and then we can go home."

"Hey, kid," he said to CJ, "Take my stuff to your wheels. Then, if you're not busy, you can give me a tour of this metropolis." He dropped back into the wheelchair and covered his legs with the quilt, feigning feebleness and adding, "Pretty please."

"It would be an honor, Graybeard. If you allow my…" CJ stumbled over the word, "…daughter to accompany us." Whoops and whistles exploded from my room. Conversations are easily overheard through an open doorway.

"My beard is not gray," Dad muttered.

The corners of my mouth curled into a grin even as my brows furrowed as I wondered about my complicated future. And then the solution to Felipe's strange riddle about walking a maze with a truth-telling guide and a lying guide came to me. "I would ask," I said to the four walls, "which door would the other guard say leads out?"

MRS. C'S LONG ISLAND ICED TEA

½ fluid ounce vodka
½ fluid ounce rum
½ fluid ounce tequila
½ fluid ounce gin
½ fluid ounce triple sec
2-1/2 fluid ounces sweet and sour mix
Cola to taste
Lemon wedge/slice
Mix first six ingredients. Pour over ice. Splash cola.
Garnish with lemon.

Thank you for taking the time to read *Rescues, Rogues, & Renegade*. If you enjoyed it please tell your friends, and I would be so grateful if you would consider posting a review. Word of mouth is an author's best friend, and very much appreciated.

Thank you,

Mary Seifert

* * *

Watch for the next books in this series, coming very soon!

Get s free recipe collection from Mary when you subscribe to her newsletter. Visit her website to find out how!

Visit Mary's website: MarySeifertAuthor.com/
Facebook: facebook.com/MarySeifertAuthor
Twitter: twitter.com/mary_seifert
Instagram: instagram.com/maryseifert/
Follow Mary on BookBub and Goodreads too!

What's next for Katie and Maverick?

Katie and Maverick are out for their walk when Maverick dashes through the moving gate at a self-storage facility and they get locked in. By the time the police respond to the silent alarms the pair have set off, the smell of exhaust fumes has begun to seep from one of the garage-sized units, and the car inside is quickly engulfed in a ball of flame. Was it a suicide that turned extra messy, or did someone rig the expensive sports car to explode and kill the woman inside?

When Katie starts to ask the tough questions, it seems there were a long list of people who didn't much care for the victim and several of them had motives for murder. But Katie also has her days full with the upcoming holiday season and her students who are participating in a mock-trial competition. Will the kids make it to the state finals under the expert coaching of a local attorney who has joined their team? And will Katie and Maverick have a wonderful Christmas this year, the first in which Katie's dad has been home since the horrific shooting incident that nearly killed him?

Join Katie, Maverick, and their newfound extended family for the holidays—mixed, of course with the usual action from their Search and Rescue operations and the breathless drama that Mary Seifert brings to all her mystery novels.

Don't miss *Tech, Trials, & Trouble* **coming soon!**

Made in the USA
Monee, IL
04 December 2023

48167466R00184